pUrSUEd

pUrSUEd

JERRY B. JENKINS
TIM LAHAYE

TYNDALE HOUSE PUBLISHERS, INC.,
WHEATON, ILLINOIS

Visit Tyndale's exciting Web site at www.tyndale.com

Discover the latest Left Behind news at www.leftbehind.com

Pursued is a special edition compilation of the following Left Behind: The Kids titles:

Published in association with the literary agency of Alive Communications, Inc., 7680 Goddard Street, Suite 200, Colorado Springs, CO 80920.

Designed by Jenny Swanson

Library of Congress Cataloging-in-Publication Data

Jenkins, Jerry B.
   Pursued / Jerry B. Jenkins ; Tim LaHaye.
     p. cm. — (Left behind: the kids)
Summary: A compilation of four stories from the Left behind: the kids series in which four teens, left behind after the rapture, battle the forces of evil. Includes "Nicolae High," "The Underground," "Busted!," and "Death Strike."
   ISBN 0-8423-8352-2 (hc)
   [1. End of the world—Fiction. 2. Christian life—Fiction.] I. LaHaye, Tim F. II. Title.
III. Series: Jenkins, Jerry B. Left behind—the kids
   PZ7.J4138Pu 2003
   [Fic]—dc21   2003008496

Printed in the United States of America

08   07   06   05   04   03
9   8   7   6   5   4   3   2   1

JUDD was stunned. Vicki was gone.

"Where is she?" he demanded.

Lionel and Ryan looked up from their spots on the floor before the TV. Ryan shrugged. "There's a note by the phone."

Judd grabbed it and read quickly. "Hitching to Michigan to see Bub. Back soon."

He slapped the note on his thigh and caught himself before he swore. What was he so mad about? This was his fault.

Vicki had asked him to drive her to see her big brother Eddie's buddy. Judd refused before he thought about it, telling her he felt responsible for Lionel and Ryan and had better stay with them.

"Let them ride along," Vicki had said.

"Nah," Judd said. "The roads are just starting to reopen. We don't really know where we're going. There are rumors school is going to open again, and I'd hate to be out of state if that happens."

"You're going back to school?"

"If it opens, sure."

"Why?"

"Because we have to."

"We have to? Judd, what are they going to do if we don't show up? They'll figure we disappeared along with thousands of others. Anyway, if Bruce is right and there's a peace treaty signed between the UN and Israel, we'll have only seven years left to live. Why would I want to spend half that time in school? To learn what? The world is going to hell, and we'd be sitting in class, trying to prepare for a future that doesn't exist."

She had a point. Judd was a junior, but Vicki was a freshman. School did seem like a waste of time, but Judd didn't know what he thought about breaking the law by refusing to go. If it came to that, he assumed they would all go, Lionel and Ryan back to Lincoln Junior High, he and Vicki to Prospect High.

Judd had underestimated how desperate Vicki was to locate Bub. She had never met him, had only seen pictures and talked to him on the phone—the last time the morning of the Rapture. Her brother had met him when he ran off to work in Michigan after high school. Eddie said he liked Bub at first because he was a wild party kind of a guy. But then Eddie became a Christian. He wasn't able to persuade Bub to quit his loose living, but he kept rooming with him anyway. It was Bub who had confirmed to Vicki that Eddie had disappeared in the Rapture.

2

"I've been having trouble reaching Bub by phone," she had told Judd. "I want to just go find him."

Judd thought it was a bad idea and said so. He even thought about telling Bruce, but the kids had agreed they weren't going to treat Bruce like a parent. If Judd had known Vicki was going to just leave and hitchhike to Michigan, he would have taken her himself. He hated to think of her out there alone on the road. He felt responsible for her, though he knew he really wasn't. The four of them were on their own now. They all lived together in Judd's house, sure, but it had been their choice to accept his invitation. The only rules were that they would always tell each other where they were. Vicki had fulfilled that requirement.

Judd missed Vicki. There was no other way to say it.

It wasn't that he was interested in her romantically. At least not yet. He hadn't decided how he felt about her in that way. But she was the easiest person in the house to talk to. She would turn fifteen before he turned seventeen, so they weren't quite two years apart. Lionel was only thirteen and Ryan twelve, so although they were boys, Judd usually chose to talk with Vicki.

But she was gone, at least for a while. He worried about her.

Judd liked having Vicki around because she was a buffer between Lionel and Ryan. They squabbled all the time. Judd told himself he didn't care, but they got on his nerves. He knew they were like brothers and that down deep they liked each other and probably loved each other as brothers in Christ. They just didn't act like it.

3

Lionel, who had been raised in a Christian home, was a know-it-all who treated Ryan like a dummy. Well, what did Lionel expect from a kid who had hardly been to church? The whole thing made Judd feel old. Here he was, suddenly without parents, and he was worried about people who lived with him and for whom he felt responsible. All this in just a couple of weeks. It was too bizarre.

Vicki feared she had made a mistake as soon as she caught the attention of the driver of an eighteen-wheeler. She had been praying that a family would give her a ride. If not a family, then a couple. If not a couple, then a woman. Vicki hesitated when the truck rumbled onto the shoulder and awaited her approach. She could have easily ignored him, but, after all, she *had* been standing there with her thumb out.

She prayed as she approached the passenger side. At the trailer park she had grown up in, a friend was a truck driver. So she knew how to mount the steps, open the door, and swing herself inside. But with the door open, Vicki froze. This driver was a man, and he already had a passenger—another man. She smelled alcohol and both men held beer cans.

"Well, well, well," the passenger said, "lookie what we got here!"

He was young and blond with close-cropped hair, and he wore a sleeveless tee shirt despite the chilly evening. He offered her his free hand, but she hesitated, one hand on the door handle, the other on the side of the cab. The man smiled and she smelled his breath. "C'mon in, honey. You can sit right here between us."

"Yeah," the driver said. "We'll take a lady like you anywhere you want to go!" He was muscular and sweaty.

"I was, uh, just wondering how far it is to Mount Prospect," Vicki said. There was no way she'd ride with these two.

"You know good and well where it is," the passenger said. "You had your thumb out there, honey. Now, where to?"

"Nowhere," she said and began to step back down.

"No you don't, sweetie," the young man said, and he pushed the door wide open. Vicki hung from the handle and dangled high off the ground. He pulled the door back toward him, and Vicki had to act. The last thing she wanted was to get close enough for him to reach her. She let go and dropped to the ground.

"Thanks anyway," she called out, heading toward the back of the truck as the door shut. But she knew that was not going to satisfy the truckers when the door opened again and the man bounded out, sloshing his beer can as he did.

Vicki slipped in the gravel and tried to run, her heart thundering. She was no match for a man that size. As she desperately prayed she realized how stupid she had been to take off on her own. What had she been thinking?

The man was gaining on her when another truck rolled off the side of the road, the skidding tires kicking up dust. Vicki found herself next to the passenger door of that vehicle as it flew open. Now what?

She was relieved to see this driver was alone and

5

older, probably in his sixties, big, barrel-chested, and with a week's growth of white whiskers. His smile disarmed her.

"You ought to be careful, hitchikin' by yourself these days, little lady," he said.

"Can you help me?" she said.

"What's the trouble?"

She pointed behind her, but when she turned, the young man had turned tail and was climbing back into the other truck. Taking no chances, Vicki leaped aboard the new truck.

"Where you going?" the old trucker said.

"Michigan," she said, noticing a leather cross dangling from the CB radio mounted above the dash.

"I can get you as far as Michigan City, Indiana," he said. "How'll that be?"

"An answer to prayer," she said.

The old man was shifting into one gear after the other every few feet, getting back up to speed as he pulled back onto the road. When he finally had the rig in the right lane and rolling with the heavy traffic, he cocked his head and stared at Vicki.

"Did you say that just to get next to me, 'cause you saw the cross? Or are you really a woman of prayer?"

"I am now," she said.

He chuckled and turned his gaze back at the road. "Aren't we all?" he said. "Call me Deacon."

"Deacon?"

"Yes, ma'am."

"Are you a deacon?"

6

"Actually no. But once I found the Lord and started telling everybody on the squawk box, they started calling me Deacon. I'm a little zealous I guess you might say."

"Me too."

"You a believer, Miss?"

"Vicki," she said. "With an *I*."

"Well, praise the Lord, Vicki with an *I*. Tell me your story and I'll tell you mine."

Vicki ran down her whole history before Deacon reached the state line. The ride was punctuated by occasional static from the CB radio, words she could just barely make out.

"That you, Deacon?" came one interruption. "This here's the Fat Fox."

"Hey, Fatty, how ya doin', come back."

"Seventy-threes to you, Deke. Still totin' the Lord?"

"That's a big four, Fats. You will be too if you wanna survive the flip side."

"I got the whole sermon the other day, Deacon," the other man said. "Just saying hey. "

"Well, hey back, Fox. Don't be making the Lord wait on you too long now, you hear? I want to be calling you brother next time I see you."

Deacon explained to Vicki that he liked to preach over the citizens' band radio. A lot of drivers were scared and curious since the vanishings. "I take a lot of heat for it from some. They tell me to put a lid on it or save it for Sunday, but it's way too late to be ashamed of God, don't you think?"

Vicki nodded. "Did you not believe before, or did you just not know?"

"I knew. My mother, God rest her soul, told me every day of her life. But I blamed God because she married the wrong man. He treated her wrong. Me too. I hated him till the day he died, and I always thought she deserved better than a man like that. I quit going to church fifty years ago and never went back. She sent me verses and reminders and letters and prayers every month until she died a couple of years ago. I almost got saved at her funeral. I knew what they were saying was the truth, but I figured that if I came to Jesus I would have too much apologizing to do. Three former wives, you know."

Vicki wondered why he thought she'd know.

"Anyway, my last wife became a Christian about six months after she left me. She wanted to come back, make things right, clean me up, get my life straightened out. I didn't want any part of it. She warned me that Jesus would come back and I wouldn't be ready. Boy, was she right! When everybody disappeared, I only needed to know one thing: Was Janice here or gone? As soon as I knew she was gone, leavin' her waitress uniform right where she stood, I knew it was true. I knew what to do, who to pray to, and what to say."

"Me too," Vicki said. "Quit drinking and smoking too."

Deacon tilted his head back and roared with laughter. "You got off the sauce and the cancer sticks when you got saved too, did you?"

"Yes, sir!"

He laughed louder. "Is that a fact?"

"Yes, it is, and I don't think it's funny. Why are you laughing?"

He wiped his eyes and down shifted. "I'm sorry, sweetheart," he said. "You just don't hit me as the hard-livin' type, if you know what I mean."

"You should have seen me three weeks ago," she said. "I never thought I would look like this, talk like this, or act like this either. Most people called me trailer trash."

"Grew up in a park?"

"Yes, sir. Prospect Gardens."

"I know the place. No garden, is it?"

"Never was. Asphalt and dirt."

"And some indoor/outdoor, right?"

"Sir?"

"That plastic indoor/outdoor carpeting that's supposed to fool people into thinking you've got a yard?"

She laughed. "We sure enough had a slab of that ourselves," she said.

Vicki told him of the trailers that had burned, and of her brother's friend Bub, who had been left behind.

Deacon was quiet for a few miles and appeared thoughtful. "Ever wonder if he doesn't want to be found?" he said finally.

Vicki shrugged. "It doesn't make any difference. It's like God put him in my heart and I have to be sure he knows the truth."

"Not everybody reacts well, you know," Deacon said.

Vicki nodded. "That's OK. I'm just supposed to tell him."

Deacon told her that he wouldn't feel right about leaving her at the Michigan state line, not knowing whether she got a ride to Portage. "I'll sit with you as long

9

as I can at the truck stop there," he said. "I want to make sure you catch a ride with somebody I know and trust."

"Thank you, Deacon," she said.

———————————————

Judd wished Vicki had told him she was going with or without him. He would have at least made her promise to call him once in a while so he'd know she was all right. Now how would he get word to her about school? Loudspeakers began blaring late Friday night, informing residents to tune in certain radio and TV emergency-broadcast stations. "Local schools will reopen a week from tomorrow," came the announcements, "and those stations will carry the details."

"What details?" Ryan said, and he and Lionel joined Judd in front of the TV.

"Listen and find out, stupid," Lionel said.

"I just figured you'd know, genius," Ryan said.

"Knock it off, you two," Judd said. "I want to hear this."

"We already know what they're going to say," Lionel said. "We know when, we know where, and we know what. School. Yuck."

"You both go to Lincoln, right?" Judd said.

Lionel nodded.

"Me too," Ryan said. "But we're not in the same classes."

"At least I have *something* to be thankful for," Lionel said.

Judd shushed them as the list of schools came up. As the names of junior highs scrolled past, Judd read,

10

"Formerly Lincoln Junior High, now Global Community Middle School."

Lionel seemed to flinch. "Why would they do that?" he said. "Change a perfectly good name. I liked going to a school named after a great president."

The phone rang.

"I'll get it," Ryan said. Judd let him as he watched the high school listings. But the station did better than just list the openings. The news of Prospect High was accompanied by film footage of the changing of the sign out front.

"It's for you," Ryan said from the kitchen phone. "Judd!"

Judd heard him but didn't respond. He stood, staring at the screen. A cherry picker and crane on the back of a truck hoisted a workman to the Prospect High sign. As Ryan nagged him from the kitchen, Judd saw the man on TV trade one sheet of plastic for another that slid in front of the lights on the sign.

Prospect High was no longer. His school would now be known as Nicolae Carpathia High. The sports mascot would also be changed. The teams formerly known as the Knights would now be the Doves.

"C'mon, Judd!" Ryan whined. "It's Bruce for you."

2

YOU been watching the news?" Bruce asked.

"Yes," Judd said, "unfortunately."

"You understand what's going on?"

"What's to understand? School starts a week from tomorrow at Nicolae Carpathia High."

Bruce laughed. "Well, it may come to that, but I meant—"

"What do you mean it *may* come to that? I was serious." Judd told him of the school announcements.

"It doesn't surprise me about their changing Lincoln to Global Community," Bruce said. "That's going to happen everywhere with the new emphasis on a one-world government. They'll want to remove nationalism and make everything planet oriented. But to already start naming things after the UN secretary-general? Wow."

"I thought you were calling to make sure I knew school was back on," Judd said.

"No, you caught that before I did. I just finished a meeting with the adult core group I told you about—the Tribulation Force."

"Yeah, the pilot and his daughter?"

"And the magazine writer. Anyway, they had not heard the big international news today, and I wanted to make sure you heard it. I have to prepare my Sunday sermon tomorrow morning, but I wondered if you four would want to come to my office early so we could talk about it."

"Three of us can. What's the news?"

"Carpathia is making himself unavailable for several days while he and his top people work on what he calls 'an understanding' between the global community and Israel, and a special arrangement between the UN and the United States."

"What does that mean?"

"That's what I'd like to talk to the Junior Trib Force about tomorrow. Sorry, the Kids Trib Force."

"How about we just call it the Young Trib Force?" Judd said.

"Sure," Bruce said. "Now, who can't make it?"

When Judd told Bruce where Vicki was, Judd was met with a long silence. "Judd," the pastor said finally, "this is not going to work."

Judd felt his neck flush. "What's not going to work?"

"You being in charge of these kids. If you can't control—"

"Controlling them is not my job!" Judd blurted. "I'm just giving them a place to stay. I'm not their parent. I can't tell them what to do."

14

"Judd, listen to me. I feel responsible for you guys too, because I know you and know where you are. You'd never get away with living alone at your ages if we weren't in the middle of a crisis. If the police weren't so busy, they'd never stand for this. I ought to call them and have them watch for Vicki, and if they don't have the manpower, I should be out looking for her myself. Where is she headed?"

"I'm not sure," Judd said, "but you're not responsible for us. We don't answer to you, and we don't have to do what you say. What are you going to do? Tell on us? Get us in trouble? What kind of a friend is that?"

Judd couldn't believe he was talking that way to a man he admired and respected as much as he did Bruce Barnes. Bruce had led all four of the kids to Christ and treated them with respect. But Judd didn't like to be lectured or told what to do. Now he sensed he had hurt Bruce, who was silent again.

"I'd like to think I'm your pastor," Bruce said at last. Judd felt guilty when he heard the emotion in Bruce's voice. He had broken the man's heart, and he knew he should apologize. Judd didn't have much experience with that, but he knew he would have to get around to it sometime soon. "Will you at least come early tomorrow morning so I can tell you what I think about what's going on?"

"Of course," Judd said, trying to sound encouraging and apologetic. "How early?"

"Like I said, I've got sermon preparation, so if you could come as early as eight, I'd appreciate it."

"We'll be there," Judd said. "All of us who are here anyway."

"You don't mind telling the younger ones what to do?"
Judd knew he had been caught in his own weak logic.

Deacon looked at his watch. Vicki was aware that they
had been getting puzzled stares from other truckers as
they ate at the counter in the truck stop. Deacon insisted
on paying, though she told him she had borrowed plenty
of money from Judd.

"Don't be saying that too loud either," he said. "You
don't want anybody knowing you're carrying a lot of cash."

"Hey, Deacon," a man said on his way out. "Keep
preachin', bro."

"Will do, Claud. Hey, you're not runnin' to Michigan
tonight, are you?"

"Nope, sorry. What's up?"

"Looking for a ride for a friend. Can't let her ride with
just anybody."

"But you'd trust her with me?" Claud said, smiling at
Vicki. "I'm flattered. If you want to see Pennsylvania
tomorrow, you can ride with me, little lady. Otherwise,
I can't help ya."

"Thanks anyway," Vicki said.

Deacon checked the time again. "I've got to get going
soon," he said, "but tell me something. Did you say your
boyfriend had wheels?"

She nodded. "He's not my boyfriend."

"But he took you and the other two in, so he's a good
friend?"

"You could say that."

16

"I need you to do me a favor, Vicki. Would you?"

"Depends."

"I want you to call your friend and have him come get you. Now don't shake your head. Hear me out. I don't think it's an accident you wound up riding in my truck tonight. I think God put us together to protect you."

"Believe me, I can take care of myself."

"Little lady, I can't even take care of *my*self in this new day, and I'm a big, old, ugly man. Who knows what kind of trouble you could get yourself into out there? Now I have to go, but I'm not leaving until I know you've got a ride home."

"But I have to get to—"

"Let me finish. I promise I'll check with some people I know, people in law enforcement who can track this guy down for you, make sure he's all right."

"But I need to talk to him face-to-face. He treats me like a little girl and wouldn't listen to me on the phone. If I was right there, he couldn't just blow me off."

"Well, then one of these days, when I know far enough in advance that I'm going to Michigan from the west, I'll let you know and you can go with me."

Vicki sat back and stared at Deacon. "You'd do that for me?"

He nodded. "What's a brother for?"

Judd was relieved to hear from Vicki, so much so that he didn't even mind the trip in the middle of the night to get her. He was not happy, however, to discover that she had given their phone number to Deacon. He seemed like a harmless and wonderful old guy, but who knew who was for real these days?

Judd was stony on the way home. Vicki badgered him to find out what was wrong.

"Bruce says this isn't working," he said, "and when you pull a stunt like this, I wonder if he might be right."

Vicki shook her head as if she was frustrated and angry. "So kick me out of the house," she said. "We don't answer to Bruce. At least I don't. And I don't answer to you either. I mean, I'm grateful for all you've done, but you're not my mom or dad."

"You didn't obey *them* either," Judd said, and he knew he had gone too far this time. "Well," he added, trying to make it better, "you told me that yourself."

3

VICKI could hardly believe herself. How could she be talking like that to the one person who had made her life bearable? She believed she had made Judd say something crueler than he had intended. The worst of it was that he was right. She was starting to talk to Judd and about Bruce the same way she had talked to and about her parents. Yet now she missed them with an ache so deep she knew it would not be soothed until she saw them with Jesus.

She wanted to apologize, but the words would not come. Bruce had taught the kids about having to deal with their old selves, their sin natures. Now she was discovering what he meant. Vicki had endured Lionel's and Ryan's bickering, passing that off as childishness and blaming it on their ages. But she and Judd should have known better. How could they let their old natures take over after all God, and Bruce, had done for them?

What had the encounter with Deacon been all about if not God showing her that he would protect her even when she did something stupid? Vicki had felt free and powerful when she started out, walking from the house out of the neighborhood and onto the main roads leading to the expressway. But then fear and foreboding had overtaken her, and she felt tense every second. Only when she finally saw Judd and was safely in his car and on the way back to the house did she realize how afraid she had been. Why couldn't she say that? Pride? Resentment at having been scolded, in essence, by both Judd and Bruce?

She opened her mouth to say something, anything, but Judd beat her to it.

"I'm sorry, Vicki," he said. "I shouldn't have said that. I don't know why I do that. I care about you, that's all. I really thought it was a bad idea for you to go to Michigan at all, but if I had known you were going to do it anyway, I'd have taken you."

"You would've?"

"Of course! I haven't been able to sleep or do anything, wondering about you, worrying about you."

She put a hand on his arm. "You're sounding more and more like a parent all the time."

"I know," he said, smiling. "And I can't believe it."

Vicki felt Judd tense under her touch and quickly pulled her hand away. She didn't want to give him the wrong idea. She appreciated him. She liked him. But getting really interested in him, interested that way, would be a mistake.

"I'm sorry too, Judd," she said. "I feel rotten when I

act so selfish. I think I had the right idea, wanting to find Bub. God really did put that in my heart. But going myself was just trying to show you I was independent or something—I don't know. It's just that I feel this desperation to tell everybody about God. There's been enough death. Nobody should still wonder what the disappearances were all about."

"I know," Judd said. "Maybe this Deacon guy can get you in touch with Bub somehow. You'll get your chance."

"I hope so."

Judd told her about the school announcements.

"Oh, brother," she said. "That sure seems like a waste of time. Aren't you going to feel squirrelly, sitting in school while the rest of the world is dying?"

He nodded but didn't say anything.

"What?" she said. "You don't agree? I mean, what will we be studying and why? I was never that good a student, but I knew I needed that diploma to get any kind of job. School was all about the future. Well, now there is no future like that, so what's the point?"

Judd was still quiet, and Vicki was intrigued. Usually she could tell when he agreed with her, and now he didn't seem to. "You going?" she said. "Back to school, I mean?"

He nodded.

"You're going to be a Carpathia Dove?"

"That I'll never be," he said, "but, yeah, I'm going to go."

"You mind saying why?"

"For the same reasons you're talking about."

"The future?"

He nodded.

21

"But don't you agree you'll be studying subjects you'll never use? Whatever kind of job you'll have will have nothing to do with what you learn in high school now."

He nodded again. Vicki sensed herself getting mad again. "So, why waste your time?" she said.

"I told you," he said. "The future. Everybody at that high school needs to know what we know. You'd rather be out telling everybody about Jesus, but what about all those kids we'll see every day? They were left behind just like we were. We'll probably meet some believers, but I'll bet not many."

He had a point. "But will we be allowed to tell them about God?" she said. "Especially if Carpathia *is* the Antichrist? I can't imagine anyone letting us do that in a building named after the guy himself. And what kind of sense does it make that we go to a school with that name?"

Judd pulled into the driveway. "It's going to seem weird," he said. "I don't guess I'll be buying a varsity jacket."

He told Vicki about the morning meeting with Bruce, then let her out of the car before pulling into the garage. "Thanks for coming to get me, Judd. I didn't deserve it."

"Yeah," he said. "Well, you're grounded."

She was too tired to smile.

Judd, on the other hand, was unable to sleep. He wandered into his father's den, where the latest monster computer sat. Judd and Marc and Marcie used to play games on it and surf the Net. Judd had enjoyed all the chat rooms, though his parents warned him about the worst ones. Those didn't even tempt him now.

He pulled the dustcover off and fired up the machine. He was stunned to see how many advertisements he found for people with schemes on how to get rich in light of the global mess. One ghastly Web site promised a listing of everybody who had died or disappeared. Judd spent an hour there, pulling up names of his own family and other acquaintances to see how accurate the thing was.

His parents were listed as having disappeared. Ryan's parents were listed as known dead. Vicki's parents were listed as killed in a trailer fire, which he knew was not true but would also be impossible to prove. Judd wanted to look up Bub for Vicki, but that wasn't enough to go on. Bub couldn't be his real first name, and even if it was, Judd had never heard a last name. Vicki had to know it, though, because she gave Deacon enough info that he was sure he could track down Eddie Byrne's friend.

Judd was amazed to see how late it was. He had promised Bruce he would bring at least Lionel and Ryan to the church in the morning. Vicki would be a pleasant surprise for Bruce.

The phone awakened Judd, and he was startled to notice that it was already ten minutes after eight. "Oh, no," he groaned, knowing the caller would be Bruce. He was right, and he quickly apologized, promising to get everybody rounded up and over there as fast as he could. Judd explained he had been up late, going to get Vicki.

23

"At least that's good news," Bruce said. "Now please respect my schedule so I can get to my sermon preparation when I need to."

Judd scolded Lionel and Ryan for not getting him up, but they, of course, blamed each other. "You never told me when the meeting was," Vicki said, sitting at the table in the kitchen. "I'm ready when you are."

Twenty minutes later, after Judd's shower, they all piled into the car. No surprise to Judd, Bruce seemed perturbed when they arrived. He didn't lecture them, but he did say he was willing to have a regular meeting time every other day and that they would be expected to be there on time and ready to study. "There's so much for you to learn, and if you're going to back to school, you're going to be in the minority there. It won't be easy."

He prayed and then opened his Bible, but before saying anything, he took a deep breath and seemed on the verge of tears. "I feel a tremendous responsibility for you all," he said. "I know you don't want me to. You want to be independent and not answer to anyone. We're all that way. But it's nothing but pride and selfishness. The Bible says that as your pastor, I am also your shepherd. That doesn't make me your parent, but if you want to be in the church and in this little group, your responsibility is to respect my authority over you.

"That's not easy for me either. I'm not used to it yet myself. I'm trying to run this church, but I'm also spending most of my days and evenings studying the Bible and commentaries so I can try to explain to you and everyone else what is going on."

"And what's to come," Judd offered.

"Exactly. I feel the press of God on me. It's hard. And I know I'm not the only one who feels it. We're all hurting, we've all lost people, we all missed the truth. I don't want to lay this all on you, but my house is so big and so cold and so lonely without my family that sometimes I don't even go home at night. I study here until I fall asleep, and I go home in the morning only to clean up and change and get back here."

Judd didn't know what to say. He hadn't seen Bruce like this. One thing was for sure: Judd wouldn't let anybody be late to these meetings again.

"One of the things I had never been good at was reading the Bible every day," Bruce continued. "I pretended to be a believer, a so-called full-time Christian worker, but I didn't care about the Bible. Now I can't get enough of it. I know what people meant when they used to say they feasted on the Word. Sometimes I sit drinking it in for hours, losing track of time, weeping and praying, forgetting to eat. Sometimes I just slip from my chair and fall to my knees, calling out to God to make it clear to me. Most frightening—and thrilling— of all, he's doing just that."

Vicki was riveted, and she could tell even the younger boys were too. They hadn't seen Bruce like this. Something was weighing on him, and it had nothing to do with the fact that the Young Trib Force had been late that Saturday morning.

"I need your prayers," Bruce continued. "God is showing me things, impressing truth on me that I can barely

keep quiet about. Yet if I say these things publicly, I will
be ridiculed and might even be in danger."

"Like what?" Vicki said.

Bruce stepped to the corner of his desk and sat on it,
towering over the kids. "We know Nicolae Carpathia is the
Antichrist. Even if the story Mr. Williams told you about
Carpathia's supernatural hypnotic power and his murder
of those two men was not true—and of course I believe it
is—there's still plenty of evidence against him. He fits the
prophecies. He's deceptive. He's charming. People are
drawn to him, flocking to support him. He has been thrust
into power, seemingly against his own wishes. He's pushing a one-world government, a one-world money system,
a treaty with Israel, moving the UN to Babylon. That alone
proves it."

Vicki's ears perked up at the mention of the treaty
with Israel. "He's said that?" she said. "On the news, I
mean? Isn't that the start of the seven-year tribulation?"

Bruce nodded. "Yesterday," he said. "His spokesman
said Carpathia would be unavailable for several days
while he conducted strategic high-level meetings."

"But did he say what they would be about?"

"He said Carpathia felt obligated to move quickly to
unite the world in a move toward peace. He's having
nations destroy 90 percent of their weaponry and
donate the remaining 10 percent to the UN in Babylon,
which he has renamed New Babylon. He's also pushing
the international money people to settle on one form of
currency for the whole world. And he wants all the religions of the world to unite as one big group that toler-

ates everybody's beliefs. I'm guessing we'll see a one-world religion."

Vicki's mind was reeling, as it had been since the day of the disappearances. At times she still wondered if this was some crazy nightmare. In an instant she had gone from a rebellious teenager to a fanatical believer in Christ. She wanted to press Bruce, to ask him about this treaty. That would be proof, if nothing else was, but how did he know? She didn't want to interrupt him.

"All I know," he was saying, "is that the closer I get to God, the deeper I get into the Bible, the heavier the burden seems on my shoulders. The world needs to know it is being deceived. I feel an urgency to preach Christ everywhere, not just here. This church is full of frightened people, and they're hungry for God. We're trying to meet that need, but more trouble is coming."

When he paused, Vicki jumped in. "But the treaty. Has he really announced a treaty?"

Bruce looked at her and nodded. "The news that really got to me yesterday was the announcement that the next major order of business for Carpathia is what he calls 'an understanding' between the global community and Israel. I don't know what form it will take or what the benefit will be to the Holy Land, but clearly this is the seven-year treaty. If that announcement says anything about a promise from Carpathia that Israel will be protected over the next seven years, it officially ushers in the Tribulation."

CAN we go soon?" Ryan asked. "I have no idea what you guys are talking about."

"Figure it out, short stuff," Lionel said. "It's only the end of the world."

Bruce leaned forward. "I understand you two haven't been getting along," he said. "Lionel, you know this stuff, don't you? Better than Ryan, I mean?"

" 'Course," Lionel said. "Doesn't everybody?"

"And is that his fault?"

"No. I was raised in church. He wasn't."

"So he's not stupid or a dummy?"

"Unless he doesn't want to learn."

"And I think he does, especially if he understands what we're talking about. You should teach him."

"Why me?"

"You're closest to his age," Bruce said. "He listens to you whether you think so or not. It's important that you're positive. He acts like he's mad at you, and sometimes maybe he doesn't like you because you keep putting him down. But he needs you, and he would look up to you if you treated him better."

Lionel looked down, and Judd hoped Bruce was getting through to him. It was a good idea—Lionel's being Ryan's teacher. The question was whether either of them would tolerate it.

"You two work it out," Bruce said.

Lionel rolled his head to gaze at Ryan, who looked back with brows raised. Judd took that to mean that both were willing to give it a try. Now that could be interesting.

Judd missed his parents and his little brother and sister, and he knew the others missed their families too. But he was excited about doing something positive, not sitting around feeling sorry for himself. They had only a few years left, and he wanted to see their group be just as eager to stand and fight as the adult Tribulation Force.

"Bruce," he said, raising his hand. "Do you have time for us, with all the other stuff you're doing, I mean?"

"I'll make the time if you'll all get serious about it. The adult Force meets here every night for two hours. I can meet with you guys after school whenever possible. I'll outline what God has revealed in the Bible. If I'm right and if the treaty with Israel comes within the next few days, we have no time to waste. I want this church to start new churches, new groups of believers. I want to go to Israel and hear the two witnesses preach at the Wailing Wall. Imagine the stories I'll come back with. By the way, you know there's a place on the Internet where you can watch what's happening at the Wall twenty-four hours a day."

"Yippee," Lionel said, and Bruce looked hard at him.

"Just kiddin'," Lionel said, "but isn't most of that in Jewish?"

Bruce smiled. "Their language is Hebrew, but often there are subtitles or even interpreters. You might find it interesting, especially when the witnesses are preaching. The Bible foretells of 144,000 Jews springing up and traveling throughout the world to preach the gospel. There will be a great soul harvest, maybe a billion or more people, coming to Christ."

"Wow!" Judd said. "Does it say there'll be that many?"

"Well, this is a good study for you. Lionel, grab that King James Bible over there. Thanks. Usually we use the New King James, or the New International, or the New Living Translation, so we can understand it better. But let's look at this in an older version and see if we can figure it out. Ryan, find Revelation 9:16, and read it to us."

Ryan took the Bible from Lionel, and Judd was pleased to hear Lionel whisper, "Last book in the whole Bible."

Ryan found the verse and read, " 'And the number of the army of the horsemen were two hundred thousand thousand: and I heard the number of them.' "

"Stop there," Bruce said. "What was the number he heard?"

"Me?" Ryan said.

"If you know."

"Anybody knows that," he said. "A thousand thousand is a million, so the number he heard was two hundred million."

"Good," Bruce said. "Now, at the risk of being too simple, would you say that army of horsemen, even though it was two hundred million, could be counted?"

"Of course," Ryan said. "The number's right here."

"Right. It's obvious. So, Judd, read Revelation 7:9."

Judd took the Bible from Ryan and read, " 'After this I beheld, and, lo, a great multitude, which no man could number, of all nations, and kindreds, and people, and tongues, stood before the throne, and before the Lamb, clothed with white robes, and palms in their hands.' "

"That's enough," Bruce said. "Anybody catch it?"

Vicki said, "I don't know who they're talking about, but it's a crowd so big nobody can number it."

"Exactly. That's how we know there will be a huge soul harvest. This is talking about people who come to Christ during the Tribulation. If an army of two hundred million can be counted, how many must there be in a crowd no man can number?"

Judd stole a glance at Ryan, who looked excited. "Is all this stuff this interesting?" Ryan said.

"That's nothing," Bruce said. "You'll be as amazed as I have been with what's in here."

"All those people becoming believers," Vicki said. "We should be thrilled."

"I *am*," Bruce said. "But we're not going to have much time to celebrate and certainly no time to rest. Remember the seven Seal Judgments Revelation talks about?"

"You said something about them, yes."

"Those will begin with the signing of the treaty. There will be eighteen months of peace, but in the three months after that—twenty-one months into the eighty-four-month Tribulation—the rest of the Seal Judgments will fall on the earth. One-fourth of the world's population will be wiped out. Do you understand what that means?"

"One-fourth of the people who have been left behind?" Lionel said.

Bruce nodded.

"I don't like the odds," Judd said. "There are four of us kids."

"One of us is going to die before even two years are up?"

Bruce didn't say anything. Judd saw him just looking at them, one by one.

"Whew!" Ryan said. "Maybe some of this isn't that interesting after all. I mean, it's interesting, but it's like stuff you don't really want to know."

"I want to know about it," Vicki said, speaking louder and more quickly than Judd had heard her before. "I want to know everything, every detail. There's no guarantee I won't be the one who's killed by the twenty-first month. I want to make sure I'm doing everything I'm supposed to be doing in the meantime."

"To earn your way to heaven," Bruce said. "Right?"

"Right! I mean, no! I know better, Bruce. I know I can't earn my way. I just want to do the right thing because it's the right thing. Millions of people are going to die in the first quarter of the Tribulation, so we have to tell them the truth as fast as we can."

"That's what I like to hear. One of the adults last night said the same thing. He said, 'We don't want to just survive; we want to take action.' "

Now they were talking Judd's language, and he was thrilled that they all seemed excited about it. There was a reason God had put them together, and they were going to do important things for him.

Vicki raised her hand. "How many people will be left at the end?"

"When Jesus returns again," Bruce said, "at the Glorious Appearing?" She nodded. "With all the judgments—fourteen more following the seven Seal Judgments—there will be war and famine and pestilence and plagues. My study tells me that several of the judgments wipe out another third of the population. That's a third of the three-fourths who are left, then a third of the two-thirds left after that, and so on. It's confusing, but if you put a calculator to it, it looks like only one of every four people who were left at the Rapture will be left standing at the Glorious Appearing."

"The rest will be in heaven or hell?" Ryan said.

"Right. And the ones in heaven will return with Christ to set up his earthly kingdom, his thousand-year reign."

Ryan looked at the others. "I'd like to be the one left standing, but if I'm not, I get to go to heaven *and* come back? That would be cool too."

That afternoon Judd worked at the computer, looking for the Temple Mount Web site in Jerusalem. Vicki sat in the kitchen with her Bible and some books Bruce had given her to study. Lionel and Ryan watched television, but Lionel also told Ryan Bible stories that were new to him.

Late in the afternoon, Lionel hollered up the stairs. "Hey, Judd, some guy on TV is talking about announcements from the UN and all that. You want to hear it?"

"I do!" Vicki said, emerging from the kitchen.

Judd joined the others in front of the TV, where a commentator said: "Moving the UN out of New York and into the ruins of Babylon, south of Baghdad, is a good thing. If Carpathia is sincere about disarming the world and stockpiling the remaining 10 percent of the weapons, I'd rather he store them in the Middle East than on an island off New York City.

"But the world will never settle on a single religion, and as streamlined as it may be, there will never be fewer than three currencies either."

"What are currencies?" Ryan asked.

"Types of money," Judd said. "Like now we have American dollars, European marks, and Asian yen. Carpathia wants to go to just dollars. Bruce thinks eventually Carpathia wants to go to no cash."

"How would they do that?"

"Everybody would have an account and a credit card. Anything you want, you just put on that card. No cash."

"Cool!"

"Yeah," Vicki said, "but what happens when they do away with the card and put a chip or a mark on you to be scanned?"

"Even better," Ryan said. "Nothing to carry."

"But these books Bruce lent me say it will be the mark of the beast, the Antichrist, and then he'll own you. It's right in the Bible."

"Not me," Ryan said. "They'd have to kill me first, so then I'd be in heaven."

As Vicki headed back to the kitchen and Judd toward the stairs, she told him, "Bruce says the only woman in the adult Tribulation Force is the daughter of the pilot."

"I know."

"And she's memorizing three books of the Bible."

"I didn't know *that*."

"She's going to be Bruce's research assistant and help him teach. Maybe she'll teach us when he's out of town."

"That'd be neat. What's she memorizing?"

"The three books with the most end-times prophecies: Ezekiel, Daniel, and Revelation."

"Those are not short books."

"No kidding. But what a goal. Maybe I'll try that. It would be more important than school. But you're right. If I want to tell people, there are going to be a lot of people to tell at Prospect, I mean Nicolae High."

"Nine more days and we're back to class," Judd said.

"I'm looking forward to tomorrow morning. Bruce says he's got a message that excites him. This is so weird. He told me that this woman, Chloe Steele is her name, said she never thought the Bible would interest her, and now she's reading it like there's no tomorrow. Get it?"

"Huh?"

"Like there's no tomorrow. There aren't many, are there?"

36

Back in his dad's den, Judd sat thinking. Bruce had told Vicki about Chloe Steele, and he had told Judd about Buck Williams, the magazine writer. On the way out of church, Bruce had told Judd the latest thing Buck had told him. "He said he found himself turning to the Gospels rather than the Old Testament or the Revelation prophecies. He was surprised to see what a revolutionary Jesus turned out to be."

"A revolutionary?" Judd had asked.

"You know this stuff as well as I do," Bruce had said. "You grew up with it. Buck is just learning the character, the personality, the mission of Jesus, and it fascinates him. He told me that the Jesus he had always imagined or thought he knew was an impostor. The Jesus of the Bible turns out to be a radical, a man of paradoxes. Jesus said if you want to be rich, give your money away. If you want to be exalted, humble yourself. Revenge sounds logical, but it's wrong. Love your enemies, pray for those who put you down. That kind of thing."

Judd couldn't argue with that. He only wished he'd become a radical Christian long before.

5

JUDD insisted that everyone in the house be up early and ready to go long before church Sunday morning. No one grumbled. They had somehow turned a corner and were now excited and bold about the task before them. Even Ryan and Lionel seemed to be getting along.

Judd asked that they find good seats in the sanctuary, which was already filling, and he hurried down to the office to see Bruce. Loretta, Bruce's kindly old secretary, was just arriving. She told Judd he could knock on Bruce's door.

"If it can wait, I'd appreciate it," Bruce called out.

"OK," Judd said. "Sorry." But as he walked away, Bruce came to the door. He looked disheveled, unshaven, as if he had stayed up all night.

"I didn't know it was you, Judd. What's up?"

"Nothin'," Judd said. "Just wanted to say hi."

"Glad you did. Pray for me."

"OK, but why?"

"Just feeling the responsibility of this church. Big crowd already?"

Judd nodded. "Jammed. Cars lined up around the block. People mostly look scared or sad."

"They're terrified," Bruce said. "They come here looking for hope, for answers, for God. Some are finding him, and the word is spreading. I've been studying all night. I've got to shave and get going here. You study those verses I suggested?"

"Yeah. I found the one about the quarter of the population."

"Memorize it?"

"Yup."

"Let me hear it."

"You have time?" Judd said.

"Did you really memorize it?"

Judd had to prove it. "Revelation 6:8," he began, " 'So I looked, and behold, a pale horse. And the name of him who sat on it was Death, and Hades followed with him. And power was given to them over a fourth of the earth, to kill with sword, with hunger, with death, and by the beasts of the earth.' "

"Excellent, Judd. You're a good student. Unfortunately, you're going to learn that what comes after the pale horse is worse and keeps getting worse until the end."

Vicki waited with Ryan and Lionel in the third pew from the front, in the center row. She saved a seat for Judd. When she saw him coming, she also recognized Buck

Williams across the way. He had slid in behind a tall, dark man and a pretty young woman, and they were greeting each other.

"Ryan," she whispered, "don't make a big scene, but is that Captain Steele and his daughter over there in front of Mr. Williams?"

Ryan stood to look, and Vicki cringed. "Yep," he said. "That's them. Mr. S. and Chloe."

Judd joined the kids as the music began.

He noticed that many people didn't know the songs. The words were projected on the wall, and the choruses were simple and catchy, but they were new to some people. As for those, like himself, who knew the words, he wondered how he and they had all missed the truth while singing songs like those.

Finally Bruce hurried to the pulpit—not the large one on the platform, but a small lectern at floor level. He carried his Bible, two large books, and a sheaf of papers he had trouble controlling. He smiled sheepishly.

"Good morning," he began. "I realize a word of explanation is in order. Usually we sing more, but we don't have time for that today. Usually my tie is straighter, my shirt fully tucked in, my suit coat buttoned. That all seems a little less critical this morning. Usually we take up an offering. Be assured we still need it, but please find the baskets on your way out at noon, if I indeed let you out that early.

"I want to take the extra time this morning because I feel an urgency greater even than the last few weeks. I don't want you to worry about me. I haven't become a wild-eyed madman, a cultist, or anything other than what I have been since I realized I had missed the Rapture. I have read more, prayed more, and studied more this week than ever, and I am eager to tell you what God has told me."

Bruce told his own story yet again, how he had lived a phony life for years, even as a member of the pastoral staff. When Jesus came back, Bruce had been left behind, without his wife and precious children. Judd had heard the story, but it still made him want to cry. People all over the church sobbed.

"I never want to stop telling what Christ has done for me," Bruce said. "I will never again be ashamed of the gospel of Christ. The Bible says that the Cross offends. If you are offended, I am doing my job. If you are attracted to Christ, the Holy Spirit is working.

"We've already missed the Rapture, and now we live in what will soon become the most perilous period of history. Evangelists used to warn people that they could be struck by a car or die in a fire, and thus they should not put off coming to Christ. I'm telling you that should a car strike you or a fire consume you, it may be the most merciful way you can die. Be ready this time. Be ready. I will tell you how to get ready."

Bruce announced that his sermon title was "The Four Horsemen of the Apocalypse" and that he wanted to concentrate on the rider of the first horse—the white one.

Judd had never seen him so earnest, so inspired. As Bruce spoke he referred to his notes, to the books he'd brought, and to the Bible. He often wiped sweat from his brow. Judd noticed that most people were taking notes and that everyone was following along in the Bible.

Bruce explained that the book of Revelation spoke of what was to come after Christ had raptured his church. "Does anyone doubt we're in the last days?" he thundered. "Millions disappear, and then what? Some believe the tribulation period has already begun and that it began with the Rapture. We feel the trials and tribulations from the disappearances of our loved ones, don't we? But that is nothing compared to what is to come.

"During these seven years, God will pour out three consecutive sets of judgments—seven seals in a scroll, seven trumpets, and seven bowls. If the Rapture didn't get your attention, the judgments will. And if the judgments don't, you're going to die apart from God. Horrible as these judgments are, I urge you to see them as final warnings from a loving God who is not willing that any should perish."

Judd was struck to remember that he had heard old Pastor Billings preach on these same subjects. Judd had scoffed and quit listening. It all sounded too weird, too far-fetched, too unbelievable.

"I warn you," Bruce rumbled on several minutes later, "this is not for the faint of heart. Revelation 6:1-2 says, 'Now I saw when the Lamb opened one of the seals; and I heard one of the four living creatures saying with a voice like thunder, "Come and see." And I looked, and behold, a white horse. He who sat on it had a bow; and a crown was given to him, and he went out conquering and to conquer.' "

Bruce stepped back and began clearing off the lectern.

"Don't worry," he said, "I'm not finished." People applauded. Bruce said, "Are you clapping because you want me to finish, or because you want me to go on all afternoon?"

The people clapped all the more, including the Young Tribulation Force. If the others were like Judd, they were drinking this in, and they wanted more and more. Clearly Bruce had been in tune with what God was showing him. He said over and over that this was not new truth, that the commentaries he cited were decades old, and that the doctrine of the end times was much, much older than that. But those who had said such teaching was not to be taken literally, well, they had been left behind. All of a sudden it was all right to take Scripture at its word! If nothing else convinced people, losing so many to the Rapture had finally reached them.

Bruce stood before the bare lectern now with only his Bible in his hand. "I want to tell you now what I believe the Bible is saying about the rider of the white horse, the first horseman of the Apocalypse. I will not give my opinion. I will not draw any conclusions. I will simply leave it to God to help you draw any parallels that need to be drawn. I *will* tell you this in advance: This millenniums-old account reads as fresh to me as tomorrow's newspaper."

Vicki couldn't believe an hour had flown by since she'd last checked her watch. She was hungry, but she could sit there all day listening to Bruce. She knew where he was going with this imagery, but more amazing, she knew someone in the sanctuary right then who knew the rider of the white horse personally. Buck Williams had experienced the power of the Antichrist. Buck had convinced her that Nicolae Carpathia was the man, the enemy of God.

"Notice," Bruce continued, "that it is the Lamb who opens the first seal and reveals that horseman. The Lamb is Jesus Christ, the Son of God, who died for our sins, was resurrected, and recently raptured his church.

"Who is this first horseman? Clearly he represents the Antichrist and his kingdom. His purpose is 'conquering and to conquer.' He has a bow in his hand, a symbol of warfare, and yet there is no mention of an arrow. How will he conquer? Other passages say he is a 'willful king' and that he will win through smooth talking. He will usher in a false peace, promising world unity. Will he be victorious? Yes! He has a crown.

"The rider of the white horse is the Antichrist, who comes as a deceiver promising peace and uniting the world. The Old Testament says he will sign a treaty with Israel. He will appear to be their friend and protector, but in the end he will be their conqueror and destroyer."

Bruce said he could prove that he himself was not the Antichrist—not that anyone suspected him—because he would never promise peace. "The Bible is clear that we will have a year and a half of peace following the pact with Israel. But in the long run, I predict the opposite of peace. The other three horsemen are coming, and they bring war, famine, plagues, and death. That is not a popular message, not a warm fuzzy you can cling to this week. Our only hope is in Christ, and even in him we will likely suffer."

Bruce closed in prayer, and Vicki assumed everyone else felt as she did, that she could have stayed all day. She tried to get to Bruce, but he had already been intercepted in the aisle, near the Steeles. Vicki was behind him as people quizzed him.

"Are you saying Nicolae Carpathia is the Antichrist?" one said.

"Did you hear me say that?" Bruce said.

"No, but it was pretty clear. They're already talking on the news about his plans and some sort of a deal with Israel."

"Keep reading and studying," Bruce said.

"But it can't be Carpathia, can it? Does he strike you as a liar?"

"How does he strike you?" Bruce said.

"As a savior."

"Almost like a messiah?" Bruce pressed.

"Yeah!"

"There is only one Savior, one Messiah."

"I know, spiritually, but politically I mean. Don't tell me Carpathia's not what he seems to be."

"I'll tell you only what Scripture says," Bruce said, "and I urge you to listen carefully to the news. We must be wise as serpents and gentle as doves."

"That's how I would have described Carpathia," a woman said.

"Be careful," Bruce said, "about giving Christlike characteristics to anyone who doesn't align himself with Christ."

Vicki had been stopped by Bruce's comment about being wise and gentle. She couldn't wait to tell the rest of the Young Trib Force about that. Wise and gentle was what they had to be when they went back to school. So many people needed what the Young Trib Force had to offer, and yet so much danger awaited them too.

The four were strangely silent on the way home, and Vicki assumed that was because they had all been so moved by Bruce and his sermon. They ate as if they hadn't eaten for hours—which was true. Just before Vicki finished, the phone rang. Ryan, who loved to answer it, announced it was for her.

"Guy named Deacon," Ryan whispered. "Sounds old."

6

THIS Bub guy," Deacon said, "you know him well?"

"Never met him," Vicki said. "I told you. He was a friend of my brother's."

"You sure you got his name right? Beryl Gaylor, right?"

"Right. Why?"

"Are you sitting down?"

"Just tell me."

"He's dead, Vicki. When did you say you talked to him last?"

Vicki could hardly speak. "The day of the Rapture," she managed. "He was fine. What happened?"

"Here's what I heard from my friend in the police department," Deacon said. "Gaylor was missing for a few days, so they searched his and your brother's apartment. They already knew Edward—that's your brother's name, right?"

"Right."

"Had disappeared out of his car. There was no evidence Bub had disappeared, no pile of clothes, that kind of a thing. His answering machine had a message from a friend, asking him to come over and check the friend's basement with him. This guy reported a gas leak the night before. The gas company repairman came out to check the lines in the basement, and then told Bub's friend to find another place to stay for the night while he worked on it. When the guy called the gas company in the morning to see if he could move back in, he couldn't get through—you know, with the vanishings and everything.

"So he was asking Gaylor to go with him to see if his house was OK. The police went to the guy's house and found the gas truck in the driveway, the owner's car and Bub's car parked behind it. The house had blown."

Vicki let out a huge sigh. "So all three of them were killed?"

"No. It looks like the gas company guy disappeared. Because the house didn't blow until Bub and his friend got there. The cops figure the gas guy disappeared when everyone else did, before he could fix the leak. Those guys coming inside in the morning to check on him must have sparked something that ignited the gas."

Vicki didn't know what to say. "I hate this," she said finally. "It's like we have to talk to everyone right away because you never know what's going to happen to them."

"Had your brother tried to tell him?"

"Yes."

"You never know, Vicki," Deacon said. "Something may have gotten through to him, even after you talked to him."

Vicki couldn't imagine, but she could hope. She thanked Deacon and said she hoped to run into him again sometime. She moved to the couch in the living room and sat crying softly. In a few minutes, Judd came looking for her.

She told him what had happened. "You see why school is going to be such a waste of time?" she said.

He shook his head. "I know it seems that way, but more kids might listen to us there than anywhere else."

"But will we be allowed to say anything? I wonder what everybody else makes of the disappearances and Carpathia and all that."

"I wonder, who'll be there and who won't," Judd said. "How many teachers and coaches and office people were raptured, and how many students?"

Late that afternoon, as Judd surfed the Internet, he realized how dramatically his life had changed in just a couple of weeks. He used to look for reasons to do anything but study or read. Now he had become a newshound, an information freak. He read his Bible, studied his notes from Bruce's sermons and private messages. Now he was searching the Net for anything else he could find about what was going on.

He heard a ping and saw the mail icon appear at the lower right side of his screen. Judd clicked on it and found a message from Bruce. "Judd, I will tell you and perhaps Vicki things I would not feel comfortable sharing with Lionel and Ryan. It isn't that I don't trust them, but these would be highly confidential matters, potentially dangerous if spread around. The younger boys might not know how to keep secrets or understand how important that is.

"Two members of the Tribulation Force, Captain Steele and Buck Williams (whom you know), run in some very interesting circles and may be able to shed light on international matters that others wouldn't be exposed to. I won't be able to tell you everything, but when I do, I'll count on your confidence—you know what that means: total secrecy. OK?"

Judd felt special that Bruce would trust him like that. When he answered, he would assure Bruce he could be trusted. Meanwhile, Bruce told him the story of Buck Williams having met Israel's Chaim Rosenzweig, the botanist who had created a formula that allowed desert sands to bloom like a greenhouse. The result had made Israel one of the richest nations in the world. Buck Williams had interviewed him and become his friend after Rosenzweig had been named *Global Weekly's* Man of the Year. Rosenzweig had introduced Buck to Nicolae Carpathia.

"I've been most encouraged by your attitude, your intelligence, and your curiosity, Judd," Bruce wrote. "You might be interested in the text of an interview with Dr. Rosenzweig. You will find it at the following Web site."

Judd quickly clicked on it. Bruce was right. Judd found it fascinating.

Wallace Theodore of ABC TV's *Nightline* had interviewed Rosenzweig, and the text had been stored on the

site. Judd found the following most intriguing and
looked forward to when he might talk with Buck
Williams personally about it.

> **WT:** Dr. Rosenzweig, what can you tell us about
> Nicolae Carpathia?
> **CR:** I found him most impressive. So bright, so
> engaging, so articulate, so humble—
> **WT:** Excuse, me, sir. Humble?
> **CR:** Probably as humble as any leader I have ever
> met. Never have I seen a man like this.
> When he was invited to speak at the United
> Nations not a month ago, he almost declined, he felt
> so unworthy. But you heard the speech. I would
> have nominated him for Prime Minister of Israel, if
> he were eligible!
> Mr. Theodore, he has ideas upon ideas! He
> speaks so many languages that he hardly ever needs
> an interpreter, even for some of the remotest tribes.
> **WT:** How can Carpathia give away *your* formula?
> **CR:** I was more than happy to offer it. Botswana will
> soon be one of the most fertile countries in all of
> Africa, if not the world.
> **WT:** Having the formula made Israel a wealthy
> nation. Russia attacked you for the formula alone.
> **CR:** It's not about money, Mr. Theodore. I need
> none. Israel needs none.
> **WT:** Then what could Carpathia offer that is worthy
> of trade?
> **CR:** What has Israel prayed for since the beginning

of time as the chosen people of God? *Shalom*. Peace. 'Pray for the peace of Israel.'

WT: Many say God supernaturally protected you against the Russian attack. With God on your side, do you need to barter with Nicolae Carpathia for protection?

CR: We pray, we seek God, but in the meantime we believe he helps those who help themselves.

WT: And you're helping yourselves by . . . ?

CR: The formula is tied to Carpathia's disarmament policy. Once the world is disarmed, Israel should not have to worry about her borders. Any nation threatening Israel will suffer immediate extinction, using the weaponry available to the UN, 10 percent from each donating country. Imagine the firepower.

WT: But Carpathia doesn't believe in war.

CR: He also knows that the best way to keep the peace is to have the weapons to enforce it.

WT: And how long does this agreement between Israel and Carpathia last?

CR: Mr. Carpathia suggested that full rights to the formula would return to us after only seven years.

Judd froze. So there it was, the seven-year agreement between Israel and the Antichrist. Judd called Bruce at the church office. "Does this say what I think it says?"

"It sure does," Bruce said. "How many will recognize it for what it is, I can't say. But here's another tidbit for you, and please tell no one other than Vicki, and swear her to secrecy as well: Buck Williams has been invited to Israel for the signing of the treaty."

Judd shook his head. "Can you get him to tell us about it when he gets back?"

"No promises. He may have to lie low and not be seen with believers for a while. But if he can and we find a way to make it happen, I'll do my best."

On Monday a week later, Vicki awoke at the crack of dawn. Her schoolbooks had burned with her trailer, she barely remembered her class schedule, and she dreaded the thought of going back. She would miss Clarice Washington, Lionel's older sister, with whom she had sat on the school bus. Clarice had been raptured, and Vicki would not ride the bus anyway; she would ride with Judd. He would drop Lionel and Ryan off at Global Community Junior High on the way. What a joke.

She knew the first day back to high school would be chaotic when she saw what was happening at the junior high.

7

JUDD felt queasy when he joined the heavy traffic wending its way to the junior high school. Lionel had fallen strangely silent since the four kids got into the car, but Ryan had kept up a steady stream of chatter. The only thing Vicki had said was that she wondered if anyone would recognize her. Judd did not recall noticing her in the past, but there was a vast difference between the hard-looking, black-lipped, and black-eyelidded girl he had met and this preppy version that sat beside him now.

For many of the junior highers, this merely looked like the first day of school again. Everyone seemed carefully dressed and equipped, and their mothers or fathers dropped them off, watching anxiously as they headed inside.

"Wonder how many kids lost parents," Ryan said. "Man, have I got something for show-and-tell."

"They still do show-and-tell?" Vicki asked.

"No, but for sure everybody's gonna want to be telling

where they were and what they saw and who they know who's gone and all that."

Judd glanced in the rearview mirror and noticed Lionel nodding, but he was gazing out the window. Judd spoke softly to Vicki. "You gonna go to the office and see about getting new books?"

"I guess," she said. "They'll probably charge me."

"If you need any mon—"

"I know, Judd," she said quickly. "Thanks. I'll let you know. But I'm going to find a job soon."

"You don't have to do that."

"Oh, yes I do. I'm not a freeloader or a charity case."

"Let me get out here!" Ryan said. "I see some of the guys!"

"Just wait," Judd said. "We've got to talk about what you're going to say about your situation."

"My situation? What do you mean? My parents are dead. How else can I say it? You think I'm going to start crying or something? I don't think I can cry anymore."

Judd pulled into the line circling the entrance, and they crawled along. "Both you and Lionel have to come up with some story about where you're staying."

"You mean lie?"

" 'Course not. But you don't have to tell people you're living with other kids. Just say you're staying with someone from church."

"Good idea," Lionel said. "I'm not sure I'm ready to tell everybody that I'm the only one left in my family. But I'll bet they try to get us talking about what we think happened. If they ask me, I'll tell 'em."

Judd pulled over and shifted into Park. "You guys are sure you want to walk all the way home after school?"

"It's not that far," Lionel said. "Anyway, it's either wait here for you for an hour or go home. Nothing else to do."

Judd nodded. Vicki said, "We're going to want to hear all about it, so try to remember everything."

"All right, all right," Ryan said. "Let's go already! Unlock the doors."

"They might ask kids whose parents are gone to fill out new emergency forms," Judd said.

"And we'll put down Bruce Barnes's name and the church's phone number," Ryan said. "We've been through this a gazillion times."

Judd unlocked the doors, and it seemed Lionel was out as quickly as Ryan. "All of a sudden I feel like a parent," Judd said, pulling back into traffic. "I could've waited ten years to start worrying about what a couple of junior highers are going to do all day."

Vicki just smiled and nodded. She looked tense.

In the parking lot at the former Prospect High School, teachers and coaches and office staff directed traffic and spoke through bullhorns. "Don't worry about parking stickers today! We'll deal with that later! Check the bulletin boards for class and schedule changes! We'll be on a shortened program today, starting in the field house for an all-school assembly! Sit with your class!"

"Homeroom?" Judd asked through the window.

"No, your whole class. Freshmen in the west balcony, sophomores in the east balcony, juniors in the back on the main floor, seniors in front."

Vicki appeared pale and on the verge of tears as she got out of the car. "You want to stay with me for that opening assembly?" Judd said.

She sighed. "I really would. You think they'd let me?"

"You don't look like a freshman anyway," he said. "You may have to join your class if they go together, but otherwise, what are they going to do, kick you out?"

Judd waited as she stopped to ask a teacher what she should do about her books. "If that's all you lost, girl," the teacher said, "consider yourself lucky. We'll deal with that at the assembly. Don't be late."

The halls were as crowded as ever until they got into the field house. When the opening bell rang it was clear that the place, usually jammed for an all-school assembly, was only 70 to 75 percent filled. The teaching staff was depleted by about the same percentage, made obvious because they were sitting in rows on the platform behind the lectern.

As Judd and Vicki sat with the juniors, the principal, Mrs. Laverne Jenness, stepped to the microphone. "Welcome back," she said. "I'm proud to announce, in case you were under a rock and missed the news or the brand-spanking-new sign out front, that you are no longer Prospect Knights. You are Nicolae Carpathia Doves!"

She may have expected an enthusiastic response, because she appeared taken aback at a smattering of boos and laughter. But when the teachers jumped to their feet in applause, most of the students began cheering too. Judd thought at first that they were just mocking the teachers—as usual—but it soon became clear the celebrants were serious.

Mrs. Jenness beamed. "I'm so pleased that you're pleased," she said. "We recognize that this decision was made without your input, but there was nearly unanimous support at the administrative level. Really, your response is most gratifying. There had long been talk that our school name, steeped in history as it was, was unimaginative, merely echoing the name of the town in which we reside. And a knight is, of course, a warrior, which has long been an offensive mascot.

"To be named after so great and humble a leader and pacifist like UN Secretary-General Nicolae Carpathia, well, that should make us all proud."

The students chanted, "Nicolae High! Nicolae High! Nicolae High!"

Mrs. Jenness smiled, then raised her hands for silence. "I recognize that we reconvene only weeks after the most tragic event to ever curse our planet. Many of you lost friends and loved ones and will be grieving. Thank you for recognizing the importance of returning for your education, regardless. As you can imagine, the counseling services offered by our school district have been taxed beyond their limits. But as you see a need for a professional to talk to, please put your name on the waiting list. Don't be ashamed or afraid to ask. We're all trying to get through this."

Judd felt a nudge, and Vicki nodded toward a couple of seniors several rows ahead. "Are those Bibles?" she said.

"Looks like it," Judd said. "You know them?"

Vicki shook her head. "Hey, look."

A football coach Judd recognized approached the seniors and knelt in the aisle. He spoke earnestly to them, smiling, but came away with both Bibles. As he hurried past, Judd reached out and whispered, "What was that all about, Coach Handlesman?"

"Mind your own business, Thompson," Handlesman said. "We haven't allowed Bibles here since before you were born."

"But even now, after what happened?"

"Especially now," the coach said, moving on.

"Remember what they look like, Vicki," Judd said. "We're going to need all the friends we can get."

Mrs. Jenness droned on about the difficulties and trauma, the mixed classes, the complicated inconveniences. "Bear with us as we try to regroup and reschedule. The ratio of missing students and faculty seems fairly even, so class size should remain approximately the same as before.

"Those of you who lost textbooks, deal with that in each class and make your purchases in the bookstore by Friday. Now before I dismiss you, I would like to ask for your help. After an international tragedy that has struck so close to home, it's only natural to want to talk about it. It's therapeutic, and our counselors have advised me to let you have at it. Today in your abbreviated classes, we have asked faculty to get the housekeeping announcements out of the way, the book business taken care of, and any outlining of new class expectations dealt with quickly. Then they are free to supervise group discussions.

Some of you will need to tell your stories of loss and fear. Others may choose not to speak of their ordeals. Please be respectful of those students and don't badger them for details before they're ready to be forthcoming.

"Now, here's what you can do for me. As you know, there has been widespread speculation about the cause of the vanishings. According to our consultants, part of the healing process—the making sense of this—involves forming and expressing your opinions on this. But I must remind you of the strict rule of the separation of church and state that has helped make this country great. We are a public institution, and this is not a forum in which we should espouse religious views.

"I am aware that one of the many explanations for what happened is religious in nature. I'm not saying it has no validity. Like most of you, I lost extended family members. Their closest relatives reminded me that those who disappeared predicted this and told us exactly what to make of such an occurrence.

"Though this happened among my own kin, and while those stories may even bear some scrutiny, I will not discuss them on school property during school hours. I'm asking that you not either. Even if I believed with all my heart that this was the best explanation for the disappearances—which, you may rest assured, I emphatically do not—I would maintain that this is the wrong venue in which to propagate that view. Thank you for understanding. I urge you to hold your questions until class time, unless anyone has something pressing that is appropriate to ask in front of the corporate body.

"All right, then. Oh, yes, son. A question from a junior boy. Please stand and state your name and your question loudly enough for me to hear and repeat it into the microphone. And if it is not something that pertains to the whole school, I would ask—"

"It pertains, ma'am!" Judd called out, rising, his heart thundering. "Judd Thompson, and I was just wondering if you would clarify this then!"

"Clarify which part, Mr. Thompson? What is unclear?"

"Why freedom of speech is extended only to those who hold certain views of what has happened?"

"This is not a freedom-of-speech issue, young man. It's a church-and-state issue. Thank you for raising it, but please don't make something of it that it is not. Dismissed!"

Judd was short of breath and knew his face was red as he gathered up his stuff. "I can't believe you did that," Vicki said, and he looked close to see if she was embarrassed or seemed to disapprove.

"That wasn't me," he said, shaking his head. "That was my evil twin. I've never done anything like that before in my life. I don't think I ever even paid attention in an assembly before."

"Hey, Judd, way to go, man," one of his classmates said, punching him on the shoulder. "Way to be raucous!"

Judd wanted to tell the boy he had been serious, but the guy was lost in the crowd. Coach Handlesman shouldered his way through to Judd and Vicki. "I liked you better when you made trouble by being a no-account, Thompson. Now you're angling to be a smart aleck, eh?"

"Nah. I just don't think there should be restrictions on people trying to figure out the truth."

"Cry me a river," the coach said, disappearing in the crowd.

"Be careful," Vicki said as they prepared to split up. "We don't want to be *too* conspicuous."

"What's your first class?" Judd said.

"Phys ed," she said. "Yours?"

"Psych."

"Should be interesting," she said.

Judd nodded but noticed Vicki was distracted. She was looking past him, and her face paled. "Shelly?" she said. "Shelly! Is that you?"

Judd had wanted to tell Vicki he would be praying for her, but that sounded cheesy, and she was preoccupied anyway. And his psych class with Mr. Shellenberger was at the complete other end of the school.

VICKI had not intended to ignore Judd or abandon him, but he was gone before she knew it. She had not seen or heard from her former neighbor Shelly since the day they both discovered what had happened. To Vicki's horror, Shelly looked the same as she had that day. She stared into the distance as if she had seen things unspeakable.

"Are you all right, Shel?" Vicki asked.

Shelly looked at her, flat brown hair straight and life-less, her pale green eyes vacant. "I don't know you," she said.

"Sure you do, Shelly. It's me, Vicki."

Shelly furrowed her brow and squinted. "No way," she said. "Vick, what happened to you?"

"To me?" It was out before Vicki could rein it in. Shelly was the one who didn't look like herself. Vicki may have been made up differently and dressed differently, but Shelly looked as if someone had punched her in the stomach.

"It's really you, Vicki?"

Vicki nodded. "Shelly, I know what happened. I lost my whole family, and—"

"I don't want to talk about it, OK? I really don't."

"But as awful as it was, Shelly, I—"

"Don't," she said, trembling.

"Leave her alone," an older girl said, glaring at Vicki. "Don't you know what happened to her?"

"No! What happened?"

"Don't tell her, Joyce!" Shelly said.

"You just get to class, Shelly. And don't let anybody make you say anything you don't want to say."

Shelly looked apologetically at Vicki and moved away. Joyce turned on Vicki. "Are you Byrne?"

"Yes, Joyce. Just dressing a little different these days."

"I'll say. Your trailer burned, right?"

Vicki nodded.

"So where you livin'?"

"Mount Prospect, with people from my church."

"That explains the threads. They makin' you dress that way?"

Vicki shook her head.

"So you didn't hear Shelly's story 'cause you haven't been back to the park?"

"Right."

"She was baby-sitting for the Fischers. You knew them."

Vicki nodded, moving toward the girls' locker room.

"One of the kids starts crying just when the parents get home. Shelly goes in to check on her, and the kid's really wailing. She picks her up, and that gets the little guy crying, so she picks him up too. Now she's got two squalling kids in her arms as the Fischers come in the door. She's about to explain that they just then woke up when both kids disappear and the parents too. Mom and Dad, poof, clothes in a pile right where they stood. The babies, gone with their pj's draped over Shelly's arms.

"Tell you the truth, it would have scared me to death, Vicki, but I wish I'd have seen it. Well, you know Shelly. She can't let it go. She's playing it over and over in her mind. I saw her the next afternoon, wandering through the trailer park, not saying a word to anybody."

"I saw her late that morning," Vicki said. "Same thing."

"I finally got her to tell me. Now everybody knows and nobody talks to her, figuring she doesn't want to talk about it. Which is true. But I think she feels like it was her fault somehow."

"Where you headed, Joyce?"

"Health. Next door here."

"You know what happened, don't you?"

"The disappearances? Sure. Jesus came back. What else? It's not like we haven't heard that all our lives."

"You believe that?"

"Sure, don't you?"

"Well, yeah," Vicki said, "but I didn't know you did."

"Don't worry, I'm not gonna get saved or anything. But look who went and who was left. Your mom and dad, right? And your little sister. But you were left. So was I. My whole family. How about Eddie? Bet your brother's still around."

"Gone," Vicki said.

69

"No kiddin'? Disappeared?"

Vicki nodded.

"That might prove me wrong. He was no Holy Joe, was he?"

"He became a believer after he got to Mich—"

"See? I knew it! What else could it be, Vick? Huh?"

"But that doesn't make you want to be a Christian?"

"No way! I still think the whole thing sounds wacky."

"Even though you believe it's true?"

"*Especially* because I believe it's true. Hey, I *know* it's true. If that was God's idea of how to do things, I want no part of it. How about you?"

"I believe it too. And I plan to be included when Jesus comes back again."

"Well, good for you, girl. You're not going to set your sights on me, are ya?"

"Well, I wish you would—"

"Oh, you are, aren't you? I'm going to be a project, just like my mom was to Mrs. Fischer. Save your breath. I don't need any convincing. I believe, and I've chosen. So turn those Bible guns on somebody else. Like Shelly. She'd be perfect. Gotta go."

Psychology was one class Judd had actually enjoyed, and Mr. Shellenberger was the reason. He was a tall, fleshy man with a generous nose and receding, wavy hair. He had a sonorous voice, a superior manner, and he loved to bestow his opinions on one and all. He was in rare form today.

"OK, class," he began, "listen up. Parking-lot stickers

in the office, new books in the bookstore—title, if you forgot already, is on the board. Now let's do some practical psychology. Let's vent our traumas and deepest fears for the benefit and enjoyment of all. I'll start."

The class chuckled.

"First, is there anyone in here who will turn me into the thought police if I discuss the religious theory? Anyone? No one? Don't be intimidated. If you're going to gum up the school year with an expensive lawsuit, tell me now, and I'll avoid the subject. Speak now or forever hold your peace. Very well, the God thing:

"Jesus didn't come to get the good people and leave the bad. There are some who actually believe that, you know. Anyone here want to stake claim to that view? Nothing to be ashamed of. Some very respected people have fessed up to it. Come on. Anyone? No one? Mr. Thompson! Really? I thought you acted the agitator this morning just to get a rise out of our fearless leader. That was out of character for you, though. Well, isn't this just too interesting? Do you care to discuss it?"

Judd shrugged. He was no match for an intellect, a presence, like Mr. Shellenberger. Judd had considered hiding his belief, but he wouldn't have been able to live with that much cowardice.

"I've already stated my opinion," the teacher said, "so I promise not to try to shred your belief system. Tell me, is this new for you? Apparently it is, because if you had held this belief before, and your theory is right, you'd have been taken by Jesus too, right?"

Judd nodded.

"So, who convinced you? Let me guess. A parent."

"In a way."

"Hmm. One that was left or one that was taken?"

"Both were taken."

Mr. Shellenberger suddenly grew serious, his face grave. His volume fell, and he appeared truly different. "Mr. Thompson, forgive me if I have offended you. I meant to ask at the beginning how many of you lost immediate family members in the vanishings. Let me back up and do that."

Half a dozen of the thirty kids raised their hands.

"How many lost extended family?"

Eight or ten more raised their hands.

"How many of you lost people you knew well or cared about?"

Another half dozen or so.

"And how many of you feel almost isolated from this, having lost virtually no one in your orbit?"

Four kids raised their hands.

"Now then," the teacher continued, his tone still subdued, "regardless of my personal view of this—which you may be assured I will impart—I do not take lightly the losses. Mr. Thompson, I am sorry for your losses. Did you lose other family members?"

"My brother and sister, twins."

Mr. Shellenberger stood towering over the students, his arms folded, a hand under his chin. "Mm-hm," he said. "Religious family?"

Religious was not a word Judd's family used. But he knew what the teacher was driving at. He nodded.

"And you were the only one left behind."

"Right," Judd said.

"It is not surprising at all that you find comfort in ascribing these losses to something divine. It has to make you feel better to believe your family is in heaven with God."

"Somewhat."

"I wouldn't denigrate that. You will outgrow it, but I'm sure it's of great benefit to you now. It may be years before you will be able to differentiate the very real confidence you feel from the defense mechanism your mind has provided."

"So I believe because I have to?"

"Excellent. Exactly. Don't get me wrong. Right now this is as real to you as if it were literally true. Our perceptions, as I have said many times, are our realities. If you perceive I despise you and you will never succeed in this class, that is reality to you. If you believe the opposite, regardless of what you know about me, the opposite will be real for you."

Judd wondered why he had never detected the silliness of the man's logic before.

"Let me ask you, Mr. Thompson, what you now believe is the reason that your family was taken and you were not?"

"I was never really a believer. They were."

"Really? Where did you fall short?"

"I just told you. I didn't buy into it. I knew what was being taught. When I was younger I was more devout."

"But not devout enough?"

"I never actually made the commitment to Christ."

"Mm-hm. Class, anyone? We're not arguing here, and I would be loath to try to talk Mr. Thompson out of a belief that has to be therapeutic for him, but someone tell me what he's really feeling now."

"Survivor's remorse," came a low voice from the back. "Just like soldiers who come back from war."

"Very good," Mr. Shellenberger said. "I'm not asking you to concede the point today or even this year, Mr. Thompson. But file it away. Let it work on you a little. You feel like the unworthy one, and yet you are the lone survivor."

"That's why I was the survivor! I *was* the unworthy one."

"You're asking, 'Why me?' "

"I know why."

"OK, very interesting. Someone else?"

A girl raised her hand. "You were going to tell us your opinion. You've said what it was not, so what was it?"

"Well, it was *not* a lot of things. I don't believe it was space aliens. I don't believe an enemy could be so surgical, taking certain ones and leaving others. No doubt it was something cosmic, perhaps even psychic or metaphysical. But the result was physical. I lean toward the hypothesis of Nicolae Carpathia and Dr. Chaim Rosenzweig of Israel, who ascribe the phenomenon to some nuclear reaction. We have stockpiled so many nuclear weapons that it was only a matter of time before something in the atmosphere—electricity, energy, magnetism, something—triggered a reaction.

"I should say this, however. Admittedly mine is a

personal observation and far from scientific. But it seems to me that those who were taken, generally and on the whole, mind you, were of a slightly lower intellect than those who were left. I come from an extremely intelligent and highly educated extended family. We lost no blood relatives. I did lose colleagues I respected and admired, but in fairness, I have to say they were not quite the academic equals of those left behind. I have no idea what that means."

You sure don't, Judd thought.

9

VICKI'S first-period class met in the gym normally used for volleyball practice. The girls sat on the floor and got the standard announcements about books, parking permits, and even gym clothes. Then her P.E. teacher sat on the floor and gathered the class around her. Mrs. Waltonen, in her midforties, was thin and dark with short hair and glasses.

"What do you make of all the children disappearing?" she said. "That's the part I can't figure out."

"You can figure out the rest?" someone said.

"Well, no. But if this is what a lot of people think it is, why would all the babies, even unborn babies, and toddlers and little kids be taken?"

"What do most people think it is?" a girl asked.

"You know," Mrs. Waltonen said. "The subject we aren't supposed to raise."

"Most people think it's that?" a tiny girl next to Vicki

said. "I thought that was just a few of the crazies. I don't think that, and nobody I know does."

"We're not supposed to discuss it, at any rate," Mrs. Waltonen said. "Let's just express some feelings."

"I have a question," Vicki said, raising her hand.

Mrs. Waltonen squinted at her, and Vicki knew the woman was wondering who she was.

"Vicki Byrne," Vicki said. "Um—"

"Without all the makeup," the teacher said. "I like the look."

Vicki blushed. "Thanks."

"Your makeup disappear?" someone said, and several laughed.

"What's your question, Vicki?"

"If you think most people think what happened was what you said, why can't we talk about it?"

Mrs. Waltonen shook her head and sighed. "You heard what I heard. I don't know. Seems nothing should be off-limits now. We have the freedom to talk about everything else under the sun, including stuff I never thought I'd hear in public, but not God. No way."

"Then don't!" someone called out. "If I hear another person say they think Jesus did this, I'm gonna croak!"

"All right," Mrs. Waltonen said. "Let's move on." She asked for a show of hands for those who had lost family members and so on.

Someone asked, "Did you lose anyone?"

Mrs. Waltonen pressed her lips together. "I'm, ah, trying to get through this right now," she said, her voice quavering. "We lost a grandchild."

78

To Vicki it seemed the groan of pain and sympathy came from the whole class.

"How old?"

"A baby. Not six months."

"That's awful."

"We miss her terribly. Her father, my son-in-law, also disappeared. And we lost my husband's sister and her whole family, her husband and three kids."

"No way God did that," a girl said.

Several others nodded and grunted in agreement. Vicki wanted to scream. Instead, she asked, "Anything different about your sister-in-law and her family? Any clues why them?"

"Well, see, I can't talk about that without getting in trouble."

"Talk about it!" a girl hollered. "We won't tell."

"No!" someone else said. "We're not supposed to, so let's not!"

Vicki turned to see who had said that, and while she couldn't tell, from the looks on the faces behind her, it could have been anyone. They were angry. In the back she saw a few confused, sorrowful faces.

Wasn't this just a little too obvious? The one explanation that made sense, that most people were aware of, that many had been warned about, was the one they were not allowed to discuss. And why? Because of the separation of church and state? Vicki suddenly felt very old.

Like Judd, she found herself bolder than she had ever been. She had been so lazy and lackadaisical in gym class that she usually skipped it or sat out, making up a litany

79

of complaints, illnesses, and injuries. She had never responded to Mrs. Waltonen or to any other teachers. It just hadn't been her style.

Now Vicki felt like an agitator. A rebel for another cause. She had been against the status quo before. But now she was *for* something. "If we're not going to talk about what obviously is the truth about what happened," she said, "let's hear some other explanation."

That started it. Angry words were tossed about, several girls raising their voices. "You believe it was God?" several said. "Where've you been? And why are you still here?"

Finally Mrs. Waltonen calmed them. "Vicki is right," she said. "Let's hear what others think happened."

Silence.

"Surely someone has an opinion."

A soft-spoken girl in the back said, "Who could ever know? I mean, really. Certain people disappeared; others didn't. Some in the same family. Almost as many women and men, but all babies and young children. I know a twelve-year-old who is still here, and a friend of mine said she knows a ten-year- old, but I don't know. These kids' mothers are wailing all over the place. This is like the worst horror movie you could ever see."

"Yeah, but we're *in* this one."

"Yeah."

"Personally," a girl sitting by herself said, "I think it was some big science experiment that went bad."

"That could be."

"Yeah, I never thought of that."

"Right, like a scientist figured out how to beam stuff

like in the old *Star Trek* movies, only he beamed the
wrong people and can't bring them back."

"I think they're coming back," one said.

"You do? Why?"

"I have to. I'd go nuts otherwise. If I lost somebody in
a wreck or I knew they died of some disease, that would
be one thing. But these people didn't die. At least I hope
they didn't."

"Some people died."

"Not the ones who disappeared. Just people who,
like, got run over because of someone else disappearing."

"You don't know the ones who disappeared are still
alive."

"I do," Vicki said.

"You can't know that!"

"Fine, but I do."

"You might believe it, Vicki, but you can't know."

"Then why do I know?"

"You don't. You just think you know."

"If my granddaughter is alive," Mrs. Waltonen said,
"I'd like to know that. I agree you can't really know, Vicki.
But tell me why you think so, and tell me where you
think she is."

Vicki looked around. It seemed people were actually
curious. "But isn't somebody going to get me in trouble
with the church/state police? I guess my freedom of
speech goes only so far."

"So you think Mrs. Waltonen's baby is in heaven with
Jesus."

"I know she is."

"You can't know that! And if you did, you'd be there too!"

"If I had known in advance, I would be, yes. With my parents and my brother and sister."

"Whoop, there it is!" a girl cried out. "You lost your family, so you've got to come up with some nice explanation. That's all right. You're entitled. No offense to Mrs. Waltonen, but you two can believe whatever you want so you feel better about who you lost. That's all. I'd like to know where the girls are who aren't here today. What about that fat girl who was such a good athlete? And those twins nobody could stand? And that girl with the bad face and the—"

"All right," Mrs. Waltonen said, "I think that's enough detail. I have a list here of the girls in the class who are known to have disappeared in the vanishings. The ones you mentioned are included, yes. Mary Alice—you know her? She's out sick today. And Francis also disappeared. There are two others, Barb and Sue, who are assumed to have disappeared."

The girls sat silently for a moment, a few weeping. Finally someone said, "Do you hear how this sounds? We're sitting here talking about people we knew disappearing."

And no one, Vicki thought, *seems to want to face the truth.* As wild as the truth seemed, it sure made more sense than the crazy ideas she'd heard.

"Is there anybody else who believes this was the rapture of the church?" Vicki blurted, and she scanned the group.

It seemed everyone responded at once, waving her off, groaning, saying no. But she saw the look of hope on the teacher's face, and a couple of girls at the edge of the group just looked sadly at her.

"Stop talking about it!" came a voice over the din. "We were told not to, so don't! You're pushing your personal religious beliefs on us, and that's wrong!"

Vicki was mad. "I don't accuse you of forcing your beliefs on me when you tell me it was aliens or *Star Trek* scientists. Don't you have a brain? Can't you think for yourself? Do you need to hide behind some rule about the separation of church and state, so you don't hear something that might mess up your mind?"

"Vicki!" Mrs. Waltonen said. "That's enough."

"Can I ask about the separation thing then?" Vicki said.

"It depends."

"It's just a question about the history of it. Where did it come from?"

"I've heard different theories," Mrs. Waltonen said. "I know it's not in the Constitution, but I believe it came from those who wanted to protect citizens from having their religious freedom threatened by the government. One of our freedoms is the right to believe and to worship without the government telling us what church we have to belong to."

"That's what I thought," Vicki said, knowing she had heard something about this, maybe from her dad, whom she had ignored. "So when did it get turned around to protect the government from religion?"

"I'm sorry?"

"You said the separation of church and state was designed to keep the government out of the church. Now it's used to keep the church out of the government."

Mrs. Waltonen raised her eyebrows, but several girls said things like, "That's the way it should be!"

"Even if it was a law, which it's not," Vicki said, "it would be no good if it violated the right to free speech. I have the freedom to say whatever I want, except here."

"Good!"

"Yeah, shut up!"

"Let her talk!"

"She's talked enough! And when did she start talking anyway? I don't even remember her from this class!"

"You do too! That's Vicki Byrne!"

"Well, when did she start caring about anything?"

"What's happening to us?" someone said, tears in her voice. "I thought we were supposed to discuss this to start coming to some closure."

"Closure? You sound like a talk-show host! How are we going to have closure on something like this?"

"That's right," Vicki said, "especially when certain theories are out of bounds?"

The bell rang, and the gym quickly emptied, but Vicki noticed that Mrs. Waltonen was gazing at her. When Vicki returned the glance, the teacher said nothing but did not look away. Vicki felt as if Mrs. Waltonen was trying to communicate something to her—exactly what, she did not know. The quiet girls in the back were also some of the last to leave, and they peeked at her too.

Was there something here, some core of a group that

might agree with her or at least be willing to listen? Vicki decided to spend the rest of the day bringing these issues up in every class. Maybe she wouldn't be as aggressive as she had been in gym class, but she would say enough to get people arguing about freedom of speech and whether God had anything to do with the disappearances. Somehow she would get an inkling of how many believers or potential believers there were at this school.

Vicki didn't want one more person to die before she at least had the chance to tell them what she believed.

10

ON THE way to his last class before lunch, Judd saw the two senior boys whose Bibles had been confiscated during the assembly. One was tall and blond, the other stockier and dark-haired. He didn't know their names, but if his memory was right, they were smart kids—science club, honor roll types. "Hey," he said, approaching them, "are you believers?"

They looked wary. "Why? Are you?"

He had to take the chance. "I am."

"How do we know you're not playing us, trying to get us in trouble?" the blond said.

"You don't."

"Well," Dark Hair said, "how did you become a believer?"

"Lost my family," Judd said. "I knew the truth all along."

"Then you should know what Christians are called during this period."

"You mean tribulation saints?"

The two looked at each other and smiled. They extended their hands. "John," the blond said.

"Mark," the other said.

"You're kidding, right?" Judd said. "John and Mark?"

"We're cousins."

"But I mean—"

"We know what you mean. Yeah, we were named after the disciples. Churchgoers all our lives. We lost everybody in our family except one aunt. We're living with her and going to a church in Arlington Heights. What's your story?"

Judd ran it down quickly. Then, "Gotta go, but let's talk again. We should get our church groups together sometime."

"That's for sure," John said. "Especially if they're not going to even let us carry our Bibles to school. Coach Handlesman said we might not even get them back."

"What? You're kidding!"

They shook their heads.

"Are we going to be in a police state or what?" Judd said.

"It's like martial law," Mark said.

Judd waved as he headed toward Current History. "See ya tomorrow."

"Yeah," John called after him, "if we're still free men."

"Not funny, John!" came the gruff voice of Coach Handlesman.

Judd began to wonder if he and Vicki, and even John and Mark, should be more covert and lie low. It was one thing to be a bold witness, but if they got kicked out or were known as dangerous people to be seen with, what good would they be?

His history teacher, an old spinster named Miss June, looked as if she had been through a war. Normally tidy and fastidious, today she looked disheveled. Her shoes were scuffed, her blouse wrinkled, her hair pinned in place without much thought. Her fingers trembled, and she sat behind her desk rather than standing as usual.

"Well, class, I have been through some things in my day, but I never would have dreamed that hearing everyone's stories would have been nearly as traumatic as experiencing this tragedy oneself. I'm wondering if you might agree that we have had enough talk on this subject by now, and perhaps we can talk about the rest of the quarter."

No one said anything.

"All right then?" she said.

"Um, no," a boy said from the back row. "What's to talk about? You're going to streamline the course because of the time we missed, and we'll start getting assignments tomorrow. What else is there?"

"We could talk about what we're going to be studying," she said.

"We already know that. Current History is current history. Let's talk about who's not coming back to this class."

Miss June pursed her lips and gave the boy a disgusted look. She studied her attendance printout, but when she began announcing the names of seven students who were either confirmed disappeared (four), whereabouts

89

unknown (one), and ill (two), her voice broke. Soon she could not continue.

"What in the world is wrong, Miss June?" a girl said. "How many people did you lose?"

But she could not speak. She just pressed a hand to her mouth and shook her head.

"This I've got to hear," the boy behind Judd said, and Judd glared at him.

"Give her a break," he said. "If you didn't lose anybody, at least be sensitive to those of us who did."

The boy pantomimed as if playing a violin.

"Can we talk about it among ourselves?" a girl said. Miss June nodded. "Because I know it wasn't a religious thing."

"We're not supposed to talk about that!"

"Oh, who's going to stop us?" the girl said. "Anyway, I'm saying it *wasn't* that. How can they have a problem with that?"

Judd's resolve to keep quiet disappeared. "You *know* it wasn't a religious thing?" he said.

"That's right," she said. "Not one person in my church disappeared. So what does that tell you?"

"That you don't believe in Jesus!" a husky guy in the back called out, and several laughed, including him.

"But we do!" she said. "We all do! We believe in all the sons of God."

"What does that mean?"

"We're not supposed to be—"

"Put a sock in it! I want to know what her church believes!"

"We believe that everybody's a son of God, like Jesus. Buddha, Confucius, Muhammad, Jesus, all the great moral leaders and great teachers."

Judd said, "So you believe Jesus is *a* son of God but not *the* Son of God."

"Not the only one, no. We're all children of God."

"So Jesus isn't God."

"Of course not, silly. God is God. There is only one God."

"So you don't believe the Bible."

"Of course we do. We accept all the sacred writings."

"Like what?"

"The Bible, the Torah, the Talmud, the—"

"And they all say that Jesus is God and is the only way to God?" Judd said.

"No! None of them say that! God is not the exclusive property of Christianity. There are many roads to God."

"The Bible says Jesus is God and that he's the only way to God."

"I don't believe that."

"That it's true or that the Bible says it?"

"Either one!"

"Then that's why you're still here."

"Oh!" someone shouted. "He burned you! But he's still here too, ain't he?"

"That's enough," Miss June said, rising and wiping her nose. "This is the very reason we're not to be getting into this aspect of it. Now if you're going to insist on discussing this, let's keep it nonsectarian."

"What does that mean?"

"Keep religion out of it, especially specific ones."

"Yeah," someone said, "like those ones where everyone was left behind!"

Miss June was weeping again. "I don't see any humor in this! Aren't you people the least bit scared? I'm terrified! I can make no sense of this, and there seems no recourse. If someone would come forward and take credit for it, make some demands, tell how he or she did it, we could get our minds around it. But this . . . this . . . crazy, unexplainable mystery! Every morning I wake up and pray it was a dream, that it will end, that it will all be made plain. Talk about it, kids. Talk about how it made you feel."

That served to silence the class. It was clear they didn't want to talk about it. Judd glanced around. The kids were somber again. No wisecracks. "It scared me to death," he said. "I was on an airplane when it happened."

The classroom was deathly still as Judd spoke. "The guy next to me disappeared while I was dozing. He was a big, heavy guy, and I couldn't figure out at first how he could have climbed over me without waking me. Then I saw his clothes there in a pile. Everybody else was discovering people missing at the same time. What a mess! I'm amazed there wasn't more panic. People thought their seatmates had gone to the bathroom, but too many were gone, and what was with all the piles of clothes and shoes and jewelry and glasses?"

Judd told how he had lost his whole immediate family, but he said nothing about how he knew what had happened. He just wanted to get kids talking, trying to find out who leaned his way and who might already be a believer. His own high school had already been named after the Antichrist, and he knew he and Vicki were going to need all the friends they could get.

At lunchtime Judd looked for Vicki. Juniors and freshmen shared the cafeteria, but he had not known her before and had no idea where she sat. He finally spotted her in a corner with a bunch of girls who looked the way Vicki described herself before the Rapture. They must have been friends from her trailer park.

Judd wanted to talk with her, but he didn't want to barge in either. He sat near their table and heard some of the conversation. The girls were telling Vicki they missed her and wondered what had happened to her. "I've been hammered every night since," one said. "How else do you cope with something like this?"

A heavyset girl sitting next to Vicki said, "Apparently you change your life and get preppy all of a sudden."

The others smiled. Vicki didn't. "I lost my whole family, you know," she said.

"You lost your mind too," the girl said. "Look at you."

Judd decided it was time to give Vicki an out. He walked past her table so she could see him. If she didn't want to acknowledge him, that was all right too. Maybe she didn't want to confirm that she even ran with a crowd that looked like him. That would make her transformation too complete.

Vicki was thrilled to see Judd, and she jumped at the chance to escape. "Judd!" she said. "Can I sit with you? We need to talk."

"Sure."

"What'sa matter?" a girl said. "We're not good enough for you anymore?"

"I'm not good enough for you anymore," Vicki said. "Since I'm wearing borrowed clothes and they don't look like yours—"

"They look like somebody's mother's clothes," the big girl said, but Vicki didn't respond. She and Judd took their trays outside.

"There's a reason these look like someone's mother's clothes," she whispered.

He nodded. They brought each other up to date on their mornings. "This is going to be hard, isn't it?" he said.

"You're telling me. But, Judd, I just feel like this is where we're supposed to be, doing what we're meant to be doing."

"Out loud or in secret? Sounds like neither of us got very far by being open."

"I found a few people I think might be with us, and those two seniors—"

"John and Mark," Judd said.

"Yeah. We've got to stick together somehow."

"We need more people. We can't just be a secret, private club. We've got to do something."

"I've been thinking about that, Judd," Vicki said. "I think there's something we can do."

"That won't get us kicked out of Nicolae High?"

"If we do it right. Your computer is the latest thing, right?"

"There's not much it can't do."

"Including publishing?"

"Desktop publishing? 'Course. It was made for that."

Vicki started gathering up her stuff. "Walk with me," she said as she took her tray inside. "And let's talk to Lionel and Ryan about this when we get home."

"About what?"

"An underground newspaper. We'll have to think of a good title for it, but it will tell people's stories without giving away their identities. We can use lots of prophecy and stuff from Bruce, and we can just leave piles of them around where anyone can get them. They don't have to be long, but we have to keep them coming. If Bruce is right and we can put a few predictions in there that actually come true, kids will want these. Who knows how many kids might become believers?"

Judd slid his tray onto the retrieval rack and stood back, looking at Vicki. "Why didn't I think of that?" he said.

"You like the idea?"

"It's perfect!"

"That's another thing we need more of in the Young Trib Force," she said.

"What," he said, "more perfect ideas?"

"I was thinking of more women," she said. "Same thing."

11

VICKI awoke with a start at 4 A.M. She could not push from her mind her friend Shelly. Vicki had prayed for Shelly often, but this morning was different. The more she thought of her, the more concerned she became. Was Shelly in some sort of danger?

Vicki wanted to talk to Shelly about God, but each time it was as if the door had closed. Either Shelly was busy or Shelly's friend had barged in and stopped the conversation. Vicki could tell Shelly was still in shock after the disappearances. Shelly needed the truth. Each time Vicki had called her, she either got the answering machine or someone who said Shelly couldn't talk right now. It would have been easy to give up and talk to people who wanted to hear her message, but Vicki couldn't get Shelly out of her mind. Shelly looked so lost and confused.

She dialed Shelly's number but hung up before it

rang. *This is crazy! Her mom will kill me if I wake them up at this hour for nothing.*

She picked up her journal. "Please God," she wrote, "give me a chance to speak to Shelly about you today."

———————————————

At breakfast Judd told Lionel and Ryan, "Remember to be waiting for us after school today. I don't want to be late for our study with Bruce."

"Yes sir!" Ryan said, saluting. "By the flagpole."

"Too many war movies," Lionel muttered, shaking his head.

"I'm not kidding," Judd said. "Don't be off playing soccer or basketball—"

"We'll be there," Lionel said, scowling at Ryan.

"My newspaper could be what God uses to get to students. Maybe they'll take it home to their parents."

Vicki squinted. Judd was talking as if it were his idea. She felt silly for caring. Couldn't she just be happy it was being done and that people would be reached? But Judd shouldn't care either.

"We get to help, right?" Ryan said.

"I need everybody," Judd said. "The school paper comes out on Tuesday. I want to beat them and get ours out Monday. Vicki and I will write the articles and get it on the computer, but we need you guys to help print and fold and—"

"Grunt work," Lionel said.

"There's no little job," Judd said. "We're starting with 500 copies. That'll take everybody's help."

"How are you gonna give it out?" Ryan said.

Judd shrugged. "I figure I'll take one entrance and Vicki can take another. We'll hand it out as the kids go in."

Ryan poked at his cereal and shook his head. "What if the principal and that coach, what's his name?"

"Handlesman," Vicki said.

"Yeah. What if they stop you before you get started?"

"He's right," Vicki said. "No Bibles, no talking about God, you know the drill. Everybody's scared."

"Distribution is the least of my worries right now," Judd said. "We need to write the *Underground* first."

"Is that what you're calling it?" Vicki said.

"Got a better idea?"

On the way to school Judd reminded Lionel and Ryan again to be ready after school. When they were gone, Vicki said, "You might want to go easy on them. I mean, you can come across wrong if you're not careful."

Judd cocked his head. "I want them to understand how important this is. You know how busy Bruce is, and we only have the weekend to get the paper done if we want to distribute it Monday."

Vicki didn't like having PE first thing every day. Mrs. Waltonen sometimes lost track of time, and they were barely able to dress before second period.

"Byrne!" Mrs. Waltonen shouted as the class ended.

Vicki ran over as the other girls left the gym. Thin and dark with short hair and glasses, Mrs. Waltonen had seemed shattered the week before while talking about losing her grandchild in the disappearances.

"The other day," Mrs. Waltonen said, "you said something about knowing where people were. The ones who disappeared."

Vicki nodded.

"You know I can't allow those conversations. About religious things."

"I don't want to offend anybody," Vicki said. "I won't disrupt class anymore, if that's what you mean."

"You don't understand," Mrs. Waltonen said, lowering her voice. "After class, on a personal basis, you know, one-on-one, I don't think they said anything about that."

"You want to talk about where your grandson is?"

"Granddaughter," Mrs. Waltonen said. "Not even six months old."

Vicki stared at the teacher. Mrs. Waltonen was older than Vicki's mother, and yet she was looking to Vicki for some kind of hope.

"Everybody's lost someone," Mrs. Waltonen said, "and it's left us without answers. But you're—well, better because of it. Something's different for you, Vicki."

Mrs. Waltonen suddenly seemed so soft. With her shrill whistle and the way she barked orders, she was the last person Vicki would have expected to start such a conversation.

"I *have* changed," Vicki said. "And the reason I believe I know about your—"

The bell rang. Girls ran from the dressing room.

"You have to go," Mrs. Waltonen said, touching Vicki's arm.

100

"It's OK. I want to stay and talk—"

"Maybe later. Maybe Monday."

Vicki didn't want to let the moment go, but Mrs. Waltonen urged her to dress and get to class. Vicki wondered if she would actually have the chance to lead one of her teachers to the truth.

Vicki was late for second period. She wiped her forehead and said, "I had gym." The teacher let it pass. After each class she looked for Shelly. She felt more than ever that something was wrong.

"A kid in homeroom got her Bible taken," Lionel said in the car after school. "They called it 'dangerous material.' "

"All we hear is stuff about self-esteem and peace," Ryan said. "Makes me sick."

Judd thought Bruce Barnes would be overjoyed at Vicki's news about talking with her PE teacher. But they found him weeping, his head on his desk. A young woman rose to meet them and closed Bruce's door.

"I'm Chloe Steele," she said. "You must be the Young Trib Force."

Judd, Vicki, and Lionel introduced themselves, but when Chloe saw Ryan, she hugged him tight. "I know you, don't I? You used to play with Raymie."

Ryan looked embarrassed and didn't seem to know what to do. "Raymie's her little brother," he explained.

"I'm sorry," Chloe said. "I'm helping in the office, and Pastor Barnes is not having a good day."

"What's wrong?" Judd said.

Before she could answer, the door opened and Bruce waved them inside. Judd saw tearstained pages on Bruce's desk and recognized the church directory. He picked it up and saw Bruce, a bit younger and fuller in the face with a pasted-on smile. Surrounding him were his wife and children. What a treasure Bruce had lost!

On the next page was Dr. Vernon Billings, the now departed senior pastor. Judd quickly turned to the back of the directory and found his own family. His mother and father stood behind the smiling twins, Marc and Marcie. Judd was off to the side, a few inches from the rest, straight and rigid. No smile. He looked like he wanted to be anywhere but in that picture. Judd flipped through a few other listings and saw friends and familiar faces now gone.

"Let me see," Vicki said. Ryan pointed out Raymie's picture and then grew quiet. Bruce wiped his eyes.

Bruce explained that the reporter, Cameron Williams, had discovered the directory and was impressed by the pictures of the Steele family. Chloe blushed.

"It brought it all back to me," Bruce said. "All the pain that night my wife and kids were taken."

Bruce composed himself and asked if anyone minded if Chloe joined them. No one objected.

"There's been a development with the two witnesses in Jerusalem," Bruce said. Judd noticed the others sit straighter when they heard Bruce's solemn tone. "This is going to be on the news tonight, and you may not want to watch. A half dozen thugs tried to charge the witnesses.

I don't know what they thought they could do, but they were killed. On the spot."

"What happened?" Judd said.

"They were burned to death."

Vicki gasped.

"Cool," Ryan said.

"There's nothing cool about it," Bruce said. "God judges his enemies. But you can bet this breaks his heart too. What you saw was a direct fulfillment of God's prophecy in Revelation 11. Grab a Bible and let's read what the angel tells the apostle John."

Bruce asked Vicki to read the passage.

" ' "And I will give power to my two witnesses, and they will prophesy one thousand two hundred and sixty days, clothed in sackcloth." These are the two olive trees and the two lampstands standing before the God of the earth. And if anyone wants to harm them, fire proceeds from their mouth and devours their enemies. And if anyone wants to harm them, he must be killed in this manner.' "

For the next half hour Bruce explained this and other prophecies being fulfilled before their eyes. Vicki told of Mrs. Waltonen again and also how worried she was about Shelly. "Why wouldn't God let me see her today?" she said.

"I don't know," Bruce said. "But keep praying for her. Your chance will come."

The six of them huddled to pray and ask God for opportunities to speak of their faith. Bruce prayed that people would have their eyes opened to the truth.

Over hamburgers in front of the TV, Ryan said, "We forgot something."

"Don't talk with your mouth full," Lionel said. "I can see pickles. What'd we forget?"

"We didn't ask Bruce about the *Underground.*"

Judd smashed his trash and tossed up a shot that bounced around the can and dropped in. *"Ask* him?" he said. "Since when do we need Bruce's permission?"

"Judd!" Vicki said.

"I just think it would be better to surprise him," he said. "Let's get the first issue done and see what happens."

He didn't return Vicki's gaze. "I'm tired," she said. "I'll write my story in the morning."

Judd sat at the computer in his father's den. The next time he looked up it was 3 A.M. He still wasn't satisfied with the graphics for the *Underground* logo. Creating a newspaper was going to be a lot more difficult than he imagined.

He spotted a copy of the same church directory he had seen in Bruce's office. He leafed through until he came to his family. Judd had clenched his teeth hard at Bruce's office. He had to be strong. He had to be the leader.

What he wouldn't give to have his mom and dad back! He wanted to ask questions. Life questions. Questions about the Bible. He missed his brother and sister. He just wanted to be with them and laugh again.

One picture haunted him. The youth group. All those kids sitting around a table, smiling and eating popcorn. Every one of them was now gone. All but one. All but him.

12

BY THE time Judd awoke Saturday it was nearly noon, and he felt awful for sleeping so late. He showered and dressed and found the others waiting for him downstairs.

"Why didn't you guys wake me up?"

No one looked at him. They stared at a horrifying scene on CNN. A camera mounted high above the Wailing Wall showed two old men in robes below. From the left of the screen, six figures briskly walked forward.

"Watch this," Ryan said.

One of the men in robes—whom the kids knew to be the two witnesses prophesied in the Bible—lifted a hand while the other stood like a stone. As the group neared, fire flashed from the right of the screen and engulfed the six. Immediately the flaming men fell to the ground in a flailing heap.

"Oh, that's awful," Vicki said, turning away.

CNN showed the video again, this time enhancing the

witnesses. The picture was blurry, but Judd could tell one man was talking, and then fire shot from the mouths of both. Vicki left the room.

"If you don't believe the Bible now," Lionel said, "you'll never believe it. That was exactly what we read in Revelation."

Judd turned off the television.

"Hey, I want to see that again!" Ryan said.

"This isn't a movie," Judd said. "Those were real people."

"I know," Ryan said. "I just want to see it one more time."

"Come on," Judd said, "I want to show you my newspaper."

Vicki was already in the den, staring at the screensaver. They gathered around the desk and Judd hit the mouse. A photo of Nicolae Carpathia High School appeared. Below it in bold letters: *The Underground.*

"Wow," Lionel said. "How'd you get the school's picture in there?"

"From a Web site of places recently named after Carpathia."

"Those are really cool letters too," Ryan said.

"It's new," Judd said. "I mixed a couple of fonts and finally got it right about 5 A.M."

Vicki crossed her arms but didn't speak.

"What do you think, Vick'?" Judd said.

"Uh—it's amazing. That took a lot of work. But—"

"What?" Judd assumed everyone would love what he had done.

"How are you going to print it? With all those colors, it'll take a long time, won't it? Shouldn't we go with something more low budget?"

Judd reddened. He wasn't about to see all his work go to waste.

"Why would you spend that much time on, well, the incidentals?" Vicki added.

"If you want people to read something," he said, "you have to put it in a nice package."

"But we can't physically print all that—"

"I don't want it to look cheap, like it came from some—"

"Trailer park?" Vicki said.

"No, I didn't mean that," Judd said. "Look, I'll figure it out. Just finish your article. I need to buy more supplies."

"I *am* finished. It's already on the computer." Vicki stepped in front of him. "You talk like the *Underground* was all your idea."

"Yeah," Ryan said. "You boss us around like little kids, like we can't do anything. And you get to do *everything!*"

"I'm trying to do this right, so it'll reach the most people. If you don't like it, stay out of it."

"Fine by me," Ryan said.

"You can't admit you're wrong," Vicki said.

"I'll do it myself if I have to," Judd said. "Lionel, you in?"

"What do I get to do?"

"First we have to get a lot more paper and more printer cartridges. You want to go?"

It took Judd and Lionel an hour to select all the supplies. They rolled three full carts to the front of the store.

"Look at this," Lionel said, holding up a copy of *Global Weekly*. "It's got a blurb in here about Buck Williams's article on the disappearances. Can we get it?"

Judd paid for the supplies and magazine. The scene that afternoon had left him dazed. Because he was so determined, he got things done. But being headstrong made living and working with him difficult. It had always been this way. With his parents, with his little brother and sister, his way was the right way. Always had been.

"Lionel," Judd said as he drove home, "what do you think about Ryan and Vicki?"

"I don't know, man," Lionel said. "They have a point. You were acting like king of the world this afternoon."

"I was tired. Anyway, they don't respect me."

"Hey, sometimes you have to earn respect. I mean, you don't like to be told what to do by Bruce, right? It's no different for us."

Judd sighed and shook his head. He thought when he became a Christian everything would be different. But he kept making the same mistakes. "I feel like a jerk," he said.

"You know what the Bible says," Lionel said. "First John 1:9 and all that."

Judd knew all right. He had memorized that verse as a little kid: "If we confess our sins, He is faithful and just to forgive us our sins and to cleanse us from all unrighteousness."

110

As soon as they unloaded the supplies into the house, Judd jogged up to his room and lay on the bed. "God," he prayed. "I can't do this on my own. I'm sorry. I didn't mean to hurt anybody. Please forgive me, and help the other kids to forgive me."

The house was silent when he came downstairs. Judd wondered if Vicki and Ryan had run away or were looking for another place to stay. He wanted to tell them he was sorry. He wanted the four of them to be a team again. But they were gone. Lionel was sprawled on the couch with the *Global Weekly*.

Judd wanted to grab readers and draw them in with the first few words of his article. He played with the first sentence several times and finally decided on: "My life changed forever at 30,000 feet." He told his story anonymously. Running from his family, Judd had stolen and lied. Over the Atlantic Ocean, in a plane he should have never been on, the unthinkable happened. People all around him disappeared.

Judd described his return home and his discovery that his family was gone. The loneliness and hurt came back as he wrote. He hoped anyone reading the paper would feel the same and consider the truth he had found in the Bible.

"Judd, I have an idea," Lionel said. "*Global Weekly* gives a preview of Buck's article, but it says their Web site has an advanced look at it. What if we use some of this in the *Underground*? Is that legal?"

"We can find out later," Judd said. He set Lionel up on a different computer and let him work. Even if they didn't use Buck's report, it would keep Lionel busy.

Vicki and Ryan kept walking. Vicki was upset about the blowup with Judd and knew Ryan was too.

"I don't understand it," Ryan said. "He can be your best friend, and then all of a sudden, bang, he turns into Dr. Jekyll. Or Mr. Hyde. Which was the bad guy?"

"Whatever," Vicki said.

"We ought to tell Bruce."

"What would he do—ground Judd? I don't think so."

"Somebody needs to talk to Judd."

They walked through half-empty neighborhoods. The farther they went, the bigger and more expensive the houses seemed to get. Vicki realized again how far she was from the life she had known.

"I'll bet the grass in these yards costs more than our trailer did," she said.

They came to a small lake with a playground and picnic tables. On a normal Saturday the beautiful park would have been filled with children running and playing. Now it was empty. There were no small children left.

"Do you ever stop missing them?" Ryan said.

"My family? I think about them all the time. On Saturdays my little sister used to ask me to play that memory game. You know, where you flip the cards over and try to get matches."

"I had one of those. It was animals. You had to match the mothers with their babies. Kinda boring."

"That's what I said. I told her to leave me alone. She'd

go into our room and play by herself or with Mom. I wish I had the chance—"

"I dreamed about my mom and dad the other night," Ryan said. "They were looking for me. I kept yelling at them, telling them where I was, but they couldn't hear me."

"I thought I heard somebody crying the other night," Vicki said.

"I try not to cry," Ryan said. "Sorry if I woke you up."

"It's not a problem," Vicki said. "I cry too."

"You do?"

"Yeah. And sometimes I just think about what might have been. What if I'd have believed what my family believed?"

"I've been praying that I could stop missing my mom and dad so much."

"I doubt you'll ever stop missing them," Vicki said. "But we could pray for each other that maybe it'll get easier with time."

Ryan looked embarrassed. "OK," he said.

A car passed slowly. Vicki wiped her eyes and shielded her face from the sun.

"What's the matter?" Ryan said.

"It can't be," Vicki said.

"That car?"

"Yes. It is!"

"Is what?" Ryan said.

"It's my gym teacher!"

Judd heard a car door and hurried downstairs. Vicki and Ryan quickly went to their rooms.

"Can we talk?" he called after them.

"What's to talk about?" Vicki shouted from downstairs.

Judd followed and stood awkwardly outside her door. Her room looked neat. And there was a hint of perfume.

"Who brought you home?" Judd said.

"I don't answer to you," Vicki said. "Go back to *your* paper and *your* ideas."

"Wait a minute," Judd said. "I need to say something."

"Say it," Vicki said.

"I want Ryan to be here too."

"Fine, let's go get him."

Vicki led the way into what looked like the aftermath of a tornado—socks and shirts everywhere, a half glass of milk on the nightstand, his bed a mess.

"Pretty neat about Vicki's gym teacher, huh?" Ryan said.

"Mrs. Waltonen brought you home?"

"You have a problem with that too?" Vicki said.

"As a matter of fact I do. Now she knows you don't live with family. Do you realize how dangerous that could be—for all of us?"

"I didn't tell her I lived here," Vicki said. "I told her it was a friend's house."

"Great, now you're in the clear and they're gonna come looking for me!"

"I'm not as dumb as you think I am," Vicki said.

"I don't think you're dumb, I just need you to under-stand that wasn't a very bright move."

"Something a trailer park girl would do, huh, Judd?" Vicki said. "For your information, Mrs. Waltonen asked about our church. She said she might come to hear Bruce tomorrow. She offered us a ride and I thought it would be a good chance to talk more. Satisfied?"

Judd sighed. Instead of getting better, things had gotten worse. He wanted to do the right thing, say the right thing, but everything came out wrong. Judd sat on the bed and rubbed his neck.

"I'm sorry. That's what I wanted to say. And about this afternoon, I was way out of line. Vicki, I did take credit for the idea, and I rolled over you guys like a bulldozer. I've been this way a long time, so it's not easy to change. I hope you'll forgive me."

Vicki and Ryan looked at the floor.

"Does that mean we're back on the *Underground?*" Ryan said.

"If you forgive me," Judd said. "And you'll be doing more than grunt work. I promise."

Vicki and Ryan smiled. It was more than Judd could have hoped for. The three bounded upstairs to the den where Lionel was still at work. Judd had already laid out his own article and started Vicki's on the second page.

"I like what you did, Vick'. It's a lot more personal than mine. If it's OK, I'd like to put Bible verses around the copy."

"Sounds good," Vicki said.

"You guys give me different verses, and we'll mix them with the articles. We can make them bold and put them in shaded boxes so they stand out."

"Maybe we could include the steps to knowing God that Bruce gave us," Lionel said. "You know, a prayer for salvation and stuff like that."

"Great idea," Judd said. "And we might use excerpts from the Buck Williams article in the second edition—that is, if we don't get caught and if there is a second one."

"How close are we to printing something out?" Ryan said. "I want to see what it looks like."

"Tomorrow," Judd said. "By evening we should have the first issue ready to go."

At church the next morning Vicki looked all over for Mrs. Waltonen, but she wasn't there. Vicki didn't understand. She had so hoped the woman would be there.

At home Vicki herded Lionel and Ryan into the kitchen to get some lunch on the table. Suddenly she heard Judd scream, "Oh no!" She ran to the den and found him kneeling, his face on the floor.

"What happened?"

Judd sat up. She had never seen him this way. He looked pale and nauseated.

"It's gone," Judd said.

"What's gone?"

"The whole thing. Every word of it."

"What are you talking about?"

"The *Underground*," he said. "Everything we've done is gone."

JUDD couldn't believe it. The screen was blank except for an error message. Each time he rebooted he got the same thing.

"Maybe it's a virus," he said. "I coulda picked it up off the Internet."

The four stared at the computer like it was a corpse.

"All that work," Judd said. "Gone."

"Did you save the articles and the logo on a separate disk?" Vicki said.

Judd shook his head.

"What do we do now?" Lionel said.

Judd pulled the computer tower from under his father's desk and looked at the connections. His dad had always said to check the little things. Make sure the monitor cable and power cords are tight. Everything was intact. But Judd noticed a silver sticker on the back that read: "Serviced by Donnie Moore." He dialed the number underneath.

"Oh, yeah," Mr. Moore said. "I installed that machine

about six months ago. Fastest available at the time. Your dad paid big bucks for that box."

Judd read the error message to Donnie.

"Doesn't sound good," he said. "Let me finish a couple of things, and I'll be over in a half hour, OK?"

The kids ate lunch in silence. Judd felt like someone had kicked him in the stomach. He had wasted time and energy he could never replace. And the deadline approached.

"Any chance this guy can get the stuff back?" Ryan said.

"I doubt it."

"Know what I think?" Lionel said. "It's got something to do with the devil."

Vicki laughed. "That's crazy. What are we gonna do, ask Bruce to come over and cast demons out of the computer?"

"Think about it," Lionel said. "We're putting together an underground newspaper that hundreds of kids are going to read. Hundreds of kids who aren't Christians. Now if you were the devil, would you like that? Would you want all these people reading stuff about the Bible right when they're looking for answers?"

"He's got a point," Judd said.

"Yeah," Vicki said, "but don't pin everything on Satan. Maybe God didn't want that to be our first edition. Maybe *he* made the computer crash."

"How are we ever gonna know?" Ryan said.

"I think that's what faith is about," Judd said. "Remember the passage Bruce was talking about? The one about how things work together, something like that."

"I know!" Ryan said. He ran for a Bible and brought it

to the table. Judd could tell he was excited. Ryan was the youngest and hadn't gone to church like the others, but he seemed to be absorbing Bruce's teaching like a sponge.

"Here it is," Ryan said. "Romans 8:28. 'And we know that all things work together for good to those who love God, to those who are the called according to His purpose.' "

"That's it," Judd said. "Not everything that happens is good, but God can turn it into something good."

"Even computer crashes," Vicki said.

Donnie Moore was in his late twenties, a blond with side-burns. Judd could tell he liked to talk. Donnie placed his hard-sided briefcase beside the tower and took the computer apart. As he poked inside, he told them about his business and his involvement with New Hope Village Church. He had installed phone systems and done odd jobs fixing printers and faxes for Pastor Billings and Loretta, the church secretary. But he had only attended church to expand his list of clients. His wife, Sandy, was interested in God and suggested they go. Though both heard a lot about the Bible, neither really changed. Except for Sunday mornings, Donny and Sandy lived the same as they had all their lives. After the vanishings, Donnie real-ized something about his belief in God was missing, but he wasn't sure what it was.

"I thought I just wasn't good enough," Donnie said. "The other people in the church were saints. They taught Sunday school, went to prayer meetings, and gave money to mission-aries. They even let poor people sleep in the basement of the church and cooked meals for them. I thought I'd been passed by because I didn't have enough brownie points."

Donnie ran a diagnostic program as he continued.

"Then Bruce Barnes showed me the tape Pastor Billings had left. He explained what had happened to everybody. I'd never thought about God that way, the way your mom and dad must have, Judd. I found out I didn't have to earn my way to heaven, that Jesus had already paid my way by being perfect and dying in my place. All I had to do was receive the gift. I couldn't believe I had missed it so bad. 'Course even Bruce had made the same mistake. You too, I guess, hm?"

Donnie scowled at the screen.

"A virus?" Judd said.

"Nah, the hard drive. I mean, it could've been some kind of virus or maybe an electrical spike the surge protector couldn't handle, but whatever it was, it's fried. I was able to retrieve some of your dad's old files, but everything else is toast."

"Do we need a new computer?" Judd said.

"I don't see anything wrong with the rest of the box," Donnie said. "Just replace the hard drive and you'll be in business."

"How much do we owe you?" Judd said.

Donnie stopped at the door and put down his briefcase. "Your dad bought a service contract, so it's no problem. But I gotta ask you something. Do you kids know why this happened? Do you know what's going to happen?"

Vicki explained why they were so upset about the computer crash. Donnie's eyes moistened. "Isn't that

120

something?" he said. He was still shaking his head when he walked out.

"Plan B," Judd said that evening. "We're not letting this stop us. The *Underground* will be out in the morning."

"You gotta be kidding," Ryan said. "It took us three days to get this far. How are we going to start over and be done by tomorrow?"

"What are we gonna use, crayons?" Lionel said.

"We're going to use what's already been written," Judd said.

Lionel looked puzzled. "I thought everything on the computer was lost."

"We're using your words, Lionel. Yours and Buck Williams's. Did you finish it?"

"Yeah, but—"

"That's our first edition. We'll hook your computer to the printer, and we're on our way. Vicki, I know this is a long shot, but why don't you try getting in touch with Buck. He might be able to add something really powerful."

Buck was senior editor of the most prestigious newsmagazine in the world, so his article was a masterpiece. He covered every theory for the disappearances from UFOs and alien attacks to a cosmic evolutionary cleansing. But the middle of the piece interested the kids the most. Here Buck had included the truth. Jesus Christ had returned for true believers. Buck had interviewed several Christians, including an airline pilot the four figured was Rayford Steele. The Bible was communicated simply and powerfully.

"So we let the best journalist in the world write our first edition," Vicki said. "Perfect."

———————————————

Vicki called Bruce for Buck's number, but he was reluctant to give it. Vicki said she wanted to ask some questions about his article, and Bruce gave her Buck's office number. His voice mail at *Global Weekly* gave his pager number. She left Judd's home number on his pager and was amazed when he called half an hour later.

"Using my stuff is a great idea," Buck said. "I didn't know it was on the Web yet. But don't quote me outside the article. Wouldn't be safe for me or you. Why not ask your questions and quote me as an unnamed source?"

"I'm really interested about what people from other churches think happened," Vicki said.

"Many Catholics are confused," Buck said. "While many disappeared, including the new pope, some remain. He stirred up a lot of controversy with a doctrine that seemed similar to the 'heresy' of Martin Luther."

"What was that?"

"Luther read the book of Romans and believed salvation wasn't gained through membership in the church, baptism, or doing good works. He said salvation was only by God's grace through faith. The new pope agreed with that, and it sent shock waves through the Catholic church.

"I talked with one of the leading archbishops, Peter Cardinal Mathews of Cincinnati. You might be hearing more from him in the coming months. Mathews said the vanishings were God's way of winnowing out the unfaithful. He compared it with the days of Noah when the good people remained and the evil were washed away."

"So he thinks we're the good guys and the people who vanished were bad?"

"Exactly," Buck said. "But remember, our view is that he was not a true believer. He was one who thought he could earn his way to heaven."

"What about the children and the babies?" Vicki said.

"He didn't have a good answer for that. He said he was leaving that to God."

Judd put Buck's anonymous quotes into a boxed article next to the text from *Global Weekly.* He and Vicki decided Ephesians 2:8-9 was the best passage to include there. It read, "For by grace you have been saved through faith, and that not of yourselves; it is the gift of God, not of works, lest anyone should boast."

By midnight the paper was done. It wasn't as professional as Judd wanted, and not as long, but it said what they all wanted to say. They printed and collated the pages as quickly as possible.

Vicki couldn't sleep. She had to be up in less than three hours for school. Her mind spun with fear and ideas. Might this be God's way of getting to Shelly? Would Vicki and the others be caught before even handing out the papers? If they did get the *Underground* to kids, would the kids actually read it? And what would the school do?

She put on her robe and went upstairs. Judd and Lionel were stacking the papers by the front door. Ryan was asleep in Judd's father's high-backed chair.

"I've been thinking," Vicki said. "This is bigger than all of us."

"I know," Judd said. "We couldn't have done this on our own."

The next morning in the car, Lionel pleaded with Judd. "Why can't we give out some copies at our school? Junior highers are just as important as older kids."

"I know," Judd said. "But this was written for high schoolers. If it works, we can do a version for you guys."

When they pulled up to Global Community Junior High, Ryan said, "Good luck. Or I mean, do it to it, or Godspeed, or whatever you're supposed to say."

Judd and Vicki waited until Ryan and Lionel ran into school before they laughed. Godspeed indeed.

JUDD and Vicki carried the *Underground* in brown grocery bags. They tried to stay calm. Judd knew they concealed something school officials considered nuclear. Though they were early, many other students were already on campus.

"You know the plan," Judd said. "I'll meet you in the gym just before first period."

"Be careful," Vicki said. "It only takes one person to rat on us."

Vicki went toward the back entrance and Judd the front. He passed the flagpole and glanced up. Under the American colors was the white flag of peace with the school's new symbol, a dove. The words, "Nicolae Carpathia High School" flapped in the light breeze.

Judd focused on green newspaper bins by the front door. Students were to pick up anything placed in the bins. Newspapers, school memos, and even school-approved advertisements from local businesses were first come, first served. Everything had to be preapproved by the office, but Judd wasn't about to let anyone censor or throw out the *Underground*. They had worked too hard for that.

Four younger students stood talking near the bins, so Judd walked inside to the water fountain. When he looked again, the four were gone.

He shot back out the front doors and dropped the bag in the bin. He took a quick look around and ripped the bag open from top to bottom. The first copies of the *Underground* were exposed.

Judd hurried back inside to his locker. He fumbled with the combination, looking behind him. He believed no one had seen him, but he couldn't be sure.

Judd slid a few coins into a soda machine and took a drink back outside. He sat near the flagpole and watched the bins fifty yards away.

He took a sip of soda and thought about the kids in his old youth group. He had labeled them fanatics for standing around that very flagpole and praying. They had asked him to join them, and Judd just laughed. Now he knew how brave they had been to take a stand. He silently asked God for a chance to make up for the lost opportunity.

Judd froze when he saw a student walk to the door, do a double take, and grab a copy of the *Underground*. The boy placed it between his books and went inside.

A bus stopped in front of the school, and for a moment Judd couldn't see. He moved to get a better look and saw several students take copies. He was thrilled. Everything was going as planned.

Many kids who walked or drove to school used the rear entrance. Vicki wasn't scared of being seen by them. She could blend in. She was concerned about the faculty parking lot. Though they were supposed to be early, some teachers arrived later than students and bolted through the rear door. They stayed in their cars to smoke or listen to the radio until the last minute. Vicki watched the entrance. A group of kids was kicking a Hacky Sack between them. In the parking lot the principal, Mrs. Laverne Jenness, and one of the school secretaries got out of their cars.

When the kids saw Mrs. Jenness, they grabbed their books and ran inside. Perfect, Vicki thought.

Vicki walked toward the parking lot, then doubled back and followed the women. Once they were inside, Vicki stepped to the newspaper bins and poured out the papers. She quickly folded the bag and turned to leave, nearly knocking someone over.

"Hey, watch where you're going," a man said. To her horror, Vicki found herself looking into the face of Coach Handlesman.

"Pay more attention, Red," Handlesman said.

Vicki hated that nickname. Usually she reprimanded anyone who called her that, young or old. But she bit her lip and forced a laugh.

"Sorry, coach."

Handlesman moved past her and picked up a paper

on his way in. Vicki watched over her shoulder as she casually walked away. He stopped and looked like he was holding a dead fish.

"The *Underground?*" he muttered. "What in the world?"

Judd watched another bus pull up. He guessed that about every third student had taken the *Underground.* It was a start.

"God, don't let anyone get it who shouldn't."

Suddenly the front door burst open and Coach Handlesman ran out. He went directly to the green bins and grabbed the stack. He scanned the courtyard like a quarterback searching for a receiver.

Judd tipped his soda back and drained it, hoping Handlesman would be gone when he looked again. The coach could be on top of him in seconds. He drank the last drop. Handlesman was gone. So were all the copies of the *Underground.*

Vicki waited for Judd in the gym. A few kids were playing basketball. A couple at the back of the gym was making out. A group behind her passed something between them, but Vicki couldn't see what it was. When she saw Judd, she ran to meet him.

"Over here," Judd said, pulling Vicki underneath the bleachers. "What happened?"

Vicki told him. "I thought I was dead," she said.

"Didn't anybody take a copy back there?"

"Handlesman took one and then carted the whole bunch away. How about in front?"

"I'd say at least twenty got a copy. Maybe twenty-five, tops."

"We're going to have to think of some other way," Vicki said.

The PA system crackled in the gym.

"May I have your attention, students," Mrs. Jenness said. "Someone placed an unaproved newspaper in the distribution bins this morning. We believe most were confiscated, but if you picked up a copy thinking this was an approved publication, please bring it to the office immediately. It's called the *Underground,* and those caught with copies are subject to expulsion. Those behind these papers can avoid expulsion by coming forward now too."

"I can think of worse things than expulsion," Judd said.

Mrs. Jenness ended with, "There is a reward for anyone with information about those behind this newspaper."

"Great," Judd said. "Now there's a bounty on us."

Vicki heard movement overhead. "Judd, look," she whispered.

Judd said, "I see only feet and legs. What?"

Vicki pointed. "They're reading the *Underground.* Listen."

"Must be dirty or something," one girl said. "It'd have to be for them to make such a fuss."

"Shouldn't we turn it in?" another said.

"No. Read it. Pass it around."

"What kind of reward would we get?"

The first bell rang. Vicki shook her head.

"What's wrong?" Judd said.

"It was such a good idea. I just don't understand why God let Handlesman get most of the papers."

"I'm not discouraged," Judd said. "That they were confiscated is a good sign. We're hitting a nerve."

"I wanted Shelly to get a copy."

"Maybe she did. We don't know. This just means we have to work harder. We have to be smarter now."

Vicki could think of nothing but the *Underground* all day. How would they get their message out now? Why didn't God let more kids see the paper?

Through the morning Vicki watched for signs of kids who might have seen the *Underground*. There were none. Mrs. Waltonen was nothing but business in gym class. Vicki wanted to ask her about Sunday, but Mrs. Waltonen went straight to her office after class.

Vicki's English teacher, Mr. Carlson, made a joke about the newspaper as class began.

"Anyone carrying any dangerous material today?" he said. "A copy of *Huck Finn*, a little *Catcher in the Rye*, some plutonium?"

The class laughed.

"Words are dangerous," Carlson continued. "Be careful how you use them. Some of the greatest writers in history have suffered because of their words."

"Are you saying whoever put out that newspaper was right?" a student asked.

"You have to take freedom of the press seriously," Mr. Carlson said. "But I doubt whoever's behind this paper compares to the great writers of literature."

Vicki wanted to say the Bible was the most censored book these days, and those who believed it were in the greatest danger. But she kept quiet.

At lunch Vicki couldn't find Judd. She ate alone and listened to her old friends at a nearby table. They ignored her, laughing and talking about their latest escapades. Vicki cringed. Was that what she used to be like? Did she brag about drinking and smoking and drugs? If only they knew the truth. Her life before Christ was empty. Listening to them now just made her feel sad.

She thought the day would never end. As she walked to her final class, a teacher stopped her.

"You need to go to the office immediately."

"What for?" Vicki said.

"It's an emergency. Something about a phone call from your mother."

Vicki gasped. Her mother was gone. Maybe Mrs. Jenness had discovered the truth and this was a trap.

She walked slowly to the office and found the secretary was the same woman she had seen with Mrs. Jenness that morning.

"Yes, you have an emergency call from your mother," the woman said. "You can take it over there."

Vicki picked up the phone. "I need to see you," a female voice whispered. "After school."

"OK," Vicki said tentatively. "Why?"

131

THE YOUNG TRIB FORCE

"Just get on your old school bus. Get off at your regular stop."

"I can't. I mean, I have something to do."

"You can and you will."

"You have to tell me what this is about before—"

"There were things in that paper today. You can help me—if you want to. Please."

The line went dead. Who would have known which bus she'd ridden? How did they connect her with the *Underground*? Was this a trap or an opportunity? She had to take the risk.

Judd paced in front of his car. Lionel and Ryan would be going crazy wondering where he and Vicki were. He had so much to tell her and ask her, but he couldn't find her. He walked into the school and past the office. No one was there except school employees.

As he walked back to his car, John and Mark approached. They were the cousins he had noticed carrying Bibles the first day of school. Coach Handlesman had confiscated their Bibles.

"Judd," Mark said. "Big news on campus."

"What's that?" Judd said.

"The alternative newspaper. The *Underground*."

"I heard the announcement," Judd said.

"We worked on the school paper last year," John said. "They've changed it to the *Olive Branch* now. We stopped by the editorial office today to see how they're going to cover the *Underground* in tomorrow's issue."

"Did they have a copy?" Judd said.

"Not one," John said. "And since we're upstanding citizens, we turned ours into the office this morning."

Judd was concerned, then noticed the two were smiling. "You turned your copies in?"

"That's what they said to do," Mark said. "So we went to the library, made a few condensed copies for friends and acquaintances, and handed the original in to the principal."

"We follow the rules," John said. "And since the *Olive Branch* staff didn't have a copy, we made sure one wound up on top of the editor's desk."

"They probably won't be allowed to write about the *Underground*, but it was worth a try," Mark said.

Judd leaned close. "Get in the car a second, guys. Have I got a story for you." John and Mark climbed in and seemed to drink in Judd's every word.

"Incredible," Mark said. "You guys sure know how to keep a secret."

"So," John said, "did you replace the hard drive?"

"Not yet. I need to buy one soon so we can do another edition."

"No need," John said. "We have everything at the house. Hard drives. Monitors. The huge ones. Our dad was a computer salesman for the entire Midwest."

"How are you going to distribute another edition?" Mark said. "The school's gonna clamp down."

Judd shook his head and shrugged. "I knew it was going to get dangerous. Any ideas?"

John scratched his head. "I might have one. It's a long shot, and we'd have to put it together tonight."

"We?" Mark said.

"If Judd'll let us help."

"You're in," Judd said. "But what? How?"

"Believe it or not, we might be able to get Nicolae High to distribute the *Underground* without even knowing it."

Judd took one more look around the school. Vicki was nowhere in sight.

15

AT DARK there was still no word from Vicki. Judd was frantic. He had taken John and Mark to get their computer gear and raced home, hoping to find her there. He found only Lionel and Ryan waiting for answers and not happy about having had to walk home.

"Maybe the coach got her," Ryan said.

"I don't even want to think about that," Judd said.

"She'll be OK," Lionel said. "She can take care of herself."

"I say we get Bruce to help us find her," Ryan said.

"Not yet," Judd said. "I'll give her another hour."

John told Judd he was ready to get started on the next issue. Mark wasn't so sure. "What if we're caught?" he said. "What if Coach Handlesman confronts you and asks you point-blank if you had anything to do with the *Underground?* Would you lie?"

"Either God is in this or he isn't," Judd said. "If he

135

wants us to do this, we gotta do it. He'll protect us. He'll give us the answers when we need them. We have to believe that."

"He either protects us or takes us to heaven," Ryan said. "Either way we can't lose."

"I'm not ready yet," Lionel said. "I mean, I want to be. I'd love to be a martyr, especially since I knew better and should have been ready for the Rapture, but I'm scared. I'm sorry, but I am."

The phone rang. As soon as Judd heard Bruce's voice he remembered their meeting.

"It totally slipped my mind," Judd said.

"Judd, we've talked about this before. My time is valuable. Please respect me enough to call and let me know the group's not going to be here."

Judd apologized again and set Thursday as their next meeting. "I promise we'll be there," he said.

Judd hung up, still worried sick about Vicki. Lionel had the floor. "In history today we talked about one of the big wars where a bunch of people were getting dragged away."

"World War II," Mark said. "The Nazis."

"Yeah, they came for the Jews and other people they didn't like, but some people couldn't stand what was happening and had to get involved. They hid Jewish people in attics and basements, wherever they could. I'll bet they lied to the Nazis. And they were right."

"If someone at school asks us directly," Mark said, "what are we going to do? You guys can talk about being brave, but when a teacher or Coach Handlesman is looking down at you, it's a different ball game."

"God doesn't need us to lie," Judd said. "But we also don't have to hang a sign around our necks that says, 'We're Christians, please persecute.'"

"Maybe we should do what Jesus did," Ryan said. "Bruce said the rulers asked Jesus questions before he was killed, and he didn't say *anything.*"

"We're each going to have to decide for ourselves," Judd said. "We need to pray for wisdom. I don't know what the right thing is, but I do know one thing. We have to get this message out to as many people as possible."

Vicki had sat at the back of the bus. The trip took nearly half an hour, and no one talked to her. She guessed it was because she looked so different. No makeup. New clothes. She had hoped to sit near Shelly, maybe talk with her. But Shelly never showed.

The bus wound its way around apartment buildings and back streets. Finally she saw the familiar white roofs of the trailer park, and she moved to the front. She got off at her old stop with several others, then watched as they walked home. Except for empty lots where burned trailers had been moved, things looked the same.

Vicki waited, hearing nothing but traffic and muffled stereos and televisions. Then she heard a familiar voice behind her:

"Vick'."

She turned. "Shelly!"

Vicki threw her arms around Shelly, but Shelly's hug was halfhearted and she nearly lost her balance.

"It was you on the phone?" Vicki said.

Shelly nodded. "I figured it had to be good to get you out of class. So I was your mother for a minute. Pretty good plan for a girl like me, wouldn't you say?"

Shelly didn't seem right. She had acted spacey and distant the last time Vicki saw her. "Have you been drinking?" Vicki said.

"Who, me?"

"What is it, Shel'?"

Shelly looked at the ground. "I had to see you one more time. I wanted to say good-bye."

"You're leaving?" Vicki said.

"You could say that."

"Where are you going?"

"I picked up that paper today," Shelly said. "The one we weren't supposed to read. After lunch I hitched a ride home and looked through it."

Vicki couldn't believe Shelly had actually read the *Underground.* "What'd you think?"

Shelly touched her head. "I need to sit down."

"Let's go to your house," Vicki said.

"No," Shelly said. "My mom's in there."

Shelly collapsed and hit the ground hard, but instead of even wincing, she laughed. Vicki had seen this before. She didn't want to believe it.

"What did you take, Shelly?"

"I don't know what you mean."

"Shelly, tell me!"

"I don't know. Something of my mom's. Don't tell her. She'll really be mad."

"How much did you take?"

"The whole thing," Shelly said. "I don't want to be here anymore."

Shelly's eyes looked strange. Vicki grabbed her shoulders and Shelly's head lolled to one side.

"You were a good friend, Vick'."

"You hang on, Shelly, you hear me? Hang on!"

John and Mark knew what to do and had Judd's computer up and running in less than an hour. They were even able to retrieve the original file with the first newspaper, something not even Donnie Moore had been able to do.

"Cool logo," Mark said. "The file was damaged, but it can be fixed. I'd say the second edition is ready to print."

"How many can we distribute with your plan?" Judd said.

"Enrollment before the Rapture was about 2,300," John said. "I'd say we lost a quarter of that. Maybe 500 kids. I'd print 1,800 copies."

"You're kidding," Lionel said. "You can get the *Underground* to every kid without the school knowing?"

"If my plan works," John said.

Shelly's mother was lying on an old couch with the television blaring and hardly stirred when Vicki rushed in to call 9-1-1.

Paramedics began pumping Shelly's stomach in the ambulance. Vicki didn't know if she had gotten her friend to the hospital in time until a doctor came to her in the waiting room. "She's gonna be OK," he said. "She OD'd on sleeping pills. Shelly's lucky she had you as a friend."

Vicki glanced at a clock. 8:30. She ran to a phone.

"I'm really sorry, Judd," she said. "I'm at the hospital."

"What's wrong? Are you OK?"

"It's a long story. Could you pick me up?"

"I'll be right over."

Judd was upset, but he also cared. By the time he and Vicki returned to the house, he was frustrated.

"We need a signal," he said. "Some code that lets the others know one of us is in trouble."

"I couldn't get in touch with anybody," Vicki said.

"You don't need a code," John said. "You need this."

He pulled from his front pocket what looked like a pager. It had a screen about as thick as a pizza crust and was a little bigger than a watch.

"My dad was beta testing these," John said. "It works like a pager, but it's radio-frequency controlled. You enter a message on the screen and send it to whoever you want who has a receiver. Instantly. No phone calls, no modem."

"How much?" Judd said.

"We have at least ten more at home," John said.

Printing 1,800 copies of the *Underground* took all six kids. By midnight the papers were stacked and in the trunk of Judd's car.

John said, "We have a window of about an hour. We'll need to be there and ready by 4 A.M."

"I'm ready," Lionel said.

"No," Judd said. "You and Ryan aren't coming."

"No fair!" Ryan said.

"Judd," Mark said. "With 1,800 papers, we need their help."

Judd agreed, but only if everyone went to bed immediately. He set his alarm for 3:30 A.M.

The alarm woke Judd, but just barely. His body felt like lead. The others were slow to rise as well, except Lionel and Ryan. They seemed so excited Judd wondered if they had slept at all.

"Can you drop me off at the hospital afterward?" Vicki said.

"Sure," Judd said. "What are you gonna do about school?"

"I'll get there somehow. This is a lot more important than being late for class."

The six squeezed into Judd's car and drove across town. John gave instructions, and Mark briefed each on their assigned duties.

"Pull over here," John said. Judd parked in an alley and turned off his lights.

"The loading dock is over there," John said. "They put the finished papers for the school out a little after four o'clock."

At 4:10 A.M. a shaft of light came from the building as a man lugged three huge stacks and a smaller one onto the dock. He lit a cigarette and stood by the door.

"They get a break about now," Mark said. "He could be out here awhile."

"How do you know all this?" Lionel said.

"John and I worked on the school paper last year. We had pick-up duty. We got to know some of the guys on the dock."

Finally the man threw his cigarette on the ground and went inside. Judd pulled up to the dock. He opened the trunk and the Young Tribulation Force put their plan into action. If successful, the truth about the disappearances would be available to every student in their school.

JUDD found John and Mark's plan ingenious. They tucked a copy of the *Underground* inside each school newspaper. When a student grabbed a copy of the *Olive Branch*, the *Underground* would be there as well.

"The bundles are wrapped loose enough," John whispered, "so just find the middle crease in each *Olive Branch* and slide the *Underground* in." He showed them how to push the *Underground* in so it wouldn't fold or stick out.

They began slowly and picked up speed. Lionel and Ryan stuffed as quickly as the older kids did. In a half hour they were almost through the first two stacks.

"How do we keep these from the principal and the *Olive Branch* staff?" Vicki said.

"The short bundle on the end is for the administration and news staff," John said. "Those get delivered to the office and to the teachers' mailboxes. That's the stack we leave alone."

"But if somebody rats on us," Vicki said, "we're back where we started, right?"

"True," Mark said. "But this time I'm betting most will think the school changed their minds. I say they don't find it until second period, and by then the whole school will have them."

Vicki was glad to be at the hospital instead of trying to stay awake in class. The nurse who had admitted Shelly told her, "Your friend is resting, but you can go in."

"What I'd like to do is sleep," Vicki said.

"There's no one else in the room," the nurse said. "Come on."

Shelly slept with her back to the door. The nurse gave Vicki a blanket and pillow and showed her a cushioned chair in the corner.

When she awoke, light streamed into the room and Vicki smelled breakfast. Shelly was sitting up.

"You been here all night?" Shelly said.

"I came early this morning." Vicki slid her chair closer. "How do you feel?"

"Like warmed-up death," Shelly said. "I thought I'd wake up in heaven or—you know."

Vicki wanted to ask the questions that burned inside her. She didn't want to scare Shelly away, but she was through hedging. There were no friends to distract them, no bell to stop their conversation. Now was the time.

"Why'd you do it, Shel'?"

"It's easy for you," Shelly said. "You got a whole new life."

"I lost my family and my house burned down with everything I own."

"You have people who care about you. You have all that God stuff too. All I have is—well, you saw my mom."

Vicki stood and took Shelly's hand. She looked so hardened, and yet fragile. Like a shell.

"We've known each other since we were kids. We used to be able to say anything. Everything."

Shelly looked away.

"I don't know what pushed you over the edge," Vicki said, "but I don't think you called to say good-bye. I think you hoped I would get there in time to help you. I'm here. I want to know. Nothing you say can stop me from caring. Tell me what's going on."

"I can't," Shelly said. "I don't even want to think about it."

"What does that say about me if you can't even tell me?"

Shelly stiffened. Her brown hair hung straight. Her eyes were lifeless pools. Vicki decided to be quiet and let her words sink in. She prayed silently and kept holding Shelly's hand. Finally, Shelly turned her weary gaze toward Vicki.

"I was baby-sitting at the Fischers. I had both kids in bed—everything was fine. I wasn't on the phone, didn't have anybody over. I was being good.

"The Fischers were late. Really late. And just when they pulled in the driveway, Maddie started crying. I mean really wailing. So I went to her room, but she wouldn't stop. I picked her up, and then Ben started crying. So I carried them both out—"

Shelly closed her eyes and slumped forward. Telling this story seemed to make Shelly relive it. Every word seemed to hurt.

"Ben was hanging onto my neck, and the baby was still crying, looking right at me. Remember how sweet she was, Vick'?"

"She was a doll."

Shelly stared into the distance. "It's like a dream. I remember every detail like it happened in slow motion. Mr. Fischer was parking the car under the carport, the trailer door opened, Mrs. Fischer saw I had both kids and looked like she felt sorry for me. I was glad she didn't look like she was blaming me for them being awake that late. She started towards me and reached for them as Mr. Fischer came in.

"And then the kids were gone. Both of them. It was like they jumped out of my arms, leaving their diapers and pajamas. I held my arms out and stared, then looked up at the Fischers and they had disappeared right out of their clothes too."

"It must have been awful," Vicki said.

"I didn't know what to do. I just stood there for the longest time."

Vicki could see Shelly still couldn't shake the feelings.

"Why did God have to take those kids, Vicki? They didn't do anything wrong."

"God wasn't punishing anyone, Shel'. He took them to heaven. You don't have to feel bad about that."

146

Shelly pulled her hand away. "But I do. I'm guilty."

"Why? What did you do?"

"I can't tell you. That's why I wanted to die. I wanted to make sure nobody ever knew."

Judd took a school paper from the news bin and tucked it into his backpack. Half the papers were gone now. So far, so good.

Mr. Shellenberger was late to first period psychology. He apologized and started writing on the board. A tall, fleshy man, as he moved the chalk his hair waved like limp spaghetti. Two students tittered in the corner. Mr. Shellenberger turned, his generous nose in profile.

"Something you'd like to share with the class?" he said.

The room fell silent.

"Come, come. Tell us. I'm sure we'd all like to join in the fun."

One boy shifted nervously.

"It's nothing funny. We just thought we weren't supposed to have this *Underground* thing. Now they've gone and put it in the school paper."

"What are you talking about?" Mr. Shellenberger said. "I saw nothing in my copy of the *Olive Branch*."

"Well, I've got one right here in the middle of mine," the boy said. He held up the *Underground*. Others opened their papers and found it as well.

"Let me see that," Mr. Shellenberger said.

I have to stall him, Judd thought. *Keep him from reporting this too soon.*

147

Mr. Shellenberger studied the *Underground* for a moment.

"Why would they change their policy on this?" Judd blurted. Mr. Shellenberger looked at him and shrugged, then turned back to the paper. Judd continued, "I mean, why would the school outlaw this one day and the very next day include it in all our papers? Is there something psychological going on?"

The class laughed.

"You tell me, Thompson. What do you think?"

"Maybe it's guilt," Judd said. "You know, for years we hear how important free speech is and freedom of the press. Maybe they thought it over and let this thing go through because they felt guilty about the double standard."

"Interesting," Mr. Shellenberger said. "Anyone else?"

"Whatever it is, Shelly, it isn't too bad for God to forgive."

"You don't know what I've done, Vicki."

Vicki walked to the window. "I know what *I've* done," she said. "It's as bad as anything you could ever dream. I could hardly believe God could forgive me."

"God can't forgive me," Shelly said. "I'd have to spend the rest of my life making up for what I've done."

"That's where you're wrong," Vicki said. "You can't make up for your sins. You could never do that. Just one is enough to separate you from God."

"Then how are you supposed to make it right?"

Vicki explained that Jesus came to pay the penalty for sin. Because he was perfect, he fulfilled God's demands.

148

His sacrifice allowed anyone who believed he died for them to come back to God.

"It sounds too easy," Shelly said. "You just believe something and it happens."

"Simple but not easy," Vicki said. "It cost a lot. To know what Jesus went through for you—"

"God can't forgive what I've done," Shelly said. "No way it could be that simple."

"You don't understand God. No sin is too great."

Vicki returned to the side of the bed. Shelly still looked stony.

"Is this about the baby?" Vicki said.

"Not the Fischer's baby."

"Then what? You can trust me, Shel', you know that."

"You won't tell anybody?"

"Never."

There was a knock and Shelly's doctor entered. He asked Vicki to step out while he examined Shelly.

"I'll be right back, Shelly," she said.

"Don't you have to get to school?"

"Let me worry about that."

Mr. Shellenberger had taken the class on a tour of the history of guilt, including the Puritan concept of good and evil. Whenever he seemed to be winding down, Judd asked another question and he was off again.

A student near Judd asked, "Is this going to be on the test?"

The bell rang before Mr. Shellenberger could answer.

Judd saw him take a copy of the *Underground* toward the office. Mark was right. It would be second period before officials discovered what they had distributed themselves.

Judd felt a buzz in his pocket. He pulled out the gizmo John and Mark had given him. The screen read, "Pray for Shelly." He ran into John and Mark in the hall.

"Something's up," John said. "We've just been called to the office. Anybody who worked for the school paper in the last three years has to be there."

"Looks like the *Underground* is toast," Mark said.

"Be careful," Judd said. "Remember, you don't have to volunteer information."

As he headed to his next class, Judd silently prayed that God would keep John and Mark from being found out, and then he prayed for Shelly.

Judd hit the reply button on the tiny machine. "Pray for John and Mark," he tapped in. "*Underground* discovered."

"She's been through a lot," the doctor told Vicki as he left Shelly's room. "I wouldn't push her emotionally."

"I just want to be her friend."

"Maybe the best thing is to let her rest."

"But—"

"Tell her you have to get to school," the doctor said. "You can come back this afternoon when she's had a chance to rest."

Vicki tried again but the doctor made sense. "If you care for your friend, you'll come back later."

Vicki hated leaving Shelly now, when Shelly needed
her most. She entered the room to find Shelly watching TV.

"The doc says I ought to let you rest awhile," Vicki said.

"Yeah, thanks for coming."

"I'll stay if you want."

"We can talk later," Shelly said.

So close, Vicki thought, thankful for the opportunity
but disappointed at the delay. *So close.*

17

VICKI was surprised to find the school office crowded with students. She pushed her way to the secretary's desk to report in and noticed John and Mark in the conference room. John nodded and Vicki took the hint. She sat unnoticed in the outer office where she could hear what was going on.

Coach Handlesman and Principal Jenness were talking to the English teacher, Mr. Carlson, adviser to the school newspaper. Handlesman fumed, "We had people on both sides of the school. No way anyone could have gotten to the papers without being spotted."

"This was an inside job," Mrs. Jenness said. "Someone here did this or knows who did."

"Somebody had to get to these papers before they arrived," Handlesman said. "I want to know which of you picked the papers up from the printer this morning?"

"That would be me," Mr. Carlson said sheepishly. "I

brought them in my van and some kids helped me put them in the bins. I was with them the whole time."

"How many of you kids have ever been to the print plant?" Handlesman said. "So unless someone's lying, seven of you have knowledge of when and where the papers are picked up."

Vicki assumed John and Mark raised their hands. Mr. Carlson would have been alarmed if they hadn't. She slipped into the hallway as Coach Handlesman barked something about expelling all the journalism students unless the culprits confessed. The heat was being turned up on Nicolae Carpathia High School.

At lunch she met in the cafeteria with Judd and John and Mark. The cousins were still shaken.

Mark said, "Nobody admitted anything, and I thought Jenness was going to expel us all."

"That's when the fire alarm rang," John said. "Talk about timing."

"You'd think they would have postponed the drill when they had a big meeting going," Judd said.

"It wasn't exactly a scheduled drill," Vicki said. "Somebody hit a fire alarm."

"How do you know?" Judd said.

Vicki smiled.

"No," Judd said.

"Vicki to the rescue!" Mark said, and gave her a high five.

"That sure settled things," John said. "When the fire

department gets called for nothing, the principal's not too happy. After everybody got back inside, I think they were more interested in confiscating the *Underground* than finding out who actually put the thing together."

"One of the reporters told me the office collected a few hundred copies," Mark said. "That means there're still a thousand or more out there."

"Why is this such a big deal to Handlesman?" John said. "He's the guy who took our Bibles too."

"Good question," Judd said. "What does he have to gain or lose by a couple of Bibles or the *Underground?*"

"About those Bibles," Mark said. "Last week they turned up in our lockers."

"You're kidding," Vicki said. "Are you sure they're the same ones?"

"Yeah, they have our names in them and some of the verses are highlighted."

"It's the weirdest thing," John said. "No note, no explanation. I can't figure who would have access to them."

"We'd better cool it a couple of days," Judd said. "Let's not press our luck. We'll see you two guys in a few days."

That night at home Judd filled in Lionel and Ryan, and everybody agreed it had been an amazing day. Then Bruce called.

"I need to see the four of you right away," he said.

"Something wrong?" Judd said. "We wanted to go with Vicki to—"

THE YOUNG TRIB FORCE

"I'll tell you when you get here. Come as quickly as you can."

Bruce was alone at his desk. Judd told him Vicki needed to get back to her friend at the hospital soon. "This won't take long," Bruce said. To Judd, Bruce looked as grave as he had ever seen him. "Sit down."

Bruce moved to the front of his desk and sat on the edge. "I am very concerned about what's going on at your school."

Bruce waited as if to see if anyone would explain. "I'm talking about the newspaper," he said. "I admire your desire, but I disagree with the way you've done this."

"How did you find out?" Judd said.

"Buck told me about Vicki's call and I put two and two together. But I never dreamed you were thinking about something for the whole school. You didn't seek my advice. You put each other in danger. And you've evidently gotten two other boys involved as well."

Judd exploded, "I can't believe this! Yes, we took some chances, and no, we didn't ask you to hold our hands. Sure we could have been caught, but we thought it was worth the risk."

Bruce looked stunned. Judd felt Vicki's hand on his arm, but he pulled away.

"You keep saying we don't know how much time we have left, that people need Jesus before it's too late. So we do something about it and you criticize us for taking risks!"

156

"Now, Judd—"

"I know you're our pastor, but you're not our father. I don't know what everybody else thinks, but I'm prepared to risk this and a lot more. If it means the difference between people going to heaven or hell, I don't care what happens to me."

Judd didn't realize he had risen from his chair. He looked around, embarrassed at the shocked looks. Judd sat and took a deep breath. "Bruce, you didn't even ask who Vicki was going to see in the hospital. Part of the reason Vicki even has a chance to talk with Shelly is the *Underground*."

"It's not like we didn't think this through," Vicki said. "It's hard to be criticized when so far only good has come from it."

"I'm proud of you," Bruce said, "and I know you have the right motives, but—" He sighed and ran a hand through his hair. "I don't know how much I can tell you."

"About what?" Lionel said.

Bruce pulled a copy of the *Underground* from his desk. "There is another underground believer at Nicolae High. This person believes you're all in grave danger."

"A Christian teacher?" Vicki said.

"I didn't say that," Bruce said. "I was asked not to reveal this person's identity, and I expect you to respect that."

"They know who we are?" Vicki said.

"Process of elimination," Bruce said. "This person heard about you through me. Assumptions about your identity were made when the *Underground* showed up."

157

"How do they, or you, know about the other two guys?"

"Their Bibles were confiscated and they worked for the school paper last year. They were in some meeting today?"

Judd nodded. "If whoever this is is worried about us being expelled, that's not exactly grave danger."

"Expulsion would endanger the whole group and your setup," Bruce said. "But this is worse than expulsion. Because of the high profile of the school, Global Community forces want to make this a test case. They're talking about assigning GC monitors to the school, people with the authority to make arrests."

"Why would they be worried about us?" Ryan said. "We're just a bunch of kids."

"But you're talking about things Carpathia can't tolerate. The Antichrist and his henchmen won't allow proselytizing in a school named after him."

"What's pros—"

"Proselytizing," Lionel said. "Trying to get people to believe what you believe."

"Pretty soon it'll be illegal," Bruce said.

"To even talk to people about it?" Ryan said.

"That's right."

"You think they'll start taking *all* the Bibles away?"

"That wouldn't surprise me."

Ryan shook his head. "So why don't we gather up all the Bibles we can and hide them? Later on we can give them to the people who want to read them."

"Not a bad idea," Bruce said. "Where would you hide them?"

"Not here," Ryan said, "because that's the first place they'd look. We could stash them in Judd's garage or in his basement until we find a better place."

"First we'd have to find a bunch of Bibles," Judd said.

"That's easy," Ryan said. "The people who disappeared had lots of 'em. I found some in a house the other day that looked like they'd never been used. I think the looters took everything else."

"Looks like you guys have at least one new mission," Bruce said, and Judd could tell it meant a lot to Ryan that he had come up with a plan of his own.

"Before you go," Bruce said, "tell me a little about Vicki's friend. I'm sorry I didn't ask earlier."

After Vicki told him of her conversation with Shelly, Bruce prayed for her. "And you know what, kids?" he said. "I need you to be praying for me too. As I think about the pull I feel to travel and trying to unite the little pockets of what the Bible calls the 'tribulation saints,' I don't know how I'm going to do it."

"We'll pray for you," Judd said. "And I'm sorry for blowing up like that."

"I forgive you. Like the rest of us, your strength is your weakness. You know what that means?"

Judd shook his head. "The same passion you have for God also gives you a short fuse. On one side it's a strength. On the other, it's a weakness. Something to work on."

When Vicki walked into Shelly's hospital room, Shelly's mother was by the bed. She rambled about her problems while she flipped through television channels looking for who-knew-what. She acted as if Shelly was just sick and seemed oblivious to the fact that Shelly had tried to take her own life.

"I need to grab a bite to eat," she said just before visiting hours were over. "I'll be back to say goodnight."

Shelly shook her head as her mother left. "She needs a drink. That's what she's leaving for."

Vicki couldn't wait any longer. "I promised I would keep your secret, Shelly. Whatever it is, God can forgive you. You mentioned something about a baby before I had to go?"

Shelly pulled at her fingers and looked toward the door.

"We're alone now—you don't have to worry," Vicki said.

"I never told anybody about this," Shelly said. "It's about Mom. I went with her to the doctor because she was feeling funny, and the tests came back positive. She was pregnant."

"I don't understand," Vicki said. "Why would you feel guilty for your mother being pregnant?"

"I hated her so much, Vick.' I couldn't stand living there anymore. She told me not to, but I told Dad. She said he'd move out, that he'd leave us alone, but I was so mad at her. They yelled and screamed the whole night, and the next day he was gone. It's my fault, Vick'."

"You know that's not true, Shel'," Vicki said. "People make their own decisions. Your dad would've found out anyway, right?"

"Not if she'd had an abortion."

Shelly looked like she was about to cry.

"To be honest, I was kinda excited to have a little brother or sister. I thought maybe I could take care of it, that it would make things better. I thought Mom might get some help, might sober up. But that night, when the Fischers and their babies vanished, God took my mom's baby too. He punished me for what I did."

Shelly collapsed into tears and Vicki embraced her. Shelly's mother did not return, so Vicki called Judd and told him she was staying the night. She was there, dozing in the chair, when Shelly awoke in the morning.

WE'VE all done bad things, Shel'," Vicki said as they ate breakfast together in Shelly's hospital room.

"You really think God could forgive me?"

"I know it's hard to believe, but that's what he promises. He can make you a new person."

Shelly hesitated. "Like I said, it sounds too good to be true."

"It's a gift, Shel'. We all missed it the first time around. That's why we're still here."

"But if you've hated somebody all your life, and you've split your mom and dad apart just to be mean, it doesn't seem right."

"God can forgive any sin, Shel', trust me. It's not how much we've sinned that's important—it's how much God loves us."

"What do you do to make this all happen?" Shelly said. "Do I have to kneel or something?"

"I didn't," Vicki said. "I don't think God cares, as long as your heart is in the right position. Know what I mean?"

"Yeah. I guess I want to do it, but I don't know what to say."

"You want to pray after me?"

"You mean say what you say?"

"Sure. If you mean it, God will know."

Shelly nodded and closed her eyes. She repeated each phrase after Vicki. "Dear God, I know I'm a sinner. Please forgive me. Thank you for dying on the cross for my sins so I wouldn't have to pay the penalty myself. Please come into my life and make me a new person. And thank you for promising that I will go to heaven to be with you when I die. In Jesus' name, amen."

"That's it?" Shelly said. "I don't feel any different. Don't I have to do something else?"

"The only thing you need to do now is follow him."

———————————

Vicki was thrilled later to be able to tell Judd on the way to school, "We finally have another female member of the Young Tribulation Force!"

A line of kids stretched in front of the school when Judd and Vicki arrived. Judd strained to see what was going on and finally tapped a boy on the shoulder and asked.

"They're searching everybody," he said, "I think because of that underground paper."

Judd and Vicki finally made it through the doors and found the assistant principal and a Global Community

guard going through backpacks. They were searching
every third student.

"You," the Global Community worker said to Judd,
"over here."

Vicki was waved on. She stopped at her locker and looked
back. A commotion arose. Shouting. Books flying.

"That's not mine!" someone shouted. "Let me go!"

A Global Community worker led a student away. Judd
slipped out of line unnoticed and joined Vicki.

"I think they found some booze in his backpack,"
Judd said.

"This is just what Bruce was afraid of. How are we
going to get copies through now?"

During announcements, Principal Jenness described
the searches as "unfortunately necessary. We're sorry many
were inconvenienced this morning. If we knew who the
perpetrators were, we wouldn't have to conduct such
searches. Any helpful information will be rewarded."

That night when the kids met with Bruce, Vicki loved
seeing his reaction when he heard about Shelly.

Judd said, "It makes me want to do another edition
of the *Underground* soon."

"I can imagine," Bruce said. "I wanted you to play it
safe, but now I don't know what to say. There's more
danger than ever—I know that. Let me show you what

you're up against." He turned a television monitor and pushed Play on the VCR.

A Global Community CNN reporter explained how President Gerald Fitzhugh had called upon nations of the world to study Nicolae Carpathia's proposal to do away with all weapons. As a goodwill gesture, the President gave a new 757 airplane to the United Nations.

Carpathia gazed directly into the camera, appearing to look right into the eyes of each viewer. His voice was quiet and emotional.

"I would like to thank President Fitzhugh for this most generous gesture. We at the United Nations are deeply moved, grateful, and humbled. We look forward to a wonderful ceremony in Jerusalem next Monday."

Bruce turned off the TV. "We need to pray for Rayford Steele," he said. "You know he and his daughter Chloe go to this church. We believe he will be asked to fly that plane for Carpathia."

"He'd be in almost as much danger as Judd and Vicki, wouldn't he?" Ryan joked.

"What ceremony is Carpathia talking about?" Vicki said.

"I believe it's the signing of a treaty between Israel and the new one-world government. If it is, it will signal the beginning of the seven-year Tribulation I've told you about. There are other signs. All nations are to convert their money to dollars within the year, so we'll have a one-world currency. It's almost too much to believe. There's also talk of a one-world religion, which was also prophesied in Scripture.

"Pieces of the one-world government are falling into place more quickly than I ever thought possible."

Vicki and Bruce visited Shelly at her trailer the next evening. Shelly looked pale, but there was a smile Vicki hadn't seen for ages. Shelly seemed nervous around Bruce at first, but Vicki assured her he was there only to help her understand more about the Bible.

Bruce stood when Shelly's mom walked into the room. Her hair was a mess and she smelled of alcohol. Shelly said, "You know Vicki, Mom. This is her friend, Pastor Barnes."

"A pastor? What are you doing here?"

"Just talking to Shelly about God," Bruce said. "Feel free to join us." Shelly's mother squinted warily at him but sat next to her daughter on the couch as Bruce pulled up a chair. First he told his own story, about how he'd been a phony for so many years and then lost his wife and children when he was left behind at the Rapture. He said he had finally prayed and received Christ into his life.

"Shelly made that same decision last night," Bruce said.

"I don't believe in religion," Shelly's mom said.

"This is not religion," Bruce said. "Religion is our way of trying to reach God. This is a relationship with a personal God who wants to help us."

"I don't need help."

Bruce didn't argue. He just pointed out specific Scriptures and explained them. Vicki knew he wanted Shelly to be sure she was going to heaven some day.

"In 1 John 1:9 we are told that if we confess our sins, God is faithful to forgive our sins and cleanse us from unrighteousness. And near the end of the Gospel of John, the writer says, 'These things are written that you may believe that Jesus is the Christ, the Son of God, and that by believing you may have life in His name.' The book of Romans says that everyone who calls upon the name of the Lord will be saved."

"The people who disappeared were the saved ones, Mom," Shelly said.

"That's right," Bruce said. "Just like you now, Shelly."

Shelly's mom struggled to push herself up off the couch. She looked down on Bruce. "Get out of my house," she said. "You're trying to brainwash my girl."

"Mom! Just listen!"

"I won't," she said. "Now get out!"

The next day a still-dejected Vicki walked with Ryan as he darted in and out of various neighborhoods. Though she thought it unnecessary, she carried a huge trash bag. Ryan believed he could find enough Bibles to fill it, and Vicki didn't argue. He was so excited about this adventure that she didn't want to stifle him.

Ryan would find an abandoned house and walk right in. "I found seven in here!" he would call to Vicki. He plunked them into the bottom of the bag and ran off again. *He was right,* Vicki thought. *I'll never be able to drag this home.*

They came to the brick shell of a burned-out house.

"Stay out of there," Vicki said. "It's too dangerous. Anyway, everything's burned!"

"Something's in there," Ryan shouted, running ahead. He pushed aside the charred remains of the front door and a sooty beam came crashing down, just missing him.

"Get out, Ryan!" Vicki said as she ran to the house.

"Wait!" he said. "There's somebody or something in here!"

Vicki followed him in and saw something moving in the rubble. Ryan got close and it whimpered. Black as coal, it looked like a wild animal. Ryan knelt and held out his hand, and the animal sniffed. Finally, it gingerly moved toward him. Vicki held her breath as Ryan gathered it in his arms.

"What is it?" Vicki said.

"Our new dog," Ryan said. "He looks like he hasn't eaten in weeks."

Ryan was as dirty as the pup, but it occurred to Vicki that this was the answer to her prayers. She had prayed that God would take some of the pain from him. Maybe this new companion would do just that.

"No way," Judd said. "He's not bringing that filthy thing into my house. It looks more like a rat than a dog."

Ryan handed the dog to Vicki and ran inside, returning with a piece of hot dog. "Come here, boy!"

The dog lunged at the food and nearly nipped Ryan's finger.

"Just like a rat," Judd said.

169

"Can I talk with you, Judd?" Vicki said. "In private?"

Vicki and Judd went into the den. Judd had begun the next edition of the *Underground* and the place was cluttered.

"You have to understand what this means to Ryan," she said. "What could it hurt?"

Judd shook his head. "It's not practical. We're trying to do some radical things here that take up most of our time. What happens when the dog doesn't get fed or isn't let out, and Ryan's not around?"

"Make it his responsibility. It'll be good for him. For all of us."

She was right and Judd knew it. She was in tune with Ryan in a way he could never be.

"Don't blame me if it doesn't work," he said. "The first time Ryan messes up, the dog goes."

Vicki was elated to see the change in Ryan. He went straight to work giving it a bath. Judd had invited John and Mark over to work on the next *Underground*. Everybody seemed stunned when Ryan unwrapped the dog and revealed its white fur.

"What's his name?" Mark said.

"Call him Rapture," Lionel said.

"How about Ashes?" Vicki said.

"Wait," Ryan said. "What was that bird that came out of the ashes?"

"The Phoenix," John said.

"That's it! I'll name him Phoenix."

170

Judd told John he wanted the next edition of the *Under-ground* to cover the Israel treaty. "We'll deliver it Friday and the treaty will be signed Monday. That ought to convince people we're onto something."

"How are you gonna do it," Lionel said, "with all those Global Community thugs around?"

"They aren't going to be there every day," John said. He pulled out of his pocket what looked like a tiny radio. "We put a transmitter on Mrs. Jenness's desk. It's a tiny smiley face at the end of her stapler. This receiver has to be within a hundred yards, and sometimes it doesn't work too well, but we heard her say the Global Community guys would be back Friday. That's when the *Olive Branch* gets distributed again. We can't risk that scheme again."

"I can think of only one way to get the paper to everyone," Vicki said. "And we'll have to use Ryan to do it."

"Me?" Ryan said.

"Yeah," Vicki said. "Are you willing?"

"I am," Lionel said. "I don't care what happens to me anymore."

"Me neither," Ryan said.

"*Either*," Lionel said.

LATE Thursday night, Judd drove Vicki, Lionel, and Ryan to Nicolae High, where Vicki had left a window slightly open, leading to the showers in the gym locker room.

Judd parked a few blocks away and each kid grabbed a box filled with the *Underground.*

This was their best issue yet. With John's expertise with the publishing program, it looked professionally printed. Readers of the *Underground* would learn that the Bible predicted the signing of the treaty that coming Monday. Assuming it came off as the paper outlined, readers should be convinced that the writers knew what they were talking about. They would be urged to give their lives to Christ before the beginning of the Tribulation. John and Mark had even included an untraceable E-mail address where students could write for more information and a Bible study.

The kids knew the prophecy could also backfire. If

Bruce was wrong about the signing of the peace treaty with Israel, their message wouldn't ring true. It was a risk they were willing to take.

All four wore dark clothing. Each carried a winter hat that pulled over their faces. They had heard rumors of surveillance cameras.

Judd and Lionel were to creep to the rear entrance of the school where it would be easy to hide behind the evergreens. Vicki and Ryan crawled along the rear wall to an inner courtyard. The place was well lit, so when Vicki gave the signal, they dashed to the other side, Ryan following her into the darkness.

They gingerly made their way down a few steps to what smelled like a cellar. A dim bulb above lit a huge door with bars across the window. A little farther down was a small, cobweb-filled window. "This is the one I left slightly open," Vicki said. "We're right under the gym near the showers."

Vicki pushed and the window gave way. "Can you squeeze through?"

"It's tight," Ryan said. "No wonder you didn't want to do this. Looks like the spiders are having a party."

"Yuck! Go left to the stairwell and up to the gym, across the basketball court to the back entrance. Those are the only doors I could find that don't have alarms."

Vicki returned to Judd and Lionel. They wouldn't approach the school until Ryan opened the door.

"What's taking him so long?" Lionel whispered.

"It's a long way," Vicki said. "And pretty dark. He probably has to feel his way along."

"What if a janitor or night watchman is in there?" Judd said. "Or one of the Global Community guys?"

"Don't even think about it," Vicki said.

The wind picked up. Judd and Lionel sat on the open boxes to keep the papers from flying and pulled their hats down over their faces.

"Look," Vicki said. A door opened at the end of the gym. Ryan stuck out his hand with his thumb up.

The three raced to the gym, boxes in tow. In seconds they were safely inside.

"I took a wrong turn and wound up in a big storage room," Ryan said. "It's like a dungeon. Perfect place to store my Bibles. I had to wait under the stairs when a janitor came down. He's sweeping or dusting or something in the locker room."

"Then we've got to hurry," Judd said. "And be ready to hide if you hear him."

"You'll hear him," Ryan said. "He's carrying a big ring of jangly keys."

They split into two pairs, Judd and Ryan taking one end of the school, Vicki and Lionel the other. They would meet in the middle. They folded copies of the *Underground* and slid one through the vent opening in each locker. It was slow work. It was 2 A.M. when they finally met near the front office.

"Look up there in the grate," Judd said. "They did install cameras. They'll be checking the tape tomorrow."

"Can we go now?" Ryan said. "I want to check on Phoenix and make sure he's OK."

"Ryan, wait!" Vicki said. Before she could stop him,

Ryan pushed open the fire doors at the front of the school. A shrill alarm filled the hallway. Ryan turned, wide-eyed. "I didn't mean to," he mouthed.

"This way!" Judd shouted, and they raced back to the gym. When they reached the back doors, Vicki heard the janitor's keys bouncing. He was closing in. Judd quickly opened the doors and started out, but stopped. A siren. Tires on gravel.

"We can make it," Lionel said.

"We have a better chance hiding," Judd said. "It's an open field. They'll see us out there for sure."

"The dungeon," Ryan said.

And they bolted downstairs in the darkness, putting distance between themselves and the jangling keys.

Vicki could feel the spiders. Everywhere. She shuddered and stayed close to Judd. After a few minutes their eyes adjusted to the dark. They were in an inner chamber underneath the gymnasium. Boxes of paper and school supplies were stacked around the room. The four huddled behind water-stained boxes.

"Don't worry," Ryan whispered as he swiped at the cobwebs. "These are only spider leftovers. They won't hurt you."

Judd fiddled with something in his pocket, then raised his hand for quiet. They heard footsteps overhead.

"They're in the gym," Lionel said. "I hope they don't have dogs."

"Dogs?" Vicki said.

The footsteps came closer. A beam of light waved through the hallway. A man shouted and another joined him.

176

"Here's the window they came through," one man said. "I heard 'em. I was workin' down the hall there. They probably came in to spray paint a few walls. I'll bet we scared 'em and they took off the same way they came in."

A light shone near the dungeon.

"Stinks down here," the first man said.

"Tell me about it. I'm here almost every night and I'm still not used to it. Let's get out of here."

The kids waited a few minutes, then tiptoed to the gym. The men were gone. Judd opened the back doors of the gym and motioned the others toward the car.

As the back door closed, a light flashed in their faces. Colored lights. A voice on a loudspeaker. "Police! Stop right there!"

"Scatter!" Judd yelled. "Try to get back to the car!"

Vicki ran with Ryan. The police car threw gravel and went another direction. Toward Judd, she thought. She and Ryan ran past the football field toward town. When they came near houses they stopped to catch their breath.

"Where's the car?" Ryan said.

"That way," Vicki said, gasping. "You run pretty fast."

Vicki and Ryan took the long route and made their way across lawns and through alleys. A dog startled Vicki when it snapped at them through a chain link fence. When they finally made it back to the car, neither Judd nor Lionel was in sight.

A car approached with its headlights off, so Vicki and Ryan crouched beside Judd's car.

"They're not there," a voice said.

"That's Judd," Ryan said, standing.

"Don't!" Vicki said, but it was too late.

"Hey," Judd said. "You made it."

"How did you?" Vicki said, standing. Judd and Lionel were in the backseat, John and Mark in the front.

"I got Judd's SOS on the gizmo," John said, "and we got here just in time to see these two running for their lives."

Judd found sleep impossible. He wandered down to the living room and found the others so keyed up that they were sitting around the living room talking. "We're all running on empty," he said. "Too many short nights in a row. Even if we can't sleep, we need to get to bed and at least rest. Tomorrow Nicolae High is going to get its strongest dose yet of the *Underground.*"

Judd finally fell asleep just before dawn and made everybody late for school. As he and Vicki hurried in, she said, "I thought the GC guys would be searching everybody again."

Judd shrugged. "Me too," he said, just as they came upon hundreds of students lined up in the hallway. School administrators and Global Community monitors went from locker to locker with garbage bags searching for copies of the *Underground.* Mr. Handlesman barked at kids and banged on their lockers if they were too slow.

"Students with lockers in the east hallway only, report there immediately," Mrs. Jenness said over the loudspeaker. "Everyone else, remain in your class."

John rushed up to Judd and Vicki. "Everybody who went

to their lockers before first period got one," John whispered. "Now the office is in damage-control mode. You should hear students, though, Judd. Everybody's talking about it."

———————————

Vicki's gym class sat in the bleachers, still dressed. Mrs. Waltonen conferred with an assistant as the girls sat and talked. Vicki sat near the front and listened.

"Why don't they want us to read this stuff?" one girl said.

"It's dangerous," another said.

"It says there's going to be some treaty signed Monday. It's supposed to be predicted in the Bible."

"I never understood the Bible."

"This says you can, though. It makes sense to me."

All around Vicki girls were whispering, "I want to read it. I don't care what they say. If I find one, I'm keeping it." She was ecstatic. This was just what the Trib Force had been hoping for.

At the end of the period, Mr. Handlesman's voice came over the loudspeaker.

"We've just witnessed the last incident of rebellion at Nicolae Carpathia High School. We *will* find those responsible, and we will find them *today*. Anyone with any information that can help us should report to the office now."

Kids walked through the halls carefully, as if through a war zone. Vicki knew better but felt people looked at her strangely, like they knew of her involvement.

In Vicki's English class, Mr. Carlson asked, "How many have actually read this underground paper?"

A few raised their hands. Vicki knew there had to be more but couldn't tell if they were afraid or really hadn't looked at the *Underground*.

"Why do you think this publication is so threatening to those in charge here?" Mr. Carlson said.

"There are a lot of kooks out there," a girl said. Vicki knew she was on the staff of the *Olive Branch*. "Maybe they're trying to manipulate us by scaring us about Mr. Carpathia being the Antichrist."

"Kooks is right," someone else said. "I thought all those people were gone."

"And what if one of those kooks is one of you?" Carlson said. "A schoolmate? A classmate?"

Kids looked around the room, laughing and pointing at each other. Vicki felt her cheeks flush. Mr. Carlson tried to restore order, but he was unsuccessful until Coach Handlesman entered with two Global Community guards. The room got deathly quiet. The guards stood by the door as Handlesman spoke to Mr. Carlson.

"You have to be kidding," Carlson said with a laugh. "There must be a mistake."

Coach Handlesman turned to the class. "Which one of you is Vicki Byrne?"

Vicki held her breath as everyone turned and looked at her.

"Come with us, Miss Byrne," the coach said.

"Why?" she said. "What?"

Coach Handlesman approached her desk. He leaned inches from her face.

"We know," he said. "It's over."

20

BETWEEN classes Mark found Judd and pulled him into an audiovisual department closet down the hall from the front office. John had hooked a small speaker to the receiver. "I got a message from Vicki that she had been found out," he said.

Judd looked at his own message receiver. It was off. "Oh no."

"She's not in the office yet," John said, his ear near the speaker. "At least I haven't heard anybody yet."

"My battery must be dead," Judd said. "Tell Lionel and Ryan to pray for Vicki." Mark punched in the message. "And just in case, add a line to tell Vicki we're with her."

"Wait, I hear something," John said. "Somebody just came in and sat down." They all huddled closer. Judd heard crying and hoped that wasn't Vicki. He knew she was tougher than that.

A woman's voice cut through the static. "Stop blubbering. Tell them what you know and get the money."

"Nobody said the reward was money, Mom," a girl said. "Why are you making me do this?"

"It'll be money, all right. Tell them everything. I want to get out of here too. I got places to go."

Judd felt helpless. He wished he had been caught. Instead, Vicki was about to take the blame for them all.

"How did they find Vicki?" Mark said.

"Somebody must have turned her in," Judd said.

Two GC guards sat behind Vicki and in front of the closed door to Principal Jenness's inner office. Vicki felt a vibration and peeked at the tiny screen in her pocket.

"Pray for Vicki—Caught," it read. Then, "If you see this, hang in, Vick'."

She prayed silently, "Please give me the right words. And thank you for my friends."

Coach Handlesman and Mrs. Jenness entered. He pulled a chair near her, letting it scrape across the floor. Mrs. Jenness leaned against a file cabinet, arms folded. The two adults stared at her for what seemed an eternity.

"Why'd you do it?" Handlesman said.

"What did I do?"

"You know what you did," Mrs. Jenness said. "Why did you trip the alarm the other day?"

Vicki stared at her.

"C'mon, Byrne," Handlesman said. "We saw it on tape, and we also compared the video of the kids who broke into the school last night. It was you, Vicki.

There's no use trying to hide it any longer. Tell us about it."

She knew they couldn't have seen her face the night before. They were trying to scare her into confessing.

Mrs. Jenness moved to a desk near Vicki and sat. She smiled and tried to sound reassuring.

"You're just misguided," she said. "We don't want to punish you. We just want to find out who's behind this."

Right, Vicki thought. *It had to be somebody else. A girl like me wouldn't have the brains to put two sentences together.*

"Just tell us who put you up to this," Mrs. Jenness said, "and this all goes away."

"Otherwise," Handlesman said, "you go with these guys. Believe me, you don't want to do that."

Vicki turned. The guards stared at her with blank faces. She cleared her throat. Her voice came out shaky. Scared.

"I'm sorry about the alarm," Vicki said. "I didn't know the fire department would come. Nobody put me up to that. I'll pay a fine or whatever."

"We can overlook a prank like that," Mrs. Jenness said. "But this newspaper—that's much more serious. Why don't you tell us about it, Vicki?"

Vicki remained silent, staring at Handlesman. The coach smiled and looked at the principal.

"She knows," he said. "She knows we couldn't see her face on the video from last night." He turned back to Vicki. "But I wonder if we sent someone to your home

183

in—he looked at a clipboard—Kings Trailer Court. Bet we'd find a mask, huh? Or maybe evidence of your part in producing the *Underground?*"

"We've gotta get her out of there," Judd said.

"We don't know what's going on," John said. "All I can hear is this girl whimpering and her mother."

"How could we get her out?" Mark said. "They've got her. Maybe it's time we faced the music and turned ourselves in."

"That's crazy," John said.

"As crazy as letting her take the fall for all of us?" Mark said. "She saved us the other day with that fire alarm. And for that she gets punished?"

The speaker crackled. Coach Handlesman was in Jenness's office, talking to the woman and the girl. He was asking about Vicki.

"It was her," the woman interrupted. "It had to be."

"She never told me that," the girl said.

"Why do you *think* it was her?" Handlesman said. "Did she mention the newspaper?"

"I brought it up," the girl said. "We talked about stuff in the paper," the girl said. "But she never actually said she was a part of it."

"You've got the guilty one," the woman said. "Can we have the money now?"

"That doesn't prove anything," Handlesman said. "No proof, no reward."

Judd said, "Mark, give me your gadget, quick."

184

Vicki felt another vibration and reached in her pocket as if peeking at her watch. It read, "Admit nothing. No proof."

How would anyone know that? she wondered, then remembered the bug in Jenness's office behind her.

"You don't need to worry about what time it is, young lady," Mrs. Jenness said. "You'd better be thinking about your future. Things could be pretty grim."

Coach Handlesman returned from Jenness's office, but Vicki couldn't turn around quickly enough to see who was in there before the door closed.

Coach Handlesman pulled up his chair again. "We know this wasn't your idea," he said. "You just got caught up in it. Somebody probably convinced you this would be a noble cause. We can understand that. If you cooperate now, tell us who's involved, we'll see things get worked out for you."

"And if I don't?"

Mrs. Jenness said, "You could be removed from your home and sentenced to a juvenile facility."

"For a fire-alarm prank?" Vicki said.

Handlesman slammed his fist on the table. "We don't care about that!" he screamed. "Tell us about the newspaper!"

"What makes you think it was me?"

Handlesman rose and stood in front of Mrs. Jenness's office. "Here's why," he said.

He opened the door and let it swing wide. Vicki gasped.

Shelly. And her mother. The woman pointed at Vicki.

"That's her," she said. "She's the one with all the crazy ideas. She came over to our house with that pastor of hers. Trying to brainwash my kid."

Shelly didn't speak. She just cried and mouthed, "I'm sorry. I'm so sorry."

Handlesman shut the door. "This is it," he said. "Either tell us the truth or face the consequences."

"I can't take it any more," Mark said. "I'm going in there and tell them it was me."

"Don't," John said. "Let this play out. Maybe you ought to call your pastor, Judd."

"I don't want to get him involved," Judd said. "He said something like this might happen."

"Hey, call him and tell him," John said. "At least he can pray for her."

"You guys really get me," Mark said, and he was out the door and down the hall before John or Judd could stop him.

Vicki was startled by a sharp knock on the office door. Coach Handlesman opened it and Mrs. Waltonen said, "May I see you and Mrs. Jenness a moment? Outside?"

"We're in the middle of something," Mrs. Jenness said.

"I think it will be worth your while," Mrs. Waltonen said.

Handlesman and Jenness left the door slightly open,

and Vicki saw Mark in the hall. She furrowed her brow and mouthed, "What are you doing?"

Mark shrugged. Handlesman said, "Unless you have business here, pal, get lost."

Mark caught Vicki's eye again and put his hand in his pocket, then scurried off. Vicki read his message: "I'll confess."

She quickly tapped back: "NO!"

"If Mark gives it up, we all have to," John said.

"She doesn't want him to," Judd said, looking at John's screen over his shoulder. "Let's keep our heads."

"If Vicki gets out of there without talking, the GC guys will be all over her to see who she hangs with."

Mark came back in. "That's one brave girl. Waltonen is talking to Jenness and Handlesman."

"What about?"

"She said she knows where Vicki hangs out. Waltonen gave them the street you live on, but she couldn't remember the address."

"I knew that would come back to haunt us," Judd said. "Handlesman will be sniffing around the neighborhood all afternoon. How did Vicki look?"

"Like she was on trial."

Vicki sat up as Mrs. Jenness and Coach Handlesman returned. Neither looked at her.

"Anything you want to say?" the coach said finally.

"I'm sorry about the alarm. I won't do it again."

He nodded to the principal.

"We're going to let you think about it overnight, Vicki," she said. "Your future depends on what you tell us. Tomorrow we want you back here with your parents."

Vicki wondered if her mom and dad would be proud of what she was doing. Could they see her? That thought overwhelmed her and she began to cry.

"It's OK, Vicki," Mrs. Jenness said, handing her a tissue. "You have a talk with your family. I'm sure they'll want you to do the right thing."

The bell rang and Coach Handlesman said, "You'd better get to your next class."

Vicki walked out into the stream of students. At the end of the hall Judd, John, and Mark turned and walked the other way. Would they desert her? Did they think she had betrayed them the way Shelly had betrayed her?

For the first time since she had met her new friends, she felt utterly alone.

21

SOMEONE was following her in a car. Vicki clutched her books to her chest and walked toward town. She didn't look back. She couldn't risk letting them know she suspected.

Mrs. Jenness had let her go. That was a surprise. But Vicki would have stayed all night without ratting on her friends. But would her friends be as faithful to her?

Seeing Shelly and her mother in the principal's office had sickened Vicki. Shelly had been sincere about her faith, hadn't she? Could it have been an act? The sight of Judd, John, and Mark turning away from her down the hall made her heart sink. Didn't they care? Or were they trying to protect her by keeping their distance?

Vicki had a good idea who was following her: someone from school assigned to see where she went. Perhaps Judd and the others had figured that out. They wouldn't have simply abandoned her.

Vicki had to get back to her friends. She had to talk with Pastor Bruce. When Mrs. Jenness discovered she had no parents, all the kids would be at risk. She needed to keep moving and stay away from Judd's house.

Vicki looked in shop windows and followed the reflection of the trailing car. When it stopped, she ducked into a drugstore. She sat at a bench in the back and tapped out a message on the tiny digital system on her wrist that looked like a watch. She asked Judd to meet her at a nearby park. She would try to shake whoever was following her and meet him there.

The front door opened. A man's voice. Loud. "Did a girl with red hair come in here?"

Vicki crouched beneath the prescription window.

"Right there," the cashier said.

Vicki looked up. The overhead mirror ran the length of the wall and angled down. The man behind the counter pointed toward her. Vicki remembered how her little sister, Jeanni, used to play hide-and-seek by sticking her head in the closet, her rear sticking out of the coats.

"Duh," Vicki said as she leapt to her feet.

"Stop!" the cashier shouted.

Vicki pushed open a door that said EMPLOYEES ONLY.

"Hey, you can't go in there!" the pharmacist barked.

"We'll get her," someone shouted.

Vicki locked the door behind her. Footsteps and shouts outside. Darkness inside. Vicki fumbled for a light switch. Keys were jangling, getting closer.

"What did she take?" someone said.

Vicki moved toward a thin strip of light on the other

pUrSUEd

side of the room. The back door! She tripped over a chair and banged her head. The doorknob jiggled behind her.

She leaned against the back door, and it swung open to blistering light. A siren rang just above her head. She staggered out. As the door swept shut she read, "Emergency Exit Only—Alarm Will Sound."

She ran.

Judd had waited in his car after school, hoping Vicki would walk that way. After twenty minutes he was about to leave for Lionel and Ryan's school when his wrist messenger vibrated and he saw Vicki's message. He quickly sent another to Lionel and Ryan: "Get home and keep watch. I'll be there as fast as I can."

The park had been a late-night teen hangout. With the rise in crime, a lot of kids were afraid to go there. Judd sat in the parking lot looking at the empty swing sets. Before the disappearances, the place would have been full of little kids. Now there were no families at picnic tables or moms and dads with strollers. It was a ghost town.

"Get the car," the loud man said. "I'll meet you at the end of the alley."

Vicki heard shuffling and then silence. She didn't want to rise up from her hiding place, but the smell was overpowering. She peeked from under the lid of the huge garbage bin. No one. Something furry moved behind her. She bolted.

191

Vicki ran down the alley. She was halfway to the main street when a car passed. A second later it was back.

"There she is!" a man said, but she didn't see his face. She was running the other way. The alley fence was way over her head—no time to climb. Every door she tried was locked. The car pulled behind her and gunned the engine.

Judd had been so focused on getting to the park and alerting Ryan and Lionel that he forgot to let Vicki know he was waiting.

He backtracked, slowing to look in shop windows and down alleys. He heard the screech of tires and swerved to miss an oncoming car barreling around a corner. He drove past the drugstore and hung a left. Judd sped past an alley and slammed on his brakes. Vicki ran toward him, the car bearing down on her.

Judd made a U-turn and opened the passenger door. Vicki jumped in. "Go, go, go!" she shouted.

"I don't mean to be rude," Judd said, speeding away, "but you look awful."

"Thanks," Vicki said, panting. "Just get me out of here!"

Judd sped through a yellow light. The car behind had a red, but it ran through the light, swerved to miss oncoming traffic, and kept gaining.

"Who is that?" Judd said.

"It's gotta be Handlesman or somebody he told to follow me. They want us bad."

Judd turned at the next light, then into an alley. They

careened around another corner and through an empty parking lot.

"Hang on," Judd said as he crossed a patch of grass and turned into a tree-lined subdivision. He flew across a bridge, spun in the entrance to a park, and came to a halt behind some shrubs. The trailing car was nowhere in sight.

"Better stay here awhile just to make sure," Judd said. "Who gave you the shiner?"

"A filing cabinet, I think," Vicki said.

Through gasps, Vicki told Judd about her interrogation at school. Judd told her they had listened to Shelly and her mother through the bug in Mrs. Jenness's office.

"What did Shelly say?" Vicki asked. "How much were you able to hear?"

"We heard Shelly crying and her mother yelling at her to give you up," he said. "Not much more."

"Then maybe they pushed her into it," Vicki said. "At least that's what I hope."

Judd sniffed. "Is it me, or is there an odor in here?"

Vicki blushed. "I hid in a garbage bin."

Judd pulled a blackened piece of banana peel from her hair. "Pretty resourceful."

"And gross," Vicki said, shuddering and rubbing her arms. "I hate goose bumps."

"Are you cold?"

She shook her head. "Judd, they told me to bring my parents tomorrow."

"They don't know about your mom and dad?"

"If they do, they're not letting on."

Judd paused. "Uh, I want to thank you. We couldn't

hear the interrogation, but we could tell you handled yourself well. We were all impressed."

"You would have done the same for me."

"Mark wanted to rescue you. Said we should give ourselves up."

"He didn't think I could handle the pressure?"

"He didn't think it was fair to put you through it."

"I could've choked Handlesman," Vicki said. "He treated me like some dumb little girl, like I'd never have the brains to put two sentences together, let alone a newspaper."

"Don't worry," Judd said. "You'll get your chance to show him Monday morning."

"You're not going through with it again, are you?"

Judd nodded. "Why not? If Bruce is right, the treaty between Israel and Carpathia will be headlined around the world. We can't pass this up. We have to tell people what's ahead."

"Bruce says the treaty signals the beginning of the Tribulation, right?"

"Exactly," Judd said.

"But how are you gonna get the *Underground* inside? You've got the guard checkpoint, cameras, and every teacher in the school on the lookout."

Judd shrugged. "We've got God on our side."

Vicki ran through all her options, and none seemed very good. Judd waited until dusk to start the car.

"Can we stop and see Bruce on the way home?" Vicki said. "I want to see what he thinks."

"He could pretend to be your father," Judd said.

"That'd be lying," Vicki said. "He'd never do that."

A few cars lined the New Hope Village Church parking lot. *Maybe the Tribulation Force is meeting,* Judd thought. He parked in front and kept the engine running. He waited while Vicki dashed inside. He flipped to a news station on the radio.

"Not a day has passed without some major development with new UN Secretary-General Nicolae Carpathia," the reporter said. "And today was no exception. Cincinnati Archbishop Peter Cardinal Mathews, who some see as successor to the vanished pope, announced a new cooperative religion that would incorporate the tenets of all major religions. He calls it the Global Community Faith."

"Our religions have caused much division and bloodshed," Cardinal Mathews droned. "From this day forward we will unite under the banner of the Global Community Faith. Our logo will contain sacred symbols from religions that represent all, and from here on will encompass all. Whether we believe God is a real person or merely a concept, God is in all and above all and around all. God is in us. God is us. We are God."

Judd shook his head. What a pack of lies.

"We will elect a pope," Mathews said. "And we expect that other major religions will continue to appoint leaders in their usual cycles. But these leaders will serve the Global Community Faith and be expected to maintain the loyalty and devotion of their parishioners to the larger cause."

The reporter continued. "United Nations Secretary-

General Nicolae Carpathia said the move toward one religion is a welcome change."

" 'We clearly are at the most momentous juncture in world history,' " Carpathia said. " 'With the consolidation to one form of currency, with the cooperation and toleration of many religions into one, with worldwide disarmament and commitment to peace, the world is truly becoming one.' "

"Another incredible development came when Nicolae Carpathia answered questions regarding the rebuilding of the Jewish temple and the future of the Islamic Dome of—"

Vicki jumped in the car and slapped the radio off.

"Go!" she shouted.

"What's going on?"

"Look," Vicki pointed.

Running toward them was an angry Coach Handlesman. Judd sped away.

"What's he doing here?" Judd said.

"Bruce's office door was kinda open, so I knocked. All of a sudden Coach Handlesman starts yelling! He accuses Bruce of crimes, says he'll have him thrown in jail. I was outta there."

"How could Coach Handlesman know about Bruce?"

Vicki shook her head. "Maybe Shelly gave them his name. Bruce went with me to her house."

"Great," Judd said. "I didn't want to drag Bruce into the middle of all this."

Judd parked near his house and watched for Coach Handlesman. When he was sure they had eluded

196

him, Judd pulled inside the garage and lowered the door.

Lionel and Ryan peppered them with questions until late.

"No lights tonight," Judd told them. And the four would take turns watching the street.

22

IT WAS midnight and Judd couldn't sleep. He sat in the dark living room with his four friends. Ryan and his dog, Phoenix, kept watch at the window.

"What should we do?" Lionel said, as if the problem were as much his as Vicki's.

"We could hide her," Ryan said. "I know a bunch of places they'll never find you, Vick."

"Get your stuff and let's get outta here," Judd said. "You can stay at a motel. Anywhere. We'll find a place for you, and when things calm down, you can come back."

"You know it's not that easy," Vicki said. "You gotta face your troubles. Running only postpones things."

"Just give us until Monday when the next edition of the *Underground* comes out," Judd said. "They'll think maybe you weren't involved in the first place."

"Yeah, then they'll believe I'm the ignorant stooge Coach Handlesman thinks I am."

Judd dialed Bruce's office. No answer. The next morning, with Ryan and Phoenix asleep by the window, he tried Bruce's home. No answer.

"I don't like this," Judd said. He was startled to hear a voice answer him.

"You're gonna like *this* even less," Lionel said. "Handlesman just pulled in."

Judd called downstairs to Vicki's room as the doorbell rang. He let Handlesman wait a moment while Lionel and Ryan hid in the den. Handlesman rang again and pounded on the door. "Come on, open up. I know you're in there!"

"Mr. Handlesman, what a nice surprise," Judd said. The coach walked in and looked around the house. Phoenix growled and barked from the den.

"Is she in there?" Coach Handlesman said.

"No, I don't think that's her bark," Judd said.

"Don't get smart with me, kid. Tell me—"

"I'm right here," Vicki said. "What's the matter? Didn't think I'd show up?"

"I'm not taking the chance."

Mr. Handlesman grabbed her arm and forced her through the door.

"Where are you taking her?" Judd shouted, but Mr. Handlesman kept going.

Lionel and Ryan came out as the car pulled away.

"We're cooked," Judd said. "It's only a matter of time until they get the rest of us."

They called it a hearing, but to Vicki it felt like a trial. Mrs. Jenness, Coach Handlesman, and Mrs. Waltonen testified against her. Vicki had admitted tripping a fire alarm, and they believed she had broken into the school and distributed the *Underground*.

Candace Goodwin of Global Community Social Services scribbled on a yellow legal pad. She was a tall, thin woman with glasses. She rarely looked up from her notes and made no eye contact with Vicki until the testimony against her was over.

"I'm in charge of custodial care," Mrs. Goodwin said. "Since there's no one with you, I'll assume you lost your parents and brother and sister in the vanishings."

"That's right."

"Do you have *any* aunts, uncles, or cousins?"

"Not that I know of," Vicki said. "I tried to get in touch with a friend of my brother's in Michigan, but he's gone, too."

"Where have you been living?"

"With friends."

"Are these the friends who published the *Underground*?"

Vicki looked at Coach Handlesman. "I'm from a trailer park. What would I know about that kind of thing?"

John and Mark joined Judd, Ryan, and Lionel at the house. The next issue of the *Underground* would be the most timely.

"Bingo!" John said, as he looked at the computer screen. "The big block against rebuilding the Jewish temple is the Islamic Dome of the Rock. Both the Jews and followers of Islam claim the site as a holy place. Carpathia says he's worked out an agreement to move the Dome to New Babylon."

"That means the Jews can rebuild the temple on the original site," Ryan said, "just like it says in the Bible."

Judd tapped the keyboard and stared out the window. "Where do you think they took her?"

"You didn't hear a word," John said.

"Yes, I did," Judd said. "I just—"

"Your mind's somewhere else," Mark interrupted. "Why don't we just stop and go look for Vicki?"

"We have to get this done," John said. "It may be our last issue anyway."

"Why don't we hide?" Mark said. "We can move everything to our house."

"Might not be a bad idea," Judd said.

"We could split up," Lionel said. "A couple of us go look for Vicki and the rest stay here."

"Vicki will get in touch if she needs us," John said.

"Wrong," Ryan said, holding up her wrist messenger. "We won't be hearing from her at all. She didn't have time to put it on."

"We have to find her then," Judd said. "I'll take Ryan, and you guys stay here."

Vicki was well into her story. She told how her parents had become Christians, what a change it had made in them, and how she felt when she was left behind.

202

Though she didn't use names, she told of the tape she had seen of a pastor who predicted exactly what had happened and told how to have a relationship with God.

"He said we are all sinners, that we deserve God's judgment, but that Jesus offers us forgiveness."

Mrs. Waltonen hung her head. At first she had been interested in Vicki's story. Mrs. Waltonen had lost a grandchild and other family members. Vicki wanted to give her hope, but now she seemed closed.

"Candace, I don't think we really need to hear this, do we?" Mrs. Jenness said.

"It's good to know motivation," Mrs. Goodwin said.

Mrs. Jenness tried to look concerned. "We're here to help you, Vicki. That's what we've tried to do all along. If you won't let us, you'll face the consequences."

"Which are . . . ?"

"Two options," Mrs. Goodwin said. "An emergency shelter called The Haven. You attend the same school, and your life stays pretty normal. Spartan, but comfortable."

"And option two?"

Mrs. Goodwin shrugged. "NDC."

"Northside?" Vicki said. "The detention center?"

Coach Handlesman nodded. "Not a nice place."

Judd and Ryan passed the school parking lot. Phoenix sat in the back and chewed on a toy. Coach Handlesman's car was there, but Vicki could have been anywhere.

"Can't we get in and listen on that bug you guys planted?" Ryan said.

"Too risky. Besides, only John has keys to that room."

Judd parked on a side street, and they left Phoenix in the car. He and Ryan went straight to the administrative wing, but the windows were high and dark. They crept a little ways along the brick wall, gingerly crunching the gravel underfoot.

"Get on my shoulders," Judd said.

Ryan pulled himself up and stretched to see inside. "Next room," he said. "Move down."

"Keep your head low," Judd said as he sneaked a few yards farther.

"It's her," Ryan whispered. "There's that coach guy and two women."

A van pulled in with NDC painted on the side. Judd dropped Ryan and dove to the ground. They lay there as a stocky woman climbed out.

"Looks like a dogcatcher's van," Ryan said. "There's a cage between the driver and the back seat."

"This might be our last chance," Judd said. "We have to get Vicki's wrist messenger to her."

"You've left us no choice, Vicki," Candace Goodwin said. "NDC is not our first choice, and I'm sure it's not yours."

"Listen, deary," the stocky woman drawled, "the kids we're talkin' about will eat you for lunch. You won't last a day. We try to keep control, but it's tough. Just tell these people what they want to know. No one will think less of you for it."

"This is your last chance, Vicki," Mrs. Goodwin said.

"Tell us who you were working with on the newspaper, and we'll take you to The Haven."

Vicki hated the thought of the detention center. But she hated giving up her friends even worse. She would not give in. Suddenly from the hall came footsteps, then a loud knock. Ryan burst in.

"Hey, have any of you seen my dog?"

"Young man, get out of this building!" Coach Handlesman said, standing. "You're not allowed in here—"

"Whoa, there he is now," Ryan said. Phoenix came bounding in, sliding past Ryan, tripping Coach Handlesman and making him stagger. Vicki laughed. Even Mrs. Waltonen smiled. Coach Handlesman started toward Ryan, who said, "Sorry! We're goin'."

Ryan had slipped Vicki's wrist gadget to her in the confusion. She slid it into her pocket as Candace Goodwin was filling out a form. "By the authority of Global Community Social Services, I give you over to the Northside Detention Center for a period to be determined by authorities there. I'm sorry about this, Vicki. You seem like a genuinely nice young lady."

Judd and Ryan watched from their car as Vicki was put in the back of the van.

"Are we gonna follow her?" Ryan said.

"We know where she's going. Let's send her a message."

He quickly tapped a few words and pressed the Send button. Phoenix barked. Someone was standing by their car. Coach Handlesman motioned for Judd to roll down his window.

"Go home now," he said. "The excitement's over."

Vicki scrunched down in the seat so Mrs. Weems couldn't see her. She held her wrist messenger like it was gold. This was her only link with her friends. A message scrolled across the screen: "We're with you, Vicki."

She looked at the words again and again until she saw the huge chain-link fence with razor wire at the top. A splintered sign read Northside Detention Center.

The guard at the gate wore a gun.

JUDD brought everybody up to date when he got home, and he brought up the subject of finding a new place to live, now that Handlesman was onto them.

Mark gave Judd an article he had written for the *Underground* from material by Dr. Marc Feinberg, the rabbi working on the new temple. "It explains why the temple is so important."

"Great," Judd said, sitting to read it.

It's important to understand the history of the Jewish temple. King David wanted to build it, but God felt David was too much of a warrior, so he let David's son Solomon complete it. Solomon's temple was magnificent. God's people would worship God there in Jerusalem. The glory of God appeared in the temple, and it became a symbol of the hand of God protecting the nation. The people felt so secure that

207

THE YOUNG TRIB FORCE

even when they turned from God, they believed Jerusalem was impregnable, as long as the temple stood.

The temple and the city of Jerusalem were
destroyed by King Nebuchadnezzar in 587 B.C.
Seventy years later a decree was given to rebuild the
city and eventually the temple. That temple served
Israel until it was desecrated by Antiochus
Epiphanes, a Greco-Roman ruler.

About 40 B.C., Herod the Great had the temple
destroyed piece by piece and rebuilt. That became
known as Herod's Temple. Titus, a Roman general,
laid siege to Jerusalem in A.D. 70. The Jews didn't
trust his promises not to destroy it, so they burned
the temple rather than allow it to fall into the hands
of unbelievers.

Today the Temple Mount, the site of the old
Jewish temple, houses the Muslim mosque called the
Dome of the Rock. The Temple Mount sits on Mount
Moriah, where it is believed Abraham expressed to
God his willingness to sacrifice his son Isaac.

Since the birth of Israel as a nation in 1948,
millions of dollars have been collected from around
the world for the rebuilding of the temple. Many
believe it will be even more spectacular than in the
days of Solomon.

"It looks good," Judd said. "But what does this mean
to the kids at Nicolae High?"

"That's where my stuff comes in," John said. "With a
little help from Bruce, I show how this whole thing was

prophesied in the Bible. Everything from the disappearances to Carpathia's covenant signing with Israel."

"Perfect," Judd said. "Now the hard part. We have to figure another way to get the *Underground* into their hands."

At Northside Detention Center Vicki was searched and relieved of her clothes, purse, Bible, and wrist messenger. "You won't need a watch in here," a matron told her. They gave her a toothbrush, a comb, and deodorant, along with a drab coverall, the uniform of the center.

"You don't have anything in navy, do you?" Vicki said.

The guard didn't smile. She led Vicki through a series of musty rooms to the residence wing. Six beds filled each room.

"Breakfast is at seven o'clock sharp," the guard snapped. "Get up late, you don't eat. Chores every day, before and after classes. Free time in the afternoon before dinner at five. Lights out at nine. Got it?"

"I guess," Vicki said. "Can I make a phone call?"

"No calls," the guard said. "We have recreation on Saturday afternoons. That's where everybody is now. Be in the dining hall in half an hour."

Vicki sat on the bed. Paint chips littered the floor. A wasp buzzed at the grimy window. She opened the top drawer of a rickety nightstand and found a Bible. It was in bad shape. *Probably stolen from some motel*, she thought.

She found Psalm 91 and read:

"He who dwells in the secret place of the Most High shall abide under the shadow of the Almighty. I will say of the Lord, 'He is my refuge and my fortress; My God, in Him I will trust. . . .' A thousand may fall at your side, and ten thousand at your right hand; but it shall not come near you. . . . No evil shall befall you, nor shall any plague come near your dwelling; for He shall give His angels charge over you, to keep you in all your ways."

When Vicki awoke the next morning the rest of the girls were asleep. They had been up late talking after lights-out. She was excited about the "religious service" she'd seen advertised on the bulletin board near the dining hall, so she quietly dressed and found the chapel.

Fifteen girls scattered around a tiny room. They sat on folding chairs. The leader was Chaplain Cindy, a young woman with a forced smile. She looked down most of the time, perhaps because most of the girls were nodding off.

Vicki couldn't believe what she was hearing.

"God is love, and love comes from God. He is in each of you, and if you want his light, you must embrace him. I encourage you to search for God in your own way. Become yourself as much as you can, and you will grow ever closer to the Divine."

When Chaplain Cindy finished, she asked if anyone had a question or comment.

Vicki raised her hand. "I don't think God is really in all of us," she said.

A murmur spread among the girls.

"If God had been *in* us, we wouldn't still be here. The

truth is, Jesus came back for his own, and we all got left behind," Vicki continued.

"Shut up."

"Yeah, stupid, sit down."

"Quiet," Chaplain Cindy said. "What's your name?"

"Vicki."

"What we try to accomplish here, Vicki, is oneness. This is not church per se. We come together in unity as part of the new movement of faith around the world."

"You mean Nicolae Carpathia's new religion."

"He's an inspired and wonderful leader," Chaplain Cindy gushed. "He follows the tenets of all the great religious teachers, including the one you mentioned."

"Jesus said that he was the *only* way to God," Vicki said. She tried to look up John 14:6, but before she could find it, she was hooted down.

Chaplain Cindy asked for order. "It's clear to me that Nicolae Carpathia is a Christian man," Chaplain Cindy said.

"You've got to be kidding," Vicki said.

"Of course! He lives by Christian principles. He's always concerned for the greater good."

Vicki was angry. She tried to steer the conversation back to Jesus, but there were more hoots as Vicki finally left the chapel.

She returned to a commotion in her room. Her roommates stood around Alice Weems, the director of NDC.

"I can smell it," Mrs. Weems said. "One of you confesses right now, or you all get punished. What's it gonna be?"

One of the girls pointed at Vicki. "It was her! She brought the weed with her when she came in yesterday."

Mrs. Weems looked at Vicki. "Well?"

"I don't know what you're talking about," Vicki said.

"Where did she stash it, Janie?" Weems said.

"In the top drawer," Janie said. "She was pretending to read some book in there."

Mrs. Weems grabbed the Bible and rifled through it until four crudely rolled cigarettes fell from a hole cut in pages in the back. She held the cigarettes up gingerly and sniffed at them.

"Come with me," she said to Vicki.

———————————

After church Sunday, Judd met Bruce in his study.

"Do we need to move?" Judd said. "If Handlesman knows where we are, I don't want to stick around the house."

"Stay put," Bruce said.

"That's it? Just stay put? After the stuff he said to you the other night?"

"Don't worry about me," Bruce said. "I can take care of myself. And you'll have to trust me. Now I have some other urgent news."

Bruce told Judd that his friend Rayford Steele had become the pilot of *Air Force One*, the plane now used by Nicolae Carpathia, the United Nations secretary-general. According to Steele, Carpathia planned to claim that plane as his own, and the pilot with it. In addition to that, *Global Weekly* writer Buck Williams had been trying to set up a meeting with the two witnesses at the Wailing Wall.

"I'd love to be there," Judd said. "The media mostly

ignores them now. I wish we could get the word out about the witnesses."

"You just may have your chance," Bruce said.

"What do you mean?"

"I'll tell you later," Bruce said. "The other urgent news concerns Vicki. I found out where she was taken and tried to see her, but they don't allow visitors in the first few days."

"I've tried to send her messages," Judd said, "but I don't think they're getting through."

"Keep praying for her," Bruce said. "I've heard disturbing things about that center."

Janie stared at the floor as she and Vicki sat in Mrs. Weems's cluttered office.

"What's your last name?" Vicki asked the girl.

"What's it to ya?"

"Look, we both know I didn't hide those joints in the Bible. But either way, I'm going to be blamed for it. I just like to know who I'm up against."

Janie scowled at Vicki. "McCanyon," she said finally.

"How long you been here?"

"A year. I got sent here for gettin' drunk. Now I'm into drugs. Go figure."

Mrs. Weems's heels clacked on the tile as she entered and cocked an arm against her hip.

"Janie, you know what happens if I find out these were yours."

"Yes, ma'am."

"You," she said to Vicki, "what do you have to say for yourself?"

Something made Vicki hold her tongue.

"I'll take that as an admission," Mrs. Weems said. "Since it's your first offense, I'll go easy. Five days in solitary confinement."

Mrs. Weems told them both to sit tight while she left to take a call.

Janie glanced sheepishly at Vicki. "Look, we do what we gotta do to get by," Janie said. "Better you than me in solitary."

"You've been there?"

"A few times." Janie squirmed. "Why didn't you put up a fight?"

"Who'd believe me? Weems knows I was searched when I got here."

"You mad at me?" Janie said.

Vicki was stunned that Janie was worried about that. "Of course, but I can let it go."

"You're strange, Vicki."

Mrs. Weems's heels clacked again.

"Someday I'll tell you why," Vicki said.

"Maybe tonight," Janie said. "I've got kitchen duty this week. I'll see if I can bring your plate."

"Back to your room, McCanyon," Mrs. Weems said. "Byrne, you're this way."

Before Bruce began their Bible teaching for the evening, Chloe Steele gave an update about her father, pilot

Rayford Steele. Rayford's first assignment was flying Nicolae Carpathia to the treaty signing in Israel.

"Does Carpathia know your dad's a Christian?" Ryan said.

"He does now," Chloe said. "He met Carpathia in New York. When my dad had the chance, he told Carpathia straight-out that he was a believer in Christ."

"Wow," Ryan said. "I hope that doesn't get him in trouble."

Chloe asked everyone to pray for Buck Williams as well. All she would say was that Buck was traveling and would be in a very dangerous situation in the next few days.

As Bruce began his teaching, Judd felt his wrist messenger buzz. "Meet me tonight at nine at school" the message read. "Don't ask questions."

24

BRUCE seemed excited but cautious as the meeting continued. Lionel, Ryan, John, and Mark soaked in every word as Bruce taught more about prophecy.

When the teaching time was over, Judd handed Bruce a fresh copy of the *Underground*. Bruce scanned the small print and gave a low whistle. "Can I share more about Buck?" Bruce asked Chloe. She nodded.

He said Buck Williams had met with Rabbi Tsion Ben-Judah, a brilliant Jewish scholar who had searched various holy books for the identity of the Messiah. Buck's aim was to get an interview with the two witnesses, and the rabbi got him through the tight security around the Wailing Wall.

"As they neared the crowd, Buck realized that each person present was hearing the witnesses in his or her own language!"

"Just like in Acts," Ryan said, "where all those tongues things came down and hit them in the head."

Bruce smiled. "Buck says a man suddenly raced through the crowd with an automatic weapon, yelling that he was on a mission from Allah. When he was within five feet of the two witnesses, he fell back like he had hit an invisible wall. One of the witnesses shouted that no one was to come near the servants of the Most High God. The other breathed fire from his mouth that killed the man instantly."

"Was Buck all right?" Judd said.

"More than all right. Dr. Ben-Judah actually talked to the witnesses. He and Buck met with them alone later that night."

"Wow," Lionel said. "What did they say?"

"Listen to this," Bruce said, turning on his answering machine. "Buck recorded the entire conversation and played it to me over the phone. The first one is Moishe, and the other is Eli."

"Many years ago," Moishe said, "there was a man of the Pharisees named Nicodemus, a ruler of the Jews. Like you, this man came to Jesus by night."

Rabbi Ben-Judah whispered, "Eli and Moishe, we know that you come from God; for no one can do these signs that you do unless God is with him."

Eli spoke. "Most assuredly, I say to you, unless one is born again, he cannot see the kingdom of God."

"How can a man be born when he is old?" Rabbi Ben-Judah said.

"This is straight out of the Bible," Ryan said. "I remember it from one of our studies. Cool."

218

"Shhhh," Lionel said.

Moishe answered, "Most assuredly, I say to you, unless one is born of water and the Spirit, he cannot enter the kingdom of God. That which is born of the flesh is flesh, and that which is born of the Spirit is spirit. Do not marvel that I said to you, 'You must be born again.' "

Eli spoke up again: "The wind blows where it wishes, and you hear the sound of it, but cannot tell where it comes from and where it goes. So is everyone who is born of the Spirit."

Right on cue, the rabbi said, "How can these things be?"

"Are you the teacher of Israel, and do not know these things?" Moishe said. "Most assuredly, I say to you, we speak what we know and testify what we have seen, and you do not receive our witness. If we have told you earthly things and you do not believe, how will you believe if we tell you heavenly things?"

The voices sounded like prophets right out of the Old Testament. "No one has ascended to heaven but He who came down from heaven," Eli said, "that is, the Son of Man who is in heaven. And as Moses lifted up the serpent in the wilderness, even so must the Son of Man be lifted up, that whoever believes in Him should not perish but have eternal life. For God so loved the world that He gave His only begotten Son, that whoever believes in Him should not perish but have everlasting life."

The kids sat shaking their heads as Moishe concluded his message.

"For God did not send his Son into the world to condemn the world, but that the world through him might be saved. He who believes in Him is not condemned; but he who does not believe is condemned already, because he has not believed in the name of the only begotten Son of God."

Rabbi Ben-Judah sounded animated now. "And what is the condemnation?"

In unison the witnesses said, "That the light has already come into the world."

"And how did men miss it?"

"Men loved darkness rather than light."

"Why?"

"Because their deeds were evil."

"God forgive us," the rabbi said.

And the two witnesses said, "God forgive you. Thus ends our message."

"Incredible," Ryan said.

"I thought most rabbis were skeptical of these preachers," John said.

Bruce turned off the machine. "Yes. But people are turning. Buck said Rabbi Ben-Judah took him to the Dome of the Rock and translated the Hebrew graffiti there. It said, 'Come, Messiah' and 'Deliver us,' and 'Come in triumph.' The Jewish people have been longing for Messiah for thousands of years. Buck says the Muslims have even built a cemetery near the Dome."

"So?" Mark said.

"Jewish tradition says that in the end times, Messiah and Elijah will lead the Jews to the temple in triumph through the gate from the east. But Elijah is a priest, and walking through a graveyard would defile him, so they put a cemetery there to make the triumphal entry impossible."

"Does this Ben-Judah guy believe Jesus is the Messiah?" John said.

"We'll find out tomorrow. He gives his conclusions on a live international TV broadcast."

The solitary confinement room was windowless, and the air stale and muggy. A large black spider hung in one corner near the high ceiling, spinning a web. Vicki tried to kill it by throwing a shoe, but gave up. If she knocked it down she'd have to find it and step on it, so she left it alone.

Late in the afternoon she heard a knock on the door. A slit opened enough to fit a dinner plate through.

"Sorry, this is all they'd let me give you," Janie said. "I put some extra peas on there."

Vicki didn't want to be ungrateful, but she wouldn't have given the meal even to Phoenix. And she hated peas.

"Weems will lock me up next to you if I'm not back soon," Janie said. "What were you going to say in the office? Why didn't you rat on me?"

Vicki held the flap open so she could see Janie's bloodshot eyes. Drugs made her look years older.

"This was something God wanted me to do," Vicki said.

"God?" Janie said. "Oh boy."

"Maybe I'm in here just to show you how much God loves you."

"OK, gotta go," Janie said.

"No, wait. Just a second."

Vicki quickly told how she had become a Christian after losing her family in the disappearances. "What I did for you today was sort of like what Jesus did for me," Vicki said.

"Yeah, whatever." Janie turned to leave.

Vicki called after her. "I didn't do anything wrong, right?"

Janie stopped. "Right."

"You were the guilty one, right?"

"Uh, OK, maybe."

"I'm taking your punishment, paying for what you did. That's what Jesus did for me. For you, too . . ."

"How do you know all this stuff?"

"It's all in the Bible. Get me one, and I'll show you."

"Did you have one with you when you came in?" Janie said.

"Yeah, a little one," Vicki said. "But don't—"

"Shh," Janie said, pushing the flap closed quietly.

"I wish I could be there to hear the witnesses myself," Judd said.

"It would be great if we could get their message to more people," John said.

"We could put the audio on the Internet," Mark said. "Or maybe Mr. Williams could get us some video."

"It's interesting you bring this up," Bruce said. "I'm looking for a volunteer."

"For what?" Ryan said. "I'll do it."

"Slow down," Bruce said. "I feel strongly that God wants me to take the small group model we've begun here and replicate it overseas."

"What's *replicate* mean?" Ryan said.

"Do the same thing over there as here," Lionel said.

"I want to go to Israel, to the Wailing Wall, to see the witnesses," Bruce continued. "I want to see where these prophecies came from. God's work in human history began there. Whatever he has for our future will begin there as well. I'd like one of you to go with me."

Vicki wished for anything to pass the time. She didn't even have pen or paper. She slept as much as she could and kept an eye on the spider when she was awake.

Her dozing made her less sleepy, and just before lights-out she worried she wouldn't sleep. Then she heard something in the hallway. Was Mrs. Weems paying her a visit? It was only a matter of time.

The loudspeaker crackled "lights-out," and the room went dark. Her plate from lunch slid from outside the door, and then the flap creaked open. Something dropped on the floor.

Maybe it was a trick. Or maybe a smoke bomb or more evidence planted to get her in deeper trouble. Vicki sat on the edge of the bed, her feet tucked underneath her, and tried to adjust to the darkness. A bit of light from under the door was partially blocked.

Vicki felt around on the floor until she found a grocery bag. Inside she felt her New Testament and something else. Her wrist messenger! Tears welled up.

When she could see clearly, she noticed a new message. It was hours old. "OK, Vicki, we'll meet you at nine at the school."

"Sure will be great to see Vicki," Mark said.

Judd had a queasy feeling about the meeting, like something wasn't right.

"Why didn't you say anything to Bruce?" Mark said. "He'd probably want to see Vicki too."

"If she wanted Bruce there, she would have said something," Judd said as he neared the school parking lot.

"Pull over!" John shouted.

"What's wrong?" Judd said.

"Another message from Vicki. She's still at NDC!"

Judd screeched to a halt and saw headlights switch on in the distance.

"The other message had to have been a trap," Lionel said. "They're trying to catch us."

"But it doesn't make sense," Mark said. "Handlesman knows Vicki was at your place. He could just come over and get us."

"Uh-oh," Mark said. "Maybe they're at the house gathering the evidence. Ryan's at home with Phoenix. They might be questioning him right now."

Judd backed up and gunned the engine. The headlights in his rearview mirror faded as Judd did a one-eighty.

An unmarked police cruiser with lights flashing blocked Judd's driveway. Ryan was on the front step talking with someone, while others from the neighborhood milled about. Judd drove past and parked a few doors down.

"We're fried," John said.

"What's going on?" Judd asked a neighbor.

"Somebody said something about a burglary," he said.

"Stay here," Judd told the others. He hurried to the front steps.

"Hey, Judd." Ryan grinned.

The officer turned, and Judd was relieved to see Sergeant Tom Fogarty. Judd and the others had helped the Chicago police officer crack a drug-and-burglary ring shortly after the disappearances. Ryan had called him in desperation.

"Looks like you had a little excitement while you were out," Sergeant Fogarty said. "Ryan says he was by himself, and somebody tried to get in. Big guy."

"Do you know who it was?" Judd said.

"Didn't get a look at his face," Ryan said. "But I'll know who he is when I see him."

"How's that?" Judd said.

"The perp got in the front door, and Ryan whacked him with a golf club."

"Yeah, and while he was kinda groggy, Phoenix bit him on the arm," Ryan added.

"You might want to get that door fixed pretty soon," Sergeant Fogarty said.

"I will," Judd said. "First thing after school."

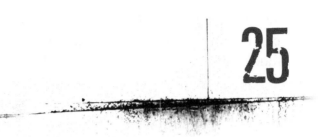

25

MONDAY morning the *Underground* made it into Nicolae High the back way. Judd went through the front and was searched, like all the other kids, while John and Mark took their stashes of paper to the side of the school. Judd pulled the small bundles through a window.

The format of this edition of the *Underground* was different. The kids had limited themselves to two pages and had shrunk the type. They cut the bright blue paper to handbill size and took it to the cafeteria.

Judd, John, and Mark left stacks of what looked like an advertisement from a popular burger place. When students picked them up, however, they found the truth about the treaty with Israel.

"If somebody doesn't bite soon," Mark said, "I'm gonna bust."

"Don't worry," John said, "it'll spread."

A girl in a running suit grabbed a flyer and walked back

to a table, where she read it to her friends. Soon another girl came to pick up a flyer, then another. Judd moved to a side entrance of the cafeteria and watched in delight.

"Judd, I've been looking for you," Vicki's friend Shelly said. Judd was wary. She had betrayed Vicki.

"How's it goin', Shelly," Judd said.

"The question is, how's Vicki?" she said.

"How would I know?"

"I thought you were kinda hangin' together."

Wary of yet another trap, Judd shrugged. "A little," he said.

"I feel awful. Please tell her I want to make it up to her, OK?"

"If I see her," Judd said.

"Oh, and nice job on the *Underground.* I mean, I know it was you guys."

"Uh . . ." Judd avoided her eyes.

"Watch this," she said. She grabbed a stack of flyers and handed them out.

"Can we trust her?" Mark said.

"I'm not sure," Judd said. "Why don't you keep an eye on her?"

Mrs. Jenness's voice came over the loudspeaker. "All students report to the auditorium. The video of the historic treaty ceremony earlier this morning in Israel will be played in its entirety."

The auditorium was filling as Judd and John arrived. Several students carried copies of the *Underground.* The audience focused on a huge screen broadcasting CNN's coverage.

"The signing ceremony was abruptly moved to the Knesset earlier this morning, Israel time," the CNN reporter said. "Some say Nicolae Carpathia was not happy with what the two preachers were saying at the Wailing Wall. What you hear behind me may be the reason. . . ."

The camera zoomed in on Eli and Moishe. With long-range, directional microphones, CNN picked up their decrying the injustice of the signing.

"This covenant signals an unholy alliance!" Moishe shouted.

"O Israel," Eli said, "you who missed your Messiah the first time have embraced a leader who denies the existence of God!"

Some kids laughed at the two, but others looked at the *Underground* and pointed to the screen. CNN flashed to the Knesset.

Judd felt helpless. No one could stem the tide of history. Bruce Barnes had taught him that there would be 144,000 Jewish converts and that the first would come from the Holy Land. The Bible said the converts would come from every part of the globe and would reap an incredible harvest—perhaps a billion souls.

Judd perked up when Buck Williams was announced as a dignitary in attendance. The loudest applause was reserved for the last five men: the chief rabbi of Israel, the Nobel Prize–winning botanist Chaim Rosenzweig of Israel, the prime minister of Israel, the president of the United States, and the secretary-general of the Global Community. As the applause crescendoed for Nicolae Carpathia, Mrs. Jenness took the podium.

"This is a great day for world peace," she said. "I hope you understand the historic moment you're witnessing. Please hold your applause so everyone can hear."

John caught Judd's eye and shook his head. "I'll try to contain myself."

"I just hope some of these people read the truth in the *Underground*," Judd said.

On the screen Nicolae Carpathia recognized those who had helped reach the agreement and ended by introducing "the Honorable Gerald Fitzhugh, president of the United States of America, the greatest friend Israel has ever had."

President Fitzhugh rose to thunderous applause; then Nicolae Carpathia beckoned him to the microphone.

"The last thing I want to do at a moment like this," President Fitzhugh said, "is to detract in any way from the occasion at hand. However, with your kind indulgence, I would like to make a couple of brief points.

"First, it has been a privilege to see what Nicolae Carpathia has done in just a few short weeks. I am certain we all agree that the world is a more loving, peaceful place because of him."

President Fitzhugh pledged his support to global disarmament. "I support the secretary-general's plan without reservation. It's a stroke of genius. We will lead the way to the rapid destruction of 90 percent of our weapons and the donation of the other 10 percent to Global Community, under Mr. Carpathia's direction.

"As a tangible expression of my personal support and that of our nation as a whole, we have also gifted Global Community with the brand-new *Air Force One*."

"There goes Rayford Steele," John said. "He'll be flying the Antichrist anywhere he wants to go."

President Fitzhugh dramatically paused. "Now I surrender the microphone to the man of destiny, the leader whose current title does not do justice to the extent of his influence, to my personal friend and compatriot, Nicolae Carpathia!"

Wild applause broke out in Jerusalem and at Nicolae High. Bruce had told Judd he thought President Fitzhugh wasn't pleased with the way Carpathia had taken over, but his speech certainly cleared that up.

Other leaders spoke of Nicolae Carpathia in glowing terms. He was a gift from God, they said. Several decorative pens were produced as television, film, video, and still cameras zeroed in on the signers. The pens were passed back and forth. There were handshakes, embraces, and kisses on both cheeks.

Judd marveled at what the kids had written. A covenant had been struck. God's chosen people had signed a deal with the devil. The seven-year "week" predicted in the Bible had begun. The Tribulation.

Mark slipped into Judd and John's row; he was out of breath. "Good news and bad news," he said. "Shelly just had a conversation with Handlesman. I think we're in trouble."

"What's the good news?" John said.

"You should see the bruise on Handlesman's head!"

Vicki awoke to the door flap creaking. Janie was back.

"I saw you didn't eat anything last night," she whispered, "so I found a couple of fresh biscuits."

Vicki took them and bit into them eagerly. "Thanks," she said. "These are great."

Janie said Vicki's Bible and watch hadn't been in the property room but in Mrs. Weems's office. "Nobody else was using them, so why shouldn't you?"

"You're taking a big risk, Janie. Be careful."

Janie looked into Vicki's eyes. "I was thinking about what you said last night."

Janie gasped, and the flap closed. "I'm sorry, I'm sorry," Janie said. "I was just giving her breakfast!"

Keys jangled, and Vicki's door swung open. Mrs. Weems bounded in, dragging Janie. "Solitary means you're alone," Mrs. Weems said. "You don't talk to anybody, you don't—"

Mrs. Weems swept the Bible and wrist messenger off the bed. She stomped on the messenger, smashing it to bits. "So much for your watch," she said.

She threw Janie toward the bed. "Now it's your turn for solitary, McCanyon! Byrne, you come with me."

Vicki picked up the Bible and followed the woman through a waiting room. A nicely dressed couple looked up and then quickly looked away.

"Get your stuff together," Mrs. Weems said after she closed the door.

"I only have this," Vicki said, holding her Bible.

"That was stolen from my office!" Mrs. Weems took the Bible and threw it in the trash. "You must know somebody important. You're getting transferred out of here to the Stein family. I don't know why they agreed to take you, but they did. Listen, one wrong move and you're back here. And believe me, Byrne, you don't wanna come back."

By the end of the treaty-signing coverage on TV, teachers were confiscating the *Underground*. Judd saw some students stuff them in their pockets.

One student raised a hand. "Weren't we supposed to see some rabbi's report too?"

"That's been canceled due to inappropriate content," Mrs. Jenness said.

"Wonder what was so inappropriate?" John said.

In class, students regarded Carpathia as everything from "cool" to "the greatest leader the world has ever known."

"I like what he's done with the media," a reporter from the school newspaper said. "I think we're going to see a lot less bias and more honest reporting now," she added.

"Interesting," the teacher said. "Many see it differently. Carpathia has accomplished something no one ever thought would happen. He's purchased newspapers, radio stations, television networks, satellite communications outlets—you name it. The Cable News Network, the Columbia Broadcast System, Time-Warner, Disney, *Newsweek*—they all now come under the auspices of the Global Community."

Judd's heart sank. The most evil man on the earth was gaining more control. No one could stop him.

26

MITCHELL and Judith Stein were a Jewish couple who had become foster parents after the loss of their daughter.

"How did she die?" Vicki said.

Silence.

"I'm sorry," she said. "I—"

"It's all right," Mr. Stein said. "It's just difficult for us to talk about."

"What was her name?" Vicki said.

The Steins didn't answer at first. Then Mrs. Stein whispered, "Chaya."

Mrs. Stein showed Vicki to a bright, cheery bedroom with a huge canopy bed and three windows that looked out on a manicured lawn. Exhausted, Vicki took a nap and was awakened by noise downstairs. She crept to the banister and watched a man on television speak about the Jewish Messiah.

Though Vicki had never seen him, she knew this must

be the rabbi Bruce had mentioned. For three years he had worked on a government project. The assignment was to read sacred books, including the Bible, and discover the identity of the Jewish Messiah. His findings had been kept secret until this broadcast.

"He is like every Orthodox Jew we know," Mr. Stein said. "He will tell us to be patient. Messiah is yet to come. We have heard this many times."

He aimed the remote control.

"Wait," Vicki said as she bounded down the staircase. "Can I watch that?"

"You are interested?" he said.

"Very."

He shrugged and left it on.

"Thank you, Vicki," Mrs. Stein said. "I would like to see this myself."

The words *Dr. Tsion Ben-Judah* flashed at the bottom of the screen. He was sitting on the edge of the table where he had displayed the several-hundred-page conclusion to his research study. He said he would tackle the question of Messiah in the broadcast. Is Messiah a real person? Has he come, or is he yet to come? The camera zoomed in on Dr. Ben-Judah's impressive features.

"I promise to not bore you with statistics, but we believe there are at least 109 separate and distinct prophecies Messiah must fulfill. They require a man so unusual and a life so unique that they eliminate all pretenders."

"He may proclaim Nicolae Carpathia as Messiah," Mrs. Stein said. "Who else could have done what he has in such a short time?"

Vicki shuddered.

"The very first qualification of Messiah, accepted by our scholars from the beginning, is that he should be born of the seed of a woman, not the seed of a man like all other human beings. We know now that women do not possess 'seed.' The man provides the seed for the woman's egg. And so this must be a supernatural birth, as foretold in Isaiah 7:14, 'Therefore the Lord Himself will give you a sign: Behold, the virgin shall conceive and bear a Son, and shall call His name Immanuel.' "

Rabbi Ben-Judah further qualified Messiah as a descendant of David, born in Bethlehem, and rejected by his own people.

Mr. Stein reddened. "I know where this is going," he said, "and I do not like it."

"Listen to him," Mrs. Stein said. "He is quoting from our scriptures, isn't he?"

After clearly explaining what the Bible said for nearly an hour, the rabbi said, "Let me close by saying that the three years I have invested in searching the sacred writings of Moses and the prophets have been the most rewarding of my life. I expanded my study to books of history and other sacred writings, including the New Testament of the Gentiles, combing every record I could find to see if anyone has ever lived up to the messianic qualifications. . . ."

"Do you see?" Mr. Stein said. "He is basing his findings on erroneous material!"

"How can you decide he is wrong if you won't even listen to him?" Mrs. Stein said.

"Was there one born in Bethlehem of a virgin," Ben-Judah continued, "a descendant of King David, traced back to our father Abraham, who was taken to Egypt, called back to minister in Galilee, preceded by a forerunner, rejected by God's own people, betrayed for thirty pieces of silver, pierced without breaking a bone, buried with the rich, and resurrected?

"According to one of the greatest of all Hebrew prophets, Daniel, there would be exactly 483 years between the decree to rebuild the wall and the city of Jerusalem 'in troublesome times' before the Messiah would be cut off for the sins of the people."

Ben-Judah looked directly into the camera. "Exactly 483 years after the rebuilding of Jerusalem and its walls, Jesus Christ of Nazareth offered himself to the nation of Israel."

"Blasphemy!" Mr. Stein shouted. "I'm turning it off!"

"What are you afraid of?" Mrs. Stein said.

"I will not subject myself to such trash!"

"Your daughter believed in this 'trash.'"

The rabbi continued. "Jesus rode into the city on a donkey to the rejoicing of the people, just as the prophet Zechariah had predicted: 'Rejoice greatly, O daughter of Zion! Shout, O daughter of Jerusalem! Behold, your King is coming to you; He is just and having salvation, lowly and riding on a donkey, a colt, the foal of a donkey.'"

"Maybe Chaya was right," Mrs. Stein said. "Maybe we should have listened while we had the chance."

"You will never use her name in this house again," Mr. Stein said. "Never!"

Vicki stood as the rabbi concluded, thrilled at the message he proclaimed. "Jesus Christ is the Messiah! There can be no other option. I had come to this answer but was afraid to act on it, and I was almost too late. Jesus came to rapture his church, to take them with him to heaven as he said he would. I was not among them because I wavered. But I have since received him as my Savior. He is coming back in seven years! Be ready!"

Dr. Ben-Judah gave a number to call for more information, but there seemed to be commotion in the TV studio.

"*Yeshua ben Yosef*, Jesus son of Joseph, is *Yeshua Hamashiach!*" the rabbi shouted quickly. "Jesus is the Messiah!"

The screen went blank.

Bruce described the message by Rabbi Tsion Ben-Judah as nothing short of miraculous. It had been broadcast live around the world. Because his findings had been kept secret, the Global Community hadn't restricted the broadcast, but Nicolae Carpathia had to be seething.

Later the four kids learned that Buck Williams was able to help the rabbi escape the television studio. Many in his own country wanted to kill the rabbi for his beliefs.

"The most exciting news is that Eli and Moishe have invited Dr. Ben-Judah to address a meeting of new believers in a large stadium in Israel. They have pledged their protection for the rabbi as he proclaims the Good News."

Mrs. Stein knocked on Vicki's door that night.

"We don't normally have outbursts like this," she said, entering the room. "But ever since we lost our daughter, things have not been the same."

Vicki nodded. "Chaya is in heaven, you know."

"I can't talk now," Mrs. Stein said. "Please, just know that you cannot bring it up with Mitchell."

"Can you tell me if I'll be able to go back to my old school?" Vicki said. "Or call my friends?"

"We were given strict guidelines. No contact with your friends. You'll attend Global Community High in Barrington."

"Why can't I talk with them?" Vicki said. "That doesn't seem fair."

Mrs. Stein looked away. "Life isn't fair."

As she turned to leave, Vicki said, "Can I ask what you thought about what the rabbi said?"

Mrs. Stein stopped and nodded. "I have been thinking about his words all evening. He seemed such an honest man. So learned. It is hard for me to believe he is trying to deceive us."

"I don't think he is," Vicki said.

"Sometimes I wonder if—"

"Judith?" Mr. Stein was at the door.

His wife quickly excused herself. But as she backed away, she held Vicki's gaze and opened the end-table drawer.

As soon as the door was shut, Vicki looked in the drawer and found a spiral notebook. "Chaya's Journal" was scrawled on the front cover. Vicki felt guilty opening it, but clearly Mrs. Stein had pointed her to it.

"The last thing I want to do is hurt Mom and Dad," Vicki read, "but I can't hide from the truth of what Tom is saying. I know there's something to this, but I don't want to believe it."

Vicki picked her way through the pages to find out who Tom was. She found an entry describing him as a "Jesus jerk." Tom had talked with Chaya about Christ.

"I told him, 'Look, I'm a Jew, lay off!' I think it worked. I haven't seen him for two days."

But it hadn't worked. Tom kept talking with her, discussing Jesus and the Bible.

"I want to dismiss this as a fable, a fairy tale by people who want to make Jesus who they want him to be. But I don't want to make a mistake, either. What if his claims are real? Didn't he fulfill all those predictions? If I can disprove his miracles, I can get Tom off my back and get on with my life."

From the journal it was clear. The more Chaya investigated, the more convinced she became that Jesus was exactly who he said he was.

Then Vicki read something that sent a chill through her. "If my mom or dad ever find out about this, I'm dead."

———————————————

Before the boys left Bruce's office, Mark brought up the militia movement. "They've been able to stockpile weapons," he said. "If there's any chance for freedom from Carpathia, it rests with them."

Bruce frowned.

Mark continued. "A guy I know says the president is cooperating with them. What if it's true? If they have President Fitzhugh's support, they can't be all wrong."

"There may be a place for military strength," Bruce said. "But I would hate to see you get involved with them."

"But why? If somebody doesn't stand up to Carpathia, we'll all be serving the devil! I don't see why you're against this."

"Our battle is different," Bruce said, flipping open his Bible. "Ephesians 6 says, 'Be strong in the Lord and in the power of His might. Put on the whole armor of God, that you may be able to stand against the wiles of the devil. For we do not wrestle against flesh and blood, but against principalities, against powers, against the rulers of the darkness of this age, against spiritual hosts of wickedness in the heavenly places.' "

"Why can't I be a Christian *and* fight with weapons?" Mark said. "The Bible is full of examples."

"Just be sure," Bruce said, "that you're doing this God's way. Zechariah 4:6 says, 'Not by might nor by power, but by My Spirit, says the Lord of hosts.' "

The last entry in Chaya's journal showed that she had studied about Jesus and concluded that he was a person of history. Chaya believed that the miracles in the New Testament were real.

"If I believe that Jesus is the Messiah," she wrote, "I

turn my back on my parents, my heritage, my ancestors, my friends. But if Jesus is the Messiah, I'm not turning my back on the God of Abraham, Isaac, and Jacob. I will meet with Tom tonight. I need to settle it once and for all."

Vicki looked at the date on that final entry. It was the same night as the disappearances!

27

THE E-mail reaction alone to the *Underground* kept the Young Trib Force busy until late Monday night. A few of the E-mails called the *Underground* a joke. More than fifty said they wanted a Bible. Judd and John answered each E-mail with a gospel outline and information about New Hope Village Church.

Ryan scurried to his hidden cache of Bibles. Judd still didn't know how many Ryan had recovered, but from Ryan's description, it had to be hundreds. Ryan made three trips and had all fifty Bibles in the back of Judd's car by midnight.

Judd knew he had to be careful. An infiltrator could pose as an eager student. So Judd made the drop points off campus. He delayed sending the E-mails as he went around town delivering copies of the Bible.

He heard a scream outside and found Lionel and Ryan wrestling on the driveway.

"He's crazy, man!" Lionel said as Judd separated them.

"You're the one who's crazy!" Ryan screamed.

Judd took them into the house. Lionel said he was stuffing the response packets into the Bibles when Ryan told him to leave them alone.

"He got all territorial on me," Lionel said. "I just put the envelopes in. He jumped me."

"He just took over," Ryan said. "He acted like those Bibles were his."

Judd asked Lionel to finish outside while he took Ryan to his room. He wanted to lay into Ryan good, but he held back. Something else was wrong.

"I know Lionel can get on your nerves," Judd said. "But he didn't deserve to be attacked. What's going on?"

Ryan pulled Phoenix close to him. "I don't know. He was being a jerk." Finally the dam broke, and the tears came. "Why did Vicki have to go away?" he sobbed.

"She's a good friend," Judd said. "I miss her too."

"And now you and Bruce are leaving, and who knows when you'll come back. Or *if* you'll come back!"

"That's not a done deal," Judd said.

"Bruce wants you to go, and you know it!"

Judd took Ryan by the shoulders. "Listen to me. When you came here I promised God I'd take care of you. I hadn't paid attention to my brother and sister, so when you came along I felt like God was giving me a second chance. If Bruce wants me to go and you don't, I'll let somebody else go."

Ryan looked stunned. "I don't want you to stay because of me. I don't want to be a wuss."

"You're not," Judd said. "I can't imagine how hard this has been for you."

"Thanks," Ryan said. "I want you to go. I'll be OK."

"You sure?" Judd said.

Ryan nodded. "I gotta go apologize to Lionel."

The next day, while in the car with Mrs. Stein, Vicki asked again, "Can you tell me how she died?"

The woman hesitated. "It is a deep wound" was all she would say.

At Mrs. Stein's doctor's appointment, she asked Vicki if she could trust her to stay in the waiting room.

"Of course," Vicki said.

As soon as Mrs. Stein left to see the doctor, Vicki approached the receptionist.

"Have the Steins been coming here a long time?" she said.

"For years."

"Chaya too?"

The receptionist stiffened. "Why?"

"I'm just curious. How old was she?"

"About eighteen. She just started university last year. Bright girl. You have to be to get into the University of Chicago."

"How did she die?" Vicki said.

The receptionist stopped typing, looked to see if anyone was listening, and beckoned Vicki closer.

Just then Mrs. Stein emerged, and the receptionist went back to her work.

Later, Vicki called the University of Chicago and discovered that Chaya had withdrawn from the school about the time of the disappearances. She hung up as Mr. Stein appeared.

"Who were you calling?"

"Just trying to reach a friend," she said.

"You know the rules," he said, pulling the phone cord from the jack.

Vicki combed through Chaya's old address books and calendars for clues. She finally came upon Tom's phone number and waited for her chance.

Vicki believed that Chaya came to Christ and had been raptured. But what if she had met with Tom and hadn't made a decision? Maybe she killed herself. That would explain the "deep wound" her mother spoke of. Chaya might also have died from an accident or even been murdered. Worst of all, Chaya could have been harmed by her parents.

Vicki had to know.

The next day, Vicki found her chance while shopping with Mrs. Stein. While the woman was in the dressing room, Vicki broke away and found a pay phone.

A groggy male voice answered.

"Hi, uh, who's this?" Vicki said.

"Look, if you're callin' for Tom, he's not here! He's gone, OK?"

"I figured," Vicki said. "I'm trying to find a friend of his. Do you remember his talking about Chaya?"

"The Jewish girl? Yeah."

"Do you know what happened to her?"

"No idea. She had an apartment in the Loop. Rode the train to school. That's all I know."

Vicki hurried back. At lunch she asked Mrs. Stein, "Why are you doing this for me? You didn't have to take me in. There are a hundred other girls you could help."

"We chose NDC because many who are there have given up hope," Mrs. Stein said. "I like to think I'm giving someone a chance for a better life."

"I'm not a charity case," Vicki said.

"That's not what drew us to you. Mrs. Weems said you were troubled but that you had spunk."

Vicki shook her head. She excused herself to go to the ladies' room and called directory information. There were two Chaya Steins in Chicago, but only one lived downtown. She put more coins in and dialed. A young lady answered.

"Sorry to bother you. I'm looking for some information about your roommate."

"Moved out about a month ago," the girl said.

"And her name was Chaya?"

"No, Gwen. I'm Chaya."

"You're Chaya Stein?" Vicki said.

"I am."

"The one from Barrington?"

"The same."

"But you're supposed to be dead!"

"You've been talking to my parents."

"Yes, they said you had died."

"I see," Chaya said. "And how do you know them?"

"I'm staying with them. Could we meet somewhere?"

They settled on a park not far from the Stein house.

"I'll meet you near the tennis courts Friday at noon," Chaya said.

Friday morning Vicki found Chaya's tennis racquet and asked Mrs. Stein if there were courts nearby.

"A few blocks away," Mrs. Stein said, "but I'm not supposed to let you go unsupervised."

"You don't trust me yet?"

Mrs. Stein hesitated. "All right. Go ahead. But don't be too long."

Vicki recognized Chaya immediately. "You look like your mother!"

Chaya's eyes misted. "This is hard."

Vicki apologized for reading her journal. Chaya said it was OK. Chaya asked about her parents and what they had said about her, but Vicki interrupted. "What happened with Tom that night?"

Chaya sat on a bench and took a deep breath. "We met in a coffee shop," she began. "He had a class the next morning, but he said he'd stay as long as I had questions. At that point I knew the truth. I had read all I needed, but I just hadn't made a decision. I knew my parents would take it hard if I went apostate, but—"

"What's that?" Vicki said.

"Becoming a heretic. Believing lies. Turning your back on everything you've been taught. I could have robbed a bank, gotten pregnant—whatever—and it wouldn't have been as terrible as becoming a Christian. A couple of years ago a friend of the family became a Christian, and I thought my parents would sit shivah for him on the day he was baptized."

"What's that?"

"Prayers for the dead," Chaya said. "My guess is that my parents don't even mention my name anymore, right?"

Vicki described the painful references to Chaya's name.

"Tell me about that night with Tom," Vicki said. "If you were that close to becoming a Christian, what happened?"

"He was walking me to my train. I was telling him what my parents might do if I converted. He quoted some verse and said no earthly pain was worth the loss of my soul. I wasn't so sure and turned to say so. His book bag fell to the sidewalk. His clothes lay in a heap on the ground. I screamed."

"How awful," Vicki said.

"It was like a movie," Chaya said. "People came running. They picked up his clothes and book bag, somebody tried to lift a manhole cover, but there was nothing they could do. He was gone."

"Did you know what had happened?"

"You mean the Rapture? No. Tom had told me Jesus was coming back, but we hadn't gotten that far. That night when I finally got home I watched the news about all the vanishings. I wanted to look up the verse he had talked about, but all I could remember was that it was in Matthew. I read the first sixteen chapters until I came to it: 'For what profit is it to a man if he gains the whole world, and loses his own soul?' "

"Tom had given me other materials," Chaya continued. "I read from Romans 10, 'If you confess with your mouth the Lord Jesus and believe in your heart that God has raised Him from the dead, you will be saved.' And later it says, 'For whoever calls on the name of the Lord shall be saved.' I begged God to save me. And he did."

Then Vicki told her own story, right up to going to the NDC and being assigned to the Steins.

Chaya wept as she said that the most difficult thing in her life had been telling her parents. "My father yelled, my mother wailed, and before they closed the door behind me, they disowned me."

Vicki put a hand on her shoulder and looked past her to the street. Chaya's mother stood by her car, watching.

28

JUDD left school early. He went home and packed and led Phoenix to the car. There was still much to do before getting to the airport. It was 2:15 P.M. Everything was going as planned.

When Chaya stood, Mrs. Stein jumped into her car and pulled away. Chaya bit her lip, then composed herself. "Come on," she said. "I'll run you home."

"I'd rather see my friends," Vicki said. "Your parents are sure to send me back to the detention center."

At 2:15 Vicki and Chaya arrived at Nicolae High and waited for the end of the school day in hopes of seeing the guys. Vicki saw a familiar face in a girls' gym class— Shelly. Vicki waved.

"I'm so glad to see you," Shelly said, running over to the car. "Did you get my message?"

"I've been kinda out of touch for a few days," Vicki said. She introduced Chaya to Shelly.

"Are you with the foster family?" Shelly said.

"How did you know that?" Vicki said.

"From a friend. I'm really sorry about what happened. I wouldn't have done that to you for anything. But you know Mom."

Vicki nodded.

"You should have seen what the guys did with the *Underground* Monday," Shelly said.

Vicki had never told her who was involved with the paper. Could she trust Shelly? Shelly had been the one responsible for her being sent to the detention center. How did she know all these things?

"Wait right here," Shelly said. "You're not going to believe this. I'll be right back, OK?"

A few moments later Shelly burst out the door, pulling someone behind her. Vicki looked in horror. Coach Handlesman.

———————————

Judd picked up Ryan and Lionel from their school.

"You got all our stuff?" Lionel said.

"It's in the back," Judd said. "And John has a key in case you guys need anything while I'm gone."

"Your house is gonna be a ghost town," Ryan said.

Judd dropped them off at John and Mark's house by

2:45. Lionel and Ryan would stay with the boys and their aunt until Judd returned.

"What are you doing here?" Coach Handlesman said.

Vicki couldn't speak. Shelly had betrayed her again.

Mrs. Jenness and a Global Community guard were at the car. The door opened. Vicki felt numb, like in a dream. The guard pulled her from the car and whisked her inside the school.

"What's going on?" Chaya shouted. "Where are you taking her?"

Shelly ran after them but was turned back when they reached Mrs. Jenness's office. "All right, where is he?" Mrs. Jenness demanded. "Where is Judd Thompson?"

"He's not here?"

"Enough! We know you helped Thompson with that newspaper. We have proof!"

Coach Handlesman burst in. "What proof?" he shouted.

"So, you're all concerned about your little project," Mrs. Jenness said.

Vicki was confused.

"Where's Thompson?" Mrs. Jenness said, eyeing the coach.

"I don't know either," he said.

"We have the proof we need," Mrs. Jenness said as the girls' gym teacher, Mrs. Laverne Waltonen, entered. Mrs. Jenness motioned to her secretary. "Get the superintendent on the phone."

Coach Handlesman moved toward the door, but a guard blocked his way.

"We'll get to the bottom of this," Mrs. Jenness said. "And your career is in jeopardy," she added to Coach Handlesman.

"What?" Vicki said. "The coach? Why?"

"You ought to know!" Mrs. Jenness said.

"Enough!" Coach Handlesman shouted. "Leave her alone. I'll tell you everything."

Bruce, Judd, and John hit traffic as they neared O'Hare Airport. An overturned trailer had spilled its contents on the expressway. Bruce had wanted to get there an hour and a half before takeoff, but they weren't going to be close. It was nearly 4:00 P.M., and they were still miles away.

The superintendent of Global Community Schools, Gerald Pembroke, arrived at 4:05 P.M. He was a large man with thin lips, and he talked precisely. Vicki was still reeling.

Superintendent Pembroke asked where "the Thompson boy" was. Coach Handlesman looked at his watch and again said that he didn't know. Mrs. Weems arrived to escort Vicki out, but Coach Handlesman stopped her. "Vicki stays," he said. "If you want the whole story, I want her right here."

Mrs. Weems looked to Mrs. Jenness. She nodded. "Sit down. You can stay."

Coach Handlesman took the floor.

"Don't blame Vicki. And quit following her around and punishing her for something that's my fault. This is my doing, and I'm ready to take whatever punishment you want to give."

"You let an innocent girl be sent to a place like Northside?" Mr. Pembroke said.

"I'm not proud of it," Coach Handlesman said. "I'm saying I want to clear things up."

"You printed and distributed those papers yourself?" Superintendent Pembroke said.

"I'm telling you, it was my fault. I'm sure Mrs. Waltonen has told you my views."

"She said you came on pretty strong."

"It's true. I'm a born-again Christian. I want to reach as many kids as possible. That's all I have to say."

Mrs. Jenness's secretary buzzed. "Rumor has it that the Thompson kid is going to the airport. Somebody said he's headed to Israel."

Israel, Vicki thought. *Why? And who's he with?*

The Global Community guard picked up the phone. "Get me El Al Airlines at O'Hare."

Bruce and Judd consolidated their clothing as John drove. They would be allowed only two carry-on bags.

"We'll never make it on time to check our luggage," Bruce said. "We take what we can run with."

"That means we leave the recording equipment," Judd said.

"We'll have to," Bruce said.

John screeched to a halt, and the two flew into the international terminal. They were breathless when they reached the ticket counter.

———————————

Mrs. Jenness had the guard finish his phone call in the next office. The rest of the group eagerly followed. Vicki and Coach Handlesman were alone.

"I don't buy it," Vicki said. "This is another trap you and Mrs. Jenness have cooked up, right?"

Coach Handlesman looked at Vicki. She wanted to believe him, but there were so many questions.

"You were against us from the start," Vicki said. "You took John's and Mark's Bibles."

"They got them back, didn't they?" Coach Handlesman said.

"You tried to get me to rat on my friends."

"I was trying to help you. If I got you to come clean before the GC authorities got involved, I thought I could protect you. But you kids kept it up."

"Mrs. Weems said somebody spoke up for me, got me into a foster family."

"Guilty," Coach Handlesman said. "Sometimes when you pretend to be someone else, you pretend really well. They believed every word."

"But I saw you at church! Yelling at Bruce."

"I saw you first and made it look good. Bruce is my dearest friend now. I didn't want to endanger him or you, so I tried to make it look good."

"What about Mrs. Waltonen?"

The coach shrugged. "I took a chance. She was asking questions. She wondered about her grandchild. Said you had talked with her, tried to give her answers. I thought she was sincere. I told her God was behind the disappearances. Her granddaughter's in heaven now."

"How did she react?"

"She got quiet. I thought she might break, but then she came at me like a dog. She said if God could be so mean, she'd never believe."

"And she turned you in?"

"Not then. Shelly was excited to see you and told me to come outside. Waltonen must have followed and put it all together when she saw you."

"You told Shelly about us?" Vicki said.

"I could tell she was going to break if somebody didn't. I explained that I was just trying to help, and that she shouldn't blame herself for your being taken away. You were with a foster family, and things were going OK now."

Coach Handlesman took off his hat, and Vicki saw the huge bruise on his head. "What happened?" she asked.

"That little slugger at Judd's house—what's his name? The kid with the dog?"

"Ryan?"

"Clocked me a good one with a golf club."

"What were you doing at the house?"

"Mrs. Jenness set a trap for Judd. She had Mrs. Weems send a message on that watch thing you guys have. Tried to trick them into coming to the school. I figured it was all over, so I went to Judd's house to hide the papers or whatever else might be there that would give you guys away."

"You would have destroyed the computer files?"

"No, I would have copied and hid 'em."

"So they still don't know whether Judd's guilty?"

"No hard proof."

"But if they catch him at the airport and take his files from home, he's sunk."

"Looks that way."

"Were you the one following me the other day?"

"Couldn't find you. Jenness called out the GC guards. They spotted you first."

"What about you? What happens now?"

He shrugged. "Fired. Suspended. Charged with something. I don't know."

Bruce and Judd hurried past the flight attendants as they went through their safety routines. They panted as they buckled their seat belts and settled in.

Mrs. Jenness and Superintendent Pembroke returned with grim faces.

"Thompson is gone," Mrs. Jenness said. "His plane left a few minutes ago."

Superintendent Pembroke looked sternly at Coach Handlesman. "I'm suspending you without pay. Clean out your office. We'll hold a hearing next week."

The principal pulled the others into the next room to confer. Coach Handlesman stopped her and nodded toward Vicki. "She ought to be free now, right?"

"Wrong," Mrs. Jenness said. "She's still a ward of the Global Community."

"If I go back to that place," Vicki said when she and the coach were alone again, "there's nobody to take care of Judd's files. I've got no way to reach the others."

Just then Chaya pecked at the window and motioned to Vicki. Coach Handlesman opened it, and Vicki quickly climbed through.

"I'll cover for you," Coach Handlesman said as he closed the window behind her.

Chaya drove Vicki to New Hope Village Church, where they learned that Judd and Bruce would be in Israel for two weeks. Vicki had lost her family. Now the two people closest to her were half a world away, and she was on the run. The detention center was one thing. Being alone again made her shiver. At least she had Chaya.

JUDD had not been on a plane since the disappearances. Both he and Bruce were tired, but each time one of them stretched to close his eyes, the other brought up a new topic, and they talked for hours. At one point Judd squirmed and cleared his throat.

"I was wondering what you thought about, uh, you know, dating and stuff."

"Dating and stuff?" Bruce said.

Judd felt his face flush. "Ryan calls it the mushy stuff. If we have only seven years left, should we forget about that kind of thing? I mean, wouldn't it take you away from doing what's important?"

Bruce smiled. "We've gone through this with the adult Trib Force with Chloe and Buck. Whether they get married or not is still open, but I do know they've been good for each other."

"But what about somebody my age?" Judd said. "Chloe's in college. Buck is . . . well, he's ancient."

Bruce raised his eyebrows. "Try to find friends, good friends. Don't get entangled in a romance. Dating someone doesn't make you happy or fulfilled."

"I know. But sometimes . . ."

"I know. I miss my wife like nothing else. But God has a plan. Yearn for a deeper relationship with him."

Chaya didn't want to leave Vicki alone, especially in the dead of night, but Vicki insisted. The two hugged and promised to keep in touch.

Judd's house was dark. Vicki stole to the back and rang the doorbell. Phoenix didn't bark, so she knew Ryan and Lionel weren't there. She couldn't wait for help. She would have to do this alone.

Getting into Judd's house was not easy. The windows were high. The back door, Vicki knew, had double locks. Near the deck a small, oval window led into the garage. If she managed to get through it, the basement door was next. She hoped someone had left it unlocked.

Vicki picked up a rock and tapped on the glass. Too noisy. She found a rag on the picnic table and held it up to the glass, then drove the rock through it. She stopped and listened. A dog barked nearby, then silence. One by one she picked out the remaining shards and carefully placed them aside. The hole would be just big enough for her to slip through.

A taxi let jet-lagged Judd and Bruce out near some tour buses. The two gathered their carry-on bags and hustled into the early morning crowd spilling into the street. They pressed forward but were only able to get about a hundred yards from the two witnesses.

Eli and Moishe used no amplification, but their voices rang clearly off the ancient walls.

"The last terrible week of the Lord has begun!" Eli bellowed. "Israel has turned from the true Messiah!"

Moishe took up the strain. "Israel is even now rebuilding the temple. It is a temple of rejection!"

A man in the crowd yelled, "Mercy!" and fell to the ground. Those nearby shushed him, but the more they did, the more the man wept and cried out.

Judd pointed toward the Wailing Wall. Eli and Moishe moved away from their perch and walked directly toward Bruce and Judd. The crowd parted, and Judd thought of Moses and the Red Sea. Eli and Moishe came to the place where the man lay prostrate and moaning. They wore ragged robes. Their arms were muscled and leathery. They had huge, bony hands and wore no shoes. The scent of ashes, as if from a recent fire, hung about them.

"To the one who seeks mercy, mercy will be given," Eli said. "But only one is merciful."

"The Lord God is rich in mercy," Moishe said. "He loved you so much that even while you were dead in your sins, he gave you life when he raised Christ from the dead."

The man cried out again, "Forgive me! I have rejected the holy one of God! Forgive me!"

Others fell to their knees and cried out. Judd heard someone speaking in Spanish, another in what sounded like German, and still others in languages he had never heard before.

"God's blessing upon you," Moishe said as he placed his hand on the man. "May you know the peace of Jesus Christ and the presence of the Holy Spirit. Amen."

Judd's knees went weak as the men backed away. He was speechless.

"Come with me," Bruce whispered. Judd followed him across the road to a small grove of trees.

Bruce spoke through tears. "It's beginning. The Jews, who have so long rejected Jesus as Messiah, are returning. It's as if we're on holy ground."

He motioned for Judd to follow while he hailed a cab. He gave the driver an address on a scrap of paper.

Vicki wrapped her bleeding leg with a fresh bandage from upstairs. She hadn't seen the piece of glass that cut so deeply. *I've gotta help Judd*, was her only thought.

She gathered paper and supplies and put them in a garbage bag. Then she unscrewed the computer connections. She left the printers, monitors, and other equipment and moved the computer towers to the garage.

Shelly! she thought. *If Handlesman was right, Shelly will surely help.*

Bruce rang the doorbell of a modest Israeli home. The door opened slightly, and a middle-aged woman looked at them warily.

"I was looking for the house of the rabbi," Bruce said. "Why?"

"I . . . I am a follower of Christ," Bruce said.

Judd turned as a black car passed slowly behind them.

The woman grabbed Bruce's arm. "Come in. Quickly!"

Bruce and Judd stepped inside.

"It is not safe for you here," she said.

"I'm not worried," Bruce said. "God is protecting us."

"You sound like my husband."

"Is he here?"

"Who are you? Where are you from?"

"Bruce Barnes. I'm a pastor from America."

"If you are a pastor, why were you left behind?"

Bruce quickly told her his story.

"How do I know I can trust you?" she said.

"A mutual friend gave me your address— Buck Williams, the writer."

Relief came over the woman's face. "Eli and Moishe have asked my husband to speak at Teddy Kollek Stadium," she said. "It is an honor he says he does not deserve. It is an honor I would like someone else's husband to have."

She handed Bruce a piece of paper and told him to take it to the stadium that evening. "You must be discreet," she said. "We believe anyone who goes in or out of our home is in danger."

Judd heard another car pass slowly and peeked through the curtains.

"Stay away from the front window," she said. "Why don't you join my children in the kitchen?"

Fresh bread was on the table. A boy about Judd's age sat there. He wore glasses and had close-cropped black hair. A girl who looked slightly older stood by the stove with her arms crossed. She nodded gravely to Judd.

"American?" she said.

"From Chicago. I'm Judd Thompson."

The girl introduced herself as Nina Ben-Judah and the boy as her brother, Dan.

"The rabbi is your father?" Judd said.

"Stepfather," she said. "Our father died when we were young."

"Is your mom always like this?" Judd said. "She seems really nervous."

"My father's life has been threatened," Dan said. "He is trying to arrange for armed guards."

"Just because of what he said on TV?"

Nina said, "Of course! That was blasphemy here. Many believed his message and have become followers, but most think he is a traitor to his faith."

"What about you?" Judd asked her.

She looked at him, squinting. "You first," she said. "Are you a Christian?"

"Yes, I am."

Nina looked at Dan and smiled. "We are not ashamed of the gospel of Christ," she said. "It is the power of God to salvation for everyone who believes, for the Jew first and also for the Greek."

Judd recognized the verse she quoted. "When?" he said. "How?"

"Our father told us of his study," Dan said. "He nearly became a believer before the Rapture."

"We now know our Messiah," Nina said, "but we have become prisoners in our own home. We have to sneak out to go anywhere. Would you like to see the old city?"

Judd told Bruce he would meet him that evening at Teddy Kollek Stadium.

"Why? Where are you going?"

Judd nodded toward Nina.

"No!" her mother said. "Nina, please! It is too dangerous."

"Mother! Trust me! We have an American guest."

Nina led Judd to a trapdoor under a rug in the kitchen. A small passageway led next door where neighbors hustled Nina, Judd, and Dan out a back entrance and into a car. Nina jumped behind the wheel and sped off.

"Do you have to go through there every time you leave?" Judd said.

Dan nodded. "We must not be seen."

The kids knew Hebrew custom and history well. Judd was amazed to think that Jesus actually walked these same roads, carried the cross, was crucified, and rose again in this ancient land. He was awestruck at the Garden of Gethsemane. That afternoon the Bible came alive to him.

By the end of the day Judd felt a bond with Nina and Dan he couldn't explain. He had known them less than a day, yet they were his brother and sister in Christ. As evening approached they stopped at a café. Halfway through the meal, Dan said something in Hebrew, and Nina furtively looked toward the street.

"Kollek Stadium is less than a kilometer away," she said. "There is an exit near the rest rooms in the back. Go there now. When you are outside again, follow that street. You'll make it in plenty of time."

"What are you going to do?" Judd said.

Nina kissed Judd on one cheek and then the other. He saw her tears.

"God bless you and keep you, my brother," she said, "and cause his face to shine upon you."

Judd disappeared inside the café, hoping Nina and Dan would be all right.

Teddy Kollek Stadium was filled. Judd felt both fear and excitement as Eli and Moishe spoke without an interpreter to people from around the world.

"You have been gathered from the twelve tribes of Israel, the chosen ones of the Almighty. And we have been given the high calling of proclaiming his name to every nation, every tribe, every tongue—

"We do not trust in numbers," Moishe picked up the message. "We do not trust in the power of persuasive speech. We trust in the name of the Lord, our God!"

A shout of affirmation shook the stadium.

"One day very soon," Eli said, "every knee shall bow and every tongue confess that Jesus Christ is Lord."

". . . to the glory of God, the Father," Moishe said.

"To the glory of God," they said in unison. And then the multitude, in one voice, thundered the response, "TO THE GLORY OF GOD!!!"

Eli introduced Rabbi Tsion Ben-Judah. He was

middle-aged, trim, and youthful-looking, with only a hint of gray in his dark brown hair. He wore a black suit.

"Dear ones," Ben-Judah said. "How I praise God for each of you. Throughout history we have been a scattered people. Now God is calling us together to be his vessels of reconciliation. He has chosen us to proclaim freedom to the captives! All praise and glory to the Most High God!"

Judd made his way to a glassed-in booth high in the stadium, where he looked over Bruce's shoulder as he tapped out an E-mail message to the adult Tribulation Force.

As I look into this sea of faces, he wrote, *from every conceivable background, I am moved as never before. God's Word is true. Before my very eyes I see God's plan to carry the gospel to the ends of the earth. But my friends, be warned. Though the message is being accepted like never before, though there is coming an incredible soul harvest, there is also coming great trouble. Antichrist is preparing an assault on believers. The question is how long we have.*

Vicki called Shelly, and she agreed to help. They would take the computers to Shelly's trailer or the church. Anywhere but Judd's house. Vicki heard a car in the driveway and hit the button for the automatic door. Vicki shielded her eyes from the flashing red and blue lights.

A voice boomed, "This is the police. Put your hands up and move away from the house!"

OF ALL the sights in Israel, the most amazing and frightening to Judd was the new temple. It looked magnificent. Many said it surpassed the glory of Solomon's temple of old. Judd knew this temple was not built to praise God but rather his enemy.

That evening, as Judd downloaded a day's worth of E-mail, Bruce told him he had met a man from Singapore at the stadium the night before. "He invited us to hold meetings next week in the same stadium Dr. Ben-Judah will use next month when he's there. God is answering our prayers."

"Fantastic!" Judd said. He opened an urgent message from John. Judd slumped. "Vicki's in trouble again—this time with the police."

"Police?" Bruce said.

"John also says Coach Handlesman has been detained. What in the world—?"

Bruce told Judd the truth about Coach Handlesman. Coach had prayed to receive Christ in Bruce's office, and Bruce encouraged him to take his new faith back to school. "He's been worried about you kids for so long. We'll need to get back right away and help him."

"Wait," Judd said. "If God wants you in Singapore, that's where you should go."

"I wouldn't want to abandon Vicki or Coach Handlesman when they need me most," Bruce said.

"You're not abandoning them," Judd said. "They would want you to follow God's leading. I'll go back."

Bruce shook his head, but Judd pressed. "You've said yourself that we were left here to reach those who don't know God. This is a great opportunity for you. I can handle this."

"I hate to send you back alone."

"I'll be fine. This feels right, Bruce."

"If you're sure . . ."

"I'm sure."

Vicki had tripped a silent alarm when she climbed through the window. As Vicki was led to the police cruiser, Shelly passed by. "Go home," Vicki mouthed.

Shelly nodded and kept moving.

The big problem now was the evidence. If Global Community goons found the computer files, Judd would be toast.

At the police station, Vicki was allowed one call.

An hour later a guard approached her. "There's someone to see you." She led Vicki through a packed waiting room and into a private holding area. Vicki brightened when she saw Chaya.

"Hiya, sis," Vicki said, cautious with a guard nearby.

"I'm glad you called me. I want to help, but I don't know how. Do you need a lawyer or something?"

"I think I have it figured out," Vicki said, bending to whisper to Chaya.

"No whispering," the guard said.

Chaya sat back. "I can do that."

"Good," Vicki said. She wrote a phone number on a piece of paper. "Call my friend Shelly, too. She'll be worried. Now, what about you? I've been thinking. You're all alone, and you want to learn more about the Bible."

"Exactly," Chaya said.

"Move here," Vicki said. "Get an apartment near the church. Bruce is the best teacher of the Scriptures."

The guard answered a knock at the door and stepped outside.

"It's tempting," Chaya said. "I'd have to get another job. . . ."

Chaya suddenly put a hand to her mouth. Vicki turned and saw Mrs. Weems and the Steins.

Chaya looked at her parents. Her father turned away, but her mother seemed to lock eyes with her. When Mrs. Weems led the Steins from the room, Chaya wept.

Judd found an empty row on the plane and stretched out. Leaving Bruce was hard, but he knew it was right.

At the airport Bruce had slipped a piece of paper into Judd's pocket. Judd opened it and read:

"To Judd, my son in the faith. Words can't express how much you have meant on this trip, and I will always remember your service. I hope we can one day finish a trip together.

"Hold fast to the hope you have in Christ. Fight the good fight of faith, lay hold on eternal life, to which you were also called and have confessed the good confession in the presence of many witnesses.

"If those words seem familiar, they are Paul's instructions to Timothy. Read 1 and 2 Timothy on your way home. Tell Vicki and Mr. Handlesman they are in my prayers. I remember Lionel and Ryan daily as well.

"May God's grace be with you all. Bruce."

Judd read the passages and was struck especially by 2 Timothy 3:12: "Yes, and all who desire to live godly in Christ Jesus will suffer persecution."

Finally back in Chicago, a customs officer took Judd's passport and ushered him into a waiting room.

Two hours later Judd was fuming. He banged on the door.

"What's this about?" he yelled. "I didn't bring anything back but clothes."

Finally, a tall, thin man entered. He was balding, and Judd couldn't help staring at the wrinkles in his forehead. He pulled a chair across the room close to Judd. He extended a hand, which Judd shook reluctantly.

"Stan Barkoczyk, Global Community task force. Your name came up in an investigation we're pursuing. How well do you know Mr. Handlesman?"

"Not well," Judd said.

"He hasn't helped you?"

"Helped me what? Do more chin-ups in gym? Run the mile a little faster?"

"You're a religious type, aren't you?"

"Depends on how you define *religious*."

Barkoczyk leaned toward Judd, inches from his face. Judd smelled his stale breath. Foamy beads of white formed at the corners of his mouth. "I define *religious* as undermining the Global Community. Religious types think they know more than everybody else and can't wait to show how stupid they are."

Mr. Barkoczyk leaned back and crossed his legs. Judd locked eyes with him and remained silent.

Later Mr. Barkoczyk drove Judd to a police station. Principal Jenness and Superintendent Pembroke shook hands with Mr. Barkoczyk, and the four were led into a cluttered evidence room. Judd's computers sat on a table in the middle of the room.

"Would you like to show us, or do we have to find it ourselves?" Mr. Barkoczyk said.

Judd knew they had him. When they opened his computer files, he would have to tell them everything.

———

Mrs. Weems led Vicki to the infirmary, where a nurse changed the bandage on her leg.

"I didn't have a chance to apologize about your little message machine," Mrs. Weems said. "And it looks like your boyfriend is back. He'll get his today."

"Don't bet on it," Vicki muttered. "And he's not my boyfriend."

The girls hooted when Vicki returned. "Preacher girl is back!" one girl said. "The one who got Janie in trouble."

"Where is Janie?" Vicki said.

"What's it to you?" the girl said. "She's been in the hole since the day you got sprung."

That night, Mrs. Weems showed what she called a "motivational film." It was a Global Community production targeted to troubled teens. While the girls groused about the subject, it was one of the few times they were allowed to watch TV.

The face of Nicolae Carpathia appeared on the screen.

"He's pretty cute," one girl said.

While the narrator extolled the virtues of peace and harmony, Vicki fell to her knees and crept to the back of the room. She opened the door silently and sneaked into the solitary confinement area. She tried several rooms in the dim light of the hallway. Finally, she opened a slat and saw two hollow eyes.

Vicki pushed an apple through the hole. "It's not much, but it's the least I could do after what you did for me."

"What're you doing back in?"

"Long story," Vicki said. "You OK? Can I get you anything else?"

"As soon as it's safe," Janie said, "come back and talk? I'm going crazy in here."

Judd turned on the first computer as the others inched closer. His mind raced. *Can I delete the files? Not with them watching.* Mr. Barkoczyk leaned over Judd's shoulder as the screen flickered. "System error" was all Judd could see.

"What is it?" Barkoczyk said.

"I don't know," Judd said.

Mr. Barkoczyk turned crimson and shoved Judd out of the way. He banged the keyboard and switched the computers off and on. The screens were blank. A computer technician was called in.

"Both dead, sir," the man concluded. "Hard drives crashed. Not a thing I can do for you."

Mr. Barkoczyk cursed and marched a relieved but puzzled Judd past the front desk and told him to wait in the lobby.

A few chairs away an officer put down his newspaper. "Hello, Judd," he said.

Judd couldn't believe his eyes. Sergeant Tom Fogarty.

"Just be calm," Sergeant Fogarty said. "Don't act like you know me."

"How did you know I was here?" Judd whispered.

"I've been keeping an eye on some of the Global Community reports. Vicki's friend Chaya called and asked for help. When I heard the GC was involved, I thought I'd better check it out."

"What did you do?"

Sergeant Fogarty smiled. "I took a look at your computers. I never was much good with those things. I'm afraid I may have messed up your hard drives. Hope you don't mind."

Judd sighed. "Thanks. So what happens to me now?"

"I can't imagine. They have no evidence."

Sergeant Fogarty lifted his newspaper as Mr. Barkoczyk and the others returned. Mrs. Jenness and Mr. Pembroke stared at the floor. "You're free to go, Thompson. But I'd watch my step if I were you."

Judd walked into the fading sunlight with a carton of damaged computer equipment. He would face difficult decisions soon. What about the *Underground?* What about staying in his home? Judd's senior year was approaching. What then? College seemed out of the question. Or was it? Could he rescue Vicki or even get a message to her? It felt like a lifetime since Judd had spoken to her.

Lionel and Ryan kept Judd up late, bringing him up to date and asking about his trip to Israel. They wanted to know every detail about Israel and Judd's new friends there. Judd flipped through a stack of mail as he talked. He slipped one envelope into his pocket and put the rest aside.

Before he went to sleep he retrieved an old laptop from his father's desk to go on-line. Only one E-mail interested him. It was from Bruce.

"God is at work," Judd read, "raising up house churches and small groups. The day is coming when such will be outlawed. I hope you are safe, Judd. I pray for you each day."

Judd was glad to be in his own bed, but the envelope in his pocket kept him from sleep. He couldn't tell anyone. It was a bank statement. His father's account, which he thought would easily last the next seven years, was dangerously low. They would be lucky if the money lasted seven months.

VICKI saw the flash. *A knife,* she thought. Her friend Janie turned and screamed as a girl approached with the crude object.

"I'm sorry, Darla," Janie whined. "I'll get you the stuff today. Tomorrow at the latest."

"You won't be gettin' me anything," Darla snarled. "You're goin' down."

Janie scooted under the lunch table and out the other side. Now only Vicki separated Janie from harm.

"I got no problem with you, Byrne. Outta the way."

Janie hunkered down behind Vicki. She knew the damage a homemade shank could do.

"I don't have a problem with you either, Darla," Vicki said. "Put that away. We can settle this without anybody getting hurt."

"I said I'd make her pay if she stiffed me again."

Vicki looked for a guard. Darla had waited for the right moment to bring out the knife.

"I didn't stiff you!"

"Shut up, Janie," Vicki said. She turned to Darla. "What if she gives your money back? Then everything's square, right?"

Janie tapped on Vicki's shoulder and whispered, "I don't have it."

"That's it," Darla yelled, pushing past Vicki and lunging toward Janie.

Vicki grabbed Darla's arm and pulled her down as a sharp pain invaded Vicki's side. Someone screamed. A whistle blew. Shouting. People crowded around, looking at her. A guard pushed people away.

"She's bleeding!" Janie yelled.

Vicki felt woozy. The room spun. Something warm ran from her side. The guard shouted, "Leave the knife in! You'll do more damage if you take it out!"

––––––––––––––––––

Judd passed the security gauntlet at Nicolae High. There were more Global Community guards this year. Mrs. Jenness, the principal, kept watch at the front.

Judd had vowed to become valedictorian of his class. Speeches he had heard during the most tumultuous year in history left him hollow. If he had the chance, he would use the opportunity to give a speech his classmates and their parents would never forget.

Judd had never had to work for good grades. But his newfound faith had encouraged him to study the Bible like never before, and the discipline helped in other areas. Before the disappearances, several students had been ahead of him academically. Many of them had vanished. The rest he could pass with straight A's. He set his mind toward the goal.

But Judd had problems. His father's money was quickly running out. The monthly bills, the trip to Israel, and the expense of the *Underground* had drained the account. If he didn't come up with an answer soon, he would be forced to sell the house.

Throughout the summer, Judd and the others had written Vicki. When she wrote back, she seemed hopeful, but Judd could read between the lines. Northside Detention Center was an awful place. Pastor Bruce Barnes told Judd and the others to keep praying. He was working on a plan.

Between his many trips overseas, Bruce had put the Young Tribulation Force through a rigorous discipleship program. Ryan called it Bible Boot Camp. Judd couldn't believe how much they were growing and learning. And it was fun. Each new insight and memorized verse made him feel stronger. He had once seen the Bible as difficult to understand. Now each passage was a challenge, a truth waiting to be uncovered.

When Bruce was away, Chloe Steele took them through their daily paces of study and memorization. Her friendship had meant a lot to Lionel and Ryan as well. Nothing could stop the pain of losing Vicki. They had no idea when or if she would ever return.

"Thompson, in my office," Mrs. Jenness said. "Now!"

The last time the two had been face-to-face, Judd was in a police station under suspicion for involvement with the *Underground.*

As soon as Judd was seated, Principal Jenness said, "Your friend, Coach Handlesman, is continuing his reeducation with the Global Community. He probably won't be back. At least not here."

"What does that have to do with me, ma'am?" Judd said.

"If the coach really was behind the underground newspaper as he claimed, that little problem should disappear."

"And what does that have to do with me?" Judd said without blinking.

"Maybe nothing," she said, studying him. "Just listen carefully during the assembly. The new directives from the Global Community apply doubly to you."

Vicki awoke to searing pain and cried out.

"Lie still and I'll get you something," the nurse said.

Blood stained the sheets. A bandage stretched across her wound. Vicki was afraid to look at it.

"You're lucky," the nurse said. "Didn't hit any vitals. But we had to stitch you up and give you a shot for infection. That was a pretty rusty shank."

The nurse left as Mrs. Weems came in the room. She was a large woman whose presence was felt anywhere she went.

"Care to tell me your side?" Mrs. Weems said.

"I'm fine, thank you," Vicki said.

Mrs. Weems snarled, "You're a strange kid, Byrne. You're different."

"Thank you," Vicki said.

"I hate different. To survive here you have to learn to get along."

"That's what I was doing," Vicki said. She explained what had happened.

"That was Janie's last chance," Mrs. Weems said.

"She didn't do anything."

"She was selling drugs," Mrs. Weems said. "She'll be shipped downstate to an adult facility."

Vicki had heard the hard juvenile cases were being treated as adults, but she didn't want to believe it.

"And me?"

"Come to my office as soon as you can move. I have some papers that need to be signed."

"Papers?" Vicki said.

"When you can walk, you're out of here."

"I'm going downstate too?" Vicki said, but Mrs. Weems was already out the door.

The fieldhouse was full. Incoming freshmen were required to sit in the front. Most hung on Mrs. Jenness's every word. Several times Lionel turned around and looked at Judd. Lionel rolled his eyes each time. Mrs. Jenness welcomed students and introduced key faculty members. To her right were Global Community guards in uniform.

"Looks like they're stepping up security," John whispered.

"Why do they need eight guards?" Mark said.

"It is our hope," Mrs. Jenness said, "that when you look back at Nicolae Carpathia High School twenty years from now, you will think of a time of unprecedented peace and learning."

In six years, I won't be thinking about this place at all, Judd thought.

"Last year a faculty member caused great anxiety on this campus," Mrs. Jenness said. "He is no longer with us. We are grateful that the Global Community peacekeeping forces have been given the power to enforce the new rules."

Mark caught Judd's eye. "Sounds like trouble," he said.

"Belief is a private matter. Individuals must come to their own conclusions. Our new policies include zero tolerance for those who push their beliefs on others. Any student, faculty member, or other employee doing this will suffer quick and severe punishment."

Judd saw several freshmen look at each other. They had to wonder what Mrs. Jenness was talking about.

"Students will be expelled, their records destroyed. Hopes for higher education will be lost. Those involved in any divisive activity like last year may be sent to a Global Community reeducation facility."

John leaned over and whispered, "Are these just threats?"

"See all the extra cameras in the hallway?" Judd said.

A freshman raised a hand. Mrs. Jenness shook her head. "We'll save time for questions. Now I want you to see another move toward school unity."

Two students, a boy and a girl, walked on stage and stood by the podium. The boy wore black pants and a gray shirt. The girl wore a black skirt and a gray top. On the left shoulder of both shirts was a dove, the new mascot of the school.

"I liked it better when we were the Prospect Knights," John said. "It's hard to root for a football team called the Doves."

Judd stifled a laugh.

"Beginning tomorrow," Mrs. Jenness continued, "you may purchase these uniforms in the school bookstore. Those who object to our symbol of peace may opt to wear this." She held up the same style of shirt, but in place of the dove was a huge red X.

Vicki winced with each step, but she had to know what Mrs. Weems was talking about. Blood oozed from her wound as she made it to the office.

"You should have listened to me," Mrs. Weems said. "You shouldn't have run away from the foster family."

"I didn't," Vicki said. "When I became friends with their disowned daughter, I knew they wouldn't let me stay."

Mrs. Weems leveled her eyes at Vicki. "Everyone in here is as innocent as Anne of Green Gables. Learn from this, Byrne. Don't get sent back here a third time."

Mrs. Weems shoved a stack of papers toward her. "Sign."

"What are these?"

"Adoption papers."

"What?"

"It's your choice. If you'd rather stay here—"

"No," Vicki said. "I'll sign, but—"

"You want to know where you're going?"

"Exactly."

"You'll find out tomorrow."

32

JUDD, John, and Mark debated the insignia that evening. John believed they should play it safe. "Once you wear anything other than the dove," he said, "you're a target. You can kiss the *Underground* good-bye."

"Not if every Christian takes the *X*," Mark said.

"At some point we have to stand up for what we believe," Judd said. "We've been skulking in the background, hoping we don't get caught. It's time to let our light shine."

John shook his head. "You'd rather play martyr than keep spreading the Word behind the scenes?"

"You guys are lucky," Ryan said. "At least you have a choice. We have to wear the dove."

Shelly arrived wearing the new uniform. "They let everyone who works in the office take one so we can wear it tomorrow." Shelly had removed the *X* from her shirt and rotated it a few degrees. It now looked more like a cross.

"Cool," Ryan said.

"Mrs. Jenness will have a fit," John said.

"Yeah," Mark said. "Can you fix mine that way, Shelly?"

Vicki slept fitfully and awoke bruised and sore. She skipped breakfast and skimmed magazines outside Mrs. Weems's office, but she couldn't concentrate. She would go home with someone that day, and she had no idea who or where.

Finally, Mrs. Weems's secretary ushered Vicki into a small conference room. Vicki paced until the door opened. Pastor Bruce. She was so happy to see him she hugged him despite the pain.

"You're hurt," Bruce said. "What happened?"

Vicki explained. Bruce shook his head. She was gaunt. The more he heard, the madder he became.

"I've seen animals treated better," he said.

"Mrs. Weems said someone was adopting me. Is it somebody from church?"

"Yes."

"I can't believe it," Vicki said. "Did you talk someone into it?"

"Sort of."

"Who is it?"

"I'm not sure you'll want to go with him," Bruce said. "He's a bit of a disciplinarian. Stodgy."

"If he's your friend and from the church, I won't mind. Who is it?"

"Me."

292

"You're kidding, right?"

"I wouldn't kid about that. With the great need, they've relaxed the requirements. I got the go-ahead yesterday."

Vicki wiped her eyes. Bruce's sacrifice overwhelmed her. She had felt abandoned. Now she had a home again.

Bruce broke the silence. "You'll stay at my house. I'm at the church most nights or traveling. You can take your pick of rooms upstairs or down, but you won't be alone."

"I can take care of myself," Vicki said.

"I know. But I figured you'd need someone to keep you company. Get your stuff."

"Wait," Vicki said. "Janie!"

"Who?"

Vicki told Bruce about her. "There's just something about her I can't shake," she said. "Maybe Janie is what I'd be if God hadn't found me."

While Bruce met with Mrs. Weems, Vicki found Janie.

"I'm happy for you," Janie said. "I'm going downstate, and they're going to throw away the key."

"Don't give up hope, Janie. God can help you if you'll let him."

"Save your breath, Byrne. God has a hard enough time keeping his eye on girls like you."

Judd came to Bruce's window when Ryan shouted. Bruce pulled into his driveway, and the Young Tribulation Force waited at the door. Phoenix had balloons tied to his collar.

A huge banner on the garage welcomed Vicki home. Shelly ran out first, then Lionel and Ryan. Judd waited with Mark and John until she came into the house.

"I can't believe you're really back," Judd said as he stretched out a hand. "It's good to see you."

Vicki shook it firmly. Judd felt awkward, like he should have done something more than a handshake. He was glad when Vicki was distracted by the girl behind him. Vicki squealed with delight.

"This is the surprise," Bruce said. "Meet the newest member of the Young Trib Force."

"Chaya!"

Chaya had quit her job in Chicago and moved to Mount Prospect when Bruce offered her an assistant's position working with him and Chloe Steele. Vicki and Chaya would stay together in Bruce's house.

When everyone settled down, Bruce said, "The house-church movement is exploding, and there are many more areas to reach. Someday such groups will be outlawed. I have to work quickly.

"The 144,000 Jewish evangelists are all over the world, infiltrating colleges and universities and workplaces. People are hearing the truth. Satan is working overtime, too."

"It's hard to watch the news," Chaya said. "Theft and violence are everywhere."

"And not just that," John said. "There's a lot of white collar crime, too."

"People are stealing shirts?" Ryan said.

"No," John laughed. "It means businesspeople stealing things with technology. Hackers breaking into bank computers and wiping out accounts of people who have vanished."

Judd felt sick to his stomach. That must have been what happened to his father's account.

"The enemy thinks we'll retreat," Bruce continued. "We can't. I'm going back to Israel next week for the temple dedication, and I'm taking Judd with me."

"How come he always gets to go?" Ryan said. "I want a chance."

"I hope you'll get one," Bruce said. "But not this time."

Bruce excused himself to get back to the church to prepare for Sunday.

"I have something to say," Judd said after Bruce was gone. He explained the money situation. If they scrimped and a few of them got part-time jobs, they might be able to last a few months, maybe even till the end of the school year.

"Tell Bruce," Lionel said. "He'd give you the money."

Judd shook his head. "We have to do this ourselves."

"Why don't you go to the bank and see if the account's been hacked?" John said.

"Because they might freeze the account when they find out my dad is gone. We need what little is left."

John said, "It doesn't seem right to let the weasels get away with your dad's money."

"Do you have enough money for the trip?" Vicki said.

"Barely."

"Use it and go," she said. "God will take care of us."

"Yeah," Mark said. "Exercise your faith. You've been depending on your dad's bank account."

One week later at the reopening celebration in Jerusalem, Judd and Bruce stood shoulder to shoulder with thousands who looked on from the Temple Mount. The temple was everything planners said it would be. And more. Nicolae Carpathia welcomed dignitaries from around the world and congratulated the Israelis.

"Look," Bruce said, pointing to Eli and Moishe. The two witnesses slowly walked to the temple side of the Golden Gate, much to the disdain of the crowd. They were jeered and hissed and booed, but no one dared approach, let alone try to harm them.

"This should be interesting," Bruce said. "I don't think those two have been away from the Wailing Wall more than once."

The crowd murmured as the witnesses approached. Judd thought Nicolae Carpathia sensed something.

"Israel has rebuilt the temple to hasten the return of their Messiah," Eli and Moishe suddenly shouted in unison, "not realizing that the true Messiah has already come!"

The crowd near the witnesses shrank back, while others continued their shouting against them.

"Israel has built a temple of rejection!" Eli and Moishe continued. "Israel remains largely unbelieving and will soon suffer for it!"

Carpathia's eyes flashed as he railed, "Do not let these vagabonds of violence detract from this momentous day, my friends!"

Without microphones, Eli and Moishe spoke loudly

enough for all to hear, crying out in the courtyard as they drowned out Carpathia with their words.

"Enemy of God," they called, "you yourself will one day defile and desecrate this temple!"

"Nonsense!" Nicolae said. He turned to those behind him, clearly frustrated. "Is there not a military leader in Israel with the fortitude to silence these two?"

Judd strained to hear as the Israeli prime minister stepped forward. "Sir, we have become a weaponless society."

"These two are weaponless as well!" Nicolae thundered. "Subdue them!"

But Eli and Moishe continued, "God does not dwell in temples made with hands!"

Bruce turned to Judd. "We needed to be here. The news media won't show all of this. Our Web site may be the only place people can get the true picture of what's happened."

"Do you wish to listen to me or to them?" Nicolae yelled to the crowd.

"You, Potentate! You!"

"There is no potentate but God himself!" Eli responded.

And Moishe added, "Your blood sacrifices shall turn to water, and your water-drawing to blood!"

Before leaving Israel, Judd returned to the home of Rabbi Tsion Ben-Judah to interview the rabbi's stepchildren for the *Underground.*

Dan and Nina seemed overjoyed to see Judd again, but he could tell they were nervous about something.

"We live under suspicion," Nina said. "And it has become worse. Our neighbors have stopped helping us go to and from the house."

"The threats against my father are growing," Dan said. "We have talked about the possibility of coming to your country."

Judd gave them his phone number and E-mail address. "If you need to leave, get in touch," he said. "My friends and I would love to help."

33

THE secret place. Ryan felt most at home there now. The only drawback was that he couldn't take Phoenix with him. Phoenix's bark would give them away. In the middle of stacks of Bibles, Ryan could disappear for hours. *Not that anyone would care,* he thought. *They're all so busy, they don't think about me.*

This was his place to think. To read. He kept pictures of his parents hidden away and remembered life before the world changed. He had lived through an incredible thirteenth year. His mom and dad were dead. His best friend had been raptured. And Lionel, who was both friend and foe at times, had left Global Community Middle School for Nicolae High, so Ryan felt alone. Judd was either traveling with Bruce or buried in his studies. Vicki had been gone a long time and now lived in a different house.

Ryan was changing as well. He had grown taller and

leaner over the summer, only a few inches shorter than Judd. The rest of the Young Trib Force didn't call him "little guy" anymore. His voice embarrassed him. He tried to keep it low, but at the worst times it cracked and made him want to keep quiet.

Ryan counted most on Bruce Barnes and Chloe Steele. Bruce spent his time studying, preparing for sermons, or traveling. But Chloe had occasionally taken time for Ryan while Vicki had been gone. Chloe was the older sister of his best friend, Raymie.

"Do you ever think of them?" Ryan asked one day. "Your mom and your little brother?"

"All the time," Chloe had said. "When I see you, it makes me wonder what Raymie would look like now."

"Bet it's hard to be around me," he said.

"Just the opposite," Chloe said.

Now Ryan sat alone, surrounded by Bibles he had confiscated from abandoned homes. He had been studying the book of Acts with Bruce and was fascinated with the miraculous things God had done in the lives of the early Christians. He wanted God to do the same with him.

He read in Acts 2: " 'And it shall come to pass in the last days, says God, that I will pour out of My spirit on all flesh. Your sons and your daughters shall prophesy, your young men shall see visions, your old men shall dream dreams.' "

Ryan asked Bruce later that day, "Does that mean I'm going to have a vision?"

"Not necessarily," Bruce said. "But God has already shown himself in a miraculous way in your life."

"How?" Ryan said.

"In Joel it says that God will give signs in the earth—blood and fire and clouds of smoke. The sun will darken, and the moon will become bloodred before Jesus returns."

"I'd like to see that," Ryan said.

"It'll be a terrible day," Bruce said. "But look at Acts 2:21: 'And it shall come to pass that whoever calls on the name of the Lord shall be saved.' That's what happened to you. I'd say that's a miracle."

Vicki met with Chloe Steele soon after she returned. Chloe had worked side by side with Bruce and wanted to bring Vicki up to speed on the changes within the adult Tribulation Force.

"I'm worried about my dad," Chloe said. "He lives here but flies *Global Community One* out of New York. It's hard on him. Plus, working for Carpathia is difficult."

"Why does he do it?"

"He believes that's what God wants."

"What about your relationship with Mr. Williams?" Vicki said.

Chloe shook her head. "My dad says he may be married before Buck and I are."

"Your dad? Marry who?"

"Amanda White," Chloe said. "She knew my mom. It took my dad some time, but they're getting serious."

"Buck hasn't proposed?" Vicki said.

"No, and I'm not going to push him. The night he left for New York he told me he wished I could come with him."

"Why didn't you?"

"*That* would have been appropriate," Chloe said, sarcastically. "Anyway, being apart has helped me love him even more."

"At least you know how he feels, right?"

Chloe blushed.

"What?" Vicki said. "Tell me."

"I was helping him pack. We'd held hands but never kissed. I told him he wouldn't miss me as much as I would miss him, and he dropped his packing tape and looked at me. He said there was no possible way I could care for him more than he cared for me. And then he said, 'You are my whole life. I love you, Chloe.' "

"Ohhhh," Vicki said as she scooted in her chair and rubbed her arms. "Do you think you'll get married?"

"We know the time is short," Chloe said. "If God thinks we can work better together than apart, I want it too. But I'm not going to chase him. There's too much to do to waste time looking out for myself."

Judd was impressed with how Lionel and Ryan had taken over the Web site. During studies with Bruce, the two furiously took notes. Soon Bruce's teachings were on the Web site.

They worked hard at using graphics and animation as well. Lionel and Ryan scrolled Bruce's Scripture references at the bottom of the screen. And they added icons linking news stories to the prophecies.

The Web site seemed risk-free because John and Mark had set up a system so they couldn't be traced. Lionel and

Ryan answered E-mails and sent information to those who asked. Many of the hits came from readers of the *Underground* at Nicolae High. Word had also spread to surrounding schools, and the kids saw messages from other states and even other countries.

But the *Underground* became more risky. Because of their dwindling money, the Young Tribulation Force scaled back their distribution to only once a month. And they had to be more and more creative getting it to students. One month they printed business cards with the Web site address and placed them on car windshields and in the seats of school buses. Another month they placed copies of the *Underground* inside popular magazines and books in the library. No one knew where the *Underground* would show up next.

Judd worried about the reaction to Bruce's warnings. Judd expected the Global Community to call Bruce a "kook" and even "hateful," but it seemed even many believers were tired of his gloom and doom predictions.

"I don't care what others think," Bruce said at their next meeting. "We have another year of peace before the next three horsemen of the Apocalypse appear. Once that happens, seventeen more judgments will come."

Judd handed Bruce an E-mail from the Web site. "What do we say to this guy?"

Bruce studied the paper and frowned.

"Everybody has his or her own interpretation of the Bible," the message read. "Stop trying to scare people into believing what you believe."

"Don't respond," Bruce said. "People didn't believe

Jesus was who he said he was before the Rapture. Why should it be different now?"

"Because of all that's happened," Vicki said. "I can't believe people can't see."

Bruce asked Judd to insert a video of coverage from the temple in Israel. "Remember what Eli and Moishe predicted would happen when Nicolae dedicated the temple?" Bruce said.

"Something about blood turning to water and water turning to blood, right?"

Bruce nodded. "Watch this."

Judd was amazed to see a sacrificed heifer's blood turning to water. In another ceremony, a high priest recoiled as water drawn into a pail turned dark red. The man's movement made the blood splash, and it splashed and stained his robe.

"Wow," Ryan said, "but what does all the blood and water stuff mean?"

"The Jews who don't believe Jesus is Messiah have gone back to sacrificing animals to show their devotion to God," Bruce said. "What they're doing is rejecting the sacrifice Jesus made on the cross. They're doing it their own way, and that's displeasing to God."

"But why does it have to be blood?" Ryan said.

"Blood is the symbol of forgiveness," Bruce said. "In the Old Testament it says there is no forgiveness of sin without the shedding of blood. That's why Jesus had to die. By turning the blood to water—something power-less—God is showing his disapproval of the sacrifices in the new temple."

"The Israelis are blaming the witnesses for it," Judd said.

"But it's their unbelief and rejection of Jesus as Savior that are to blame," Bruce said. "Nicolae Carpathia has urged Buck Williams to use *Global Community Weekly* to speak out against the intrusion of Moishe and Eli."

Ryan approached Bruce after the meeting. "We're gonna be together now, right?" he said. "You and Vicki and Judd and everybody from now on."

Bruce put a hand on Ryan's shoulder. "I'd like to think we'll all see the glorious appearing of Jesus at the end of the Tribulation," he said, "but I can't promise. Many will die for their beliefs before Christ returns. It's already happening."

Ryan nodded and ran to the car. "Why does Lionel always get to sit up front?" he said.

"Lionel was here first," Judd said. "Don't start."

Later in Ryan's room, Lionel said, "What's bothering you?"

"Nothin'," Ryan said, staring at the computer screen.

Lionel sat on Ryan's bed. "Lonely without me at school?"

Ryan nodded. "All the excitement's at Nicolae High."

"It's more boring than you think," Lionel said. "Judd says you're doing a good job on the Web site."

"He never told me that," Ryan said as he clicked the mouse. The images of two men appeared before a cyber Wailing Wall. Eli and Moishe quoted Scripture and proclaimed Jesus as the Messiah.

"Pretty impressive," Lionel said.

"I can do more than that," Ryan said. "Right now all I'm good for is answering E-mails and handing out used Bibles."

"Where is your stash, anyway?" Lionel said. "Am I going to have to follow you someday?"

Ryan smiled. "No way," he said. "Only one person has a clue, and I'm not telling."

34

VICKI was closely watched from the day she set foot again in Nicolae High. Judd insisted she not be part of writing or distributing the *Underground*, so when she found a copy in her gym locker, she was as surprised as anyone.

But Vicki did not stop talking about God in class or in private. Some students began to seek her out and ask questions. Others called her names. When one girl discovered she had been adopted by Bruce Barnes, Vicki became known as "Preacher's girl." Vicki only smiled.

The shock of the new year was Mrs. Waltonen. At first, Vicki wanted nothing to do with the woman, but over time, Vicki felt sorry for her. When Vicki saw her, she spoke kindly. They didn't talk one-on-one like before, but Vicki sensed a change and hoped they would.

In late November Bruce sat Vicki and Chaya down in his office. "I have a surprise for you," Bruce said. "I've been in contact with Janie."

"How is she?" Vicki said.

"You'll find out for yourself tomorrow," Bruce said. "She's coming here to live."

Bruce told them he had negotiated with the juvenile facility. He went before a judge and agreed to take full responsibility for Janie's actions while she was in his care. The system was so full of troubled kids, his offer was readily accepted by the authorities.

"But we need to set some rules," he said. "Chaya, this is where you come in."

When Janie arrived the next day, Vicki was excited. Janie seemed cautious as she walked into Bruce's house. "Nice place," she said.

Bruce laid out the rules. There would be no tobacco, no drugs, no alcohol.

Janie shrugged. "No problem."

But Janie bucked the rules. That night Vicki found her on the front step, smoking.

"Bruce said no smoking in the house," Janie said. "I'm not *in* the house."

At school, Janie quickly made friends with the druggie crowd, wore sloppy clothes, and used vulgar language.

Chaya wouldn't let Janie get away with bringing booze or drugs into the house. But Chaya couldn't be with her all day.

Janie seemed bored with the Bible and spiritual things. She sat through Bible studies and church, sighing or even sleeping. Vicki began wondering how long Bruce would let Janie stay.

"I feel responsible for her," Vicki told Bruce after a Young Trib Force meeting. "I thought she'd change."

"God loved us before we ever loved him," Bruce said. "Let's keep showing Janie a little of God's love."

Meanwhile, Vicki felt new emotions about Judd. He was something special. She had always thought so. But he'd graduate the following June, and he wasn't the kind of guy to stay home and vegetate.

Chaya had helped Vicki sort through her feelings. She tried to adopt the same attitude as Chloe Steele had toward Buck. If something happened between Vicki and Judd, fine. If God wanted something totally different for her, she would follow God. But she couldn't help sneaking a prayer in every now and then.

"Lord, if it's OK with you, I pray Judd and I would become more than just friends."

Judd invited everyone to Thanksgiving dinner, but Vicki quickly shot down that idea.

"Ever cooked a bird?" Vicki asked.

"There's a first time for everything," Judd said.

"Just bring dessert to Bruce's place," Vicki said. "I'll get Shelly to help me."

The table looked fabulous on Thanksgiving Day, which the Global Community and Nicolae High now called Fall Festival Day.

"I don't remember anything like this since my family left," Lionel said.

"Where's Janie?" Bruce asked as they stood behind their chairs.

"Still sleeping," Vicki said.

They held hands as Bruce prayed.

"Father, our country and our world no longer celebrate this day, but we do. . . ."

During the meal, talk turned to Nicolae High. They scoffed at the upcoming "winter holiday" and how far the school went to make sure the word *Christmas* was never mentioned.

"We gonna do a Christmas edition of the *Underground*?" Ryan said.

Judd nodded, smiling. "But don't tell Vicki," he whispered.

Shelly said, "No matter how much the Global Community wants people to forget, they still remember it's Christmas. What if we printed an edition that goes outside the school? I work in the office, and there's a master list of addresses for every student, parent, faculty member, and employee. We could mail it."

"Good idea," Judd said, "but the postage cost alone could sink us."

Bruce shrugged. "If God wants you to do it, he can make it happen."

"What about Shelly?" John said. "When the faculty finds out they all got the same mailing, they could trace the list to her."

"Everybody's in the phone book," Shelly said. "I'll take the risk."

Everyone turned as Janie scuffed into the room in her pajamas. She rubbed at her eyes and yawned. "Why didn't somebody tell me it was time for breakfast?"

After the Sunday morning service, Bruce pulled Judd aside. "I brought up your idea with a few church leaders," he said, "and someone's given an anonymous gift to cover the postage."

That afternoon Judd and the others went to work. They concentrated on the prophecies about Jesus' birth. In simple language they laid out the same claim Dr. Tsion Ben-Judah had made. Jesus, the son of Joseph and Mary, was God in the flesh. Not only had he come to earth and died for people's sins, but he was coming again.

The mailing went out the week before Christmas. By the twenty-fourth there were hundreds more hits on the Web page.

Ryan found Judd in the living room late on Christmas Eve. A fire crackled in the fireplace. Judd had pulled out an artificial tree from the attic, and it stood in the corner with no ornaments.

"What's up?" Ryan said, carrying a nicely wrapped box.

"Just thinking," Judd said.

"Whose name did you get for the gift exchange?" Ryan said.

311

"It's a secret," Judd said, ignoring the box. "Think you have enough Bibles for everybody who responded to the mailing?"

"Sure. People are supposed to come by the church office. Took a bunch there yesterday."

Judd stared at the tree. "Christmas used to be so important to me," he said. "I'd make a list of all the stuff I wanted. The only surprise was what color my parents wrapped the boxes."

"Man, you were lucky."

Judd closed his eyes. "My dad had the money to buy whatever I wanted," he said. "Now all I remember is my Mom playing Christmas songs on the piano. My dad on the floor playing with Marc and Marcie. Christmas Eve service. Passing out candles and lighting them, one person to the next."

"My dad never played any games with me," Ryan said. "He always brought stuff home from the office to work on. Mom worked, too. They tried to make it up to me at Christmas, so I got some pretty neat stuff. The closest I ever got to church was going over to Raymie's house."

"If I ever have kids—," Judd said.

"What?" Ryan said.

"Ah, it doesn't matter. Neither of us has to worry about being a father, good or bad."

Ryan flicked on the television and saw the leader of the new Enigma Babylon One World Faith, Pontifex Maximus Peter, formerly Peter Mathews of Cincinnati, praise the Global Community's religious unity.

"For you watching in North America," the man said,

"I applaud your embracing Enigma Babylon One World Faith. Many have abandoned the old traditions for a new belief— love and light for all people of all nations. For those who still hold to the old ways, I urge you to come to the light. Let us put away the division."

Pontifex Maximus introduced a video clip from a pastor in Maryland.

"I'm the leader of a congregation that used to tell people God could only be known one way," the pastor said. "Thankfully, we're now following a new way led by the example of Potentate Nicolae Carpathia. And I urge anyone not committed to the beliefs of the Global Community to accept them now as we begin a new year and a new era of peace."

Judd checked E-mail before going to bed. He found a message from Nina in Israel.

"There have been more threats to my father's life, but he feels God's protection. Where would we stay if we decided to come to your country?"

Judd typed a quick note saying Nina, Dan, and her parents could stay with someone in the church. He could help make it happen anytime they felt it necessary.

Christmas decorations filled Bruce's house. Late Christmas morning the Young Trib Force gathered to exchange gifts. Janie complained about not having money to buy anything good and didn't want to participate. She stayed in her room.

Vicki was chosen to open her gift first. She eyed the

slender box excitedly. It looked like jewelry, and she hoped Judd had drawn her name.

Inside she found a gold necklace with one charm—a cross. "Oh, it's beautiful," Vicki said, holding it up to her neck and looking at Judd. "I love it."

Ryan stormed from the room.

"Oh no," Vicki said. "I thought—"

Judd shook his head. "Sorry. I drew someone else's name."

Vicki heard a scream upstairs, and Ryan came running, then slammed the front door behind him.

Janie appeared at the top of the stairs. "That little creep!" she said. "He didn't even knock."

Vicki ran into the cold and followed Ryan's tracks in the snow. She found him shivering at a bus stop at the end of the street.

"She cussed at me," Ryan said. "How was I supposed to know it was her room?"

"You didn't," Vicki said. "I'm sorry about Janie. And I really do like the necklace. How'd you get the money?"

"I didn't take it—honest," Ryan said.

"I didn't think you stole it," Vicki said. "It just looks like it cost a lot."

"Saved it," Ryan said. Vicki could see his breath as Ryan looked straight ahead. "The guy at the store made me promise not to tell he sold me something with a cross on it." He sighed and shook his head. "Janie yelled at me because I caught her. She was smoking something up there."

By the time they got home, Janie had aired out the room and disposed of whatever she had been smoking.

"Ryan's a liar," Janie said. "I didn't do anything."

35

FOUR MONTHS LATER

JUDD looked at the test questions, and his heart sank. He knew the answers, but the truth wasn't what his teacher, Mr. Syncrete, wanted. Judd had had no problems all year in trigonometry or English. He had a running feud with the biology teachers over evolution, but he could back up his beliefs with scientific data. Religion class threatened his dream of becoming valedictorian.

Judd proudly wore the cross in Mr. Syncrete's class. The Global Community required religious education for graduation. Judd struggled not to make waves, but at times he couldn't keep silent.

The class had begun with an overview of the Enigma Babylon One World Faith. Mr. Syncrete praised its leader, Pontifex Maximus Peter, for ushering in what he called a "new era of tolerance and unity" among all major religions. Mr. Syncrete spent hours on Eastern religions and spoke in glowing terms of animistic beliefs—that even objects have a soul. Guest lecturers explained everything from worship of ancestors to yoga. But the teacher's demeanor soured when he covered Judaism. And when Christianity finally came up, his attitude got even worse.

"The Jews believe in one God who let them be annihilated in the Holocaust," Mr. Syncrete said with a sneer. "And the Christians have three Gods who did the same. It's an irrational, superstitious belief system."

According to Mr. Syncrete, the biggest enemies of the new one-world faith were the millions who believed Jesus was the only way to God. He scoffed at those who dared disagree. He read word for word the statement of Pontifex Maximus Peter concerning Christians:

To say arbitrarily, Pope Peter wrote, *that the Jewish and Protestant Bible, containing only the Old and New Testaments, is the final authority for faith and practice, represents the height of intolerance and disunity. It flies in the face of all we have accomplished. Those who agree with that false doctrine are hereby considered heretics.*

Spats between Judd and Mr. Syncrete were legendary. No matter what the argument, Judd came back to the Resurrection. Jesus was the only spiritual leader to prove his claims of divinity.

"You have no basis for saying that," Mr. Syncrete said once. "Give me one shred of evidence that the so-called Resurrection isn't the work of fishermen turned fiction writers."

"I'll give you the evidence," Judd said, "if you'll admit that the resurrection of Jesus, if it happened, changes everything you're teaching."

Judd had the man in a corner. If Mr. Syncrete admitted that rising from the dead would prove the claims of Christ, Judd could show that Jesus was a real person who had risen from the dead. If he didn't let Judd speak, Mr. Syncrete would look like a coward.

"We'll come back to this," Mr. Syncrete had said finally. Everyone snickered. They never got back to the question, and from that day on, Judd knew Mr. Syncrete was out to fail him.

While the Young Tribulation Force cheered Judd's efforts, Bruce cautioned him. "You don't win hearts by winning arguments. It's important to know the truth and tell it, but you can't use it to hurt. Speak the truth in love."

Judd answered the multiple-choice questions on his final. On a couple he put asterisks and wrote notes at the bottom of the page: "This is the view taught in class, not my point of view." But the final essay question made his blood boil: "Enigma Babylon One World Faith encompasses all religions and is thus superior to all individual belief systems. Explain why you believe this."

Judd rose and approached the teacher's desk.

"Sit down, Mr. Thompson," Mr. Syncrete said.

"But this is not a fair question. It assumes—"

"I said sit down!"

"It may be your job," Judd said, "but I won't be brainwashed."

"Give me your test."

Judd handed it to him.

"You are excused. The final is half your grade. You've just failed the class."

Judd went straight to Mr. Kurtz, the dean of students. Mr. Kurtz was a Santa-like figure with a big, round belly and a white beard. He could be tough, but Judd respected him. Judd explained as Mr. Kurtz stroked his beard.

"I've been watching the grade point averages, and you're a lock," Mr. Kurtz said. "The only thing that could possibly come between you and the top of your class is an F."

"I don't think it's a fair question," Judd said. "It makes the wrong assumption—that I agree."

Mr. Kurtz shrugged.

"You can go back and apologize, throw yourself on his mercy, and answer the thing, or take your lumps."

"I have no other choice?"

"You could go to the school board, but graduation would be long over by the time they could act on your complaint. Looks like you have to choose."

Judd hurried back to class. He had only five minutes left.

Toward the end of a study period, Vicki heard a commotion and followed her teacher into the hall. A Global Community guard rifled through Janie's locker. Janie stood nearby yelling, "You have no right!"

Before Vicki could get to her, Mrs. Jenness led Janie to the office.

"Back to class," the teacher said.

Vicki turned and nearly ran into Judd.

"Sorry," Judd said. "I don't have time to explain, but pray for me."

Only a handful of students were still taking the test when Judd returned. Mr. Syncrete didn't look up. Only three minutes left in the class.

"Mr. Kurtz suggested I apologize, throw myself on your mercy."

Mr. Syncrete sat back in his chair and put a pencil to his lips. He smiled. "You have been a burr in my saddle from day one. And now you have the audacity to ask for mercy?"

"I'm sorry, sir. I was wrong. I'm passionate about this, and I want people to consider what I believe. But I didn't do it the right way. Forgive me."

Mr. Syncrete looked at the clock. "It would not be fair to allow you extra time. After all, you walked out."

"Then just count the multiple choice," Judd said.

The bell rang. Others filed past and added their tests to the stack. Mr. Syncrete scratched his head, pursed his lips, and nodded.

Vicki waited for Janie outside the principal's office after school. Mrs. Waltonen nodded as she passed, then returned a few minutes later.

"She should be out in a couple of minutes," Mrs. Waltonen said.

"Thanks. They've been in there a long time."

"They found something in her locker. You probably should prepare for the worst."

Vicki hung her head. Months of trying to be Janie's friend, talking, pleading, and accepting her hadn't changed her a bit. Vicki was surprised to see Mrs. Waltonen still standing there.

"I want to say," the woman began haltingly, "that— well, I appreciate what you've tried to do for that girl."

Before Vicki could thank her, Mrs. Waltonen slipped away as Judd approached.

"Finish your last final?" Vicki said.

Judd nodded. Mr. Kurtz stepped out and waved Judd inside.

"He doesn't look happy," Vicki said.

"This is it," Judd said.

A few moments later Bruce came into the office. Vicki felt strange to greet him there. She told him what had happened in the hall.

"This has been brewing for some time," Bruce said. "We've disciplined her and done everything humanly possible. Now there have to be consequences."

"I'll wait for you," she said.

"Why would my daughter wait out here?" he said, motioning her in with him.

Mrs. Jenness told them in front of Janie that the girl had hidden drugs in her locker. Janie would be sent back to the care of the Northside Detention Center.

"They'll send me downstate," Janie said. "Please, I won't do it again."

"Can we have a moment?" Bruce said.

Mrs. Jenness stepped out. Bruce looked straight at Janie. "I've tried to help you. I've given you a home. Vicki and Chaya love you more than I could ever have imagined."

"I'll change," Janie said. "I mean it this time."

"I hope you will, Janie," Bruce said. "I pray every day that you will turn to Christ. We've done all we can for you. It's hard to let you go, knowing how you'll be treated—"

Bruce's lip quivered. "The truth will set you free. But you have to accept the truth for yourself."

Janie sobbed as she was taken away. Bruce and Vicki watched the van drive away.

Judd met them outside.

"One of the hardest things you'll ever have to do," Bruce said, "is to let go of someone you care deeply about."

Vicki asked Judd what Mr. Kurtz said.

"Good news and bad news," Judd said. "I didn't make valedictorian; I came in second. But I get to speak at graduation as salutatorian."

36

JUDD'S first draft of his speech was thirteen pages long. Single-spaced. He would have to cut more than half of it. He had only seven minutes to speak.

The valedictorian, Marjorie Amherst, wasn't a believer. Her parents sponsored a Global Community organization. Mark called them "Nicolae nuts." They had written and called Global Community headquarters for months. The rumor on campus was that Leon Fortunato, aide to Nicolae Carpathia himself, might actually attend the ceremony.

Judd was so engrossed in his speech that he had little time to think about his money problems. Everyone had pitched in, but two or three more mortgage payments, and they were sunk.

Lionel and Ryan popped in with suggestions for his speech.

"I can't wait to see you up there givin' it to 'em!" Ryan said.

"Sorry, pal," Judd said. "I get only two tickets, and I've already asked Bruce and Vicki."

"Every time—," Ryan said.

"Can't we just stand in the back?" Lionel said.

"It's nothing personal," Judd said. "Maybe you can see it on TV, especially if this Fortunato guy shows up."

Judd cut his speech to five pages. Still too long. Mrs. Jenness looked at the content, too. The next day Judd was called into her office.

"Limit your remarks to the school and what you've learned here," Mrs. Jenness said. "Cut the religious content."

"What do you consider 'religious'?"

"Mentions of God. About the disappearances being a 'wake-up call.' Don't offend any special guests."

———

Vicki asked to meet with Mrs. Waltonen during gym class. Mrs. Waltonen let the student teacher take over and showed Vicki to her office.

"About what happened," Vicki said. "I want you to know I don't hold anything against you."

"We came down hard on you," Mrs. Waltonen said. "I thought you deserved it at the time. You've healed from your wounds?"

"The stitches came out, but the detention center stays with me. At night I wake up sometimes. And I think about Janie a lot."

"Any word from her?"

"They took her downstate. I've written, but she hasn't written back."

Mrs. Waltonen lifted a snapshot from her desk.

"My granddaughter," she said. "Gone."

"I'm sorry."

"I've been thinking a lot about what you said to me last year. Coach Handlesman told me the same thing. My family members are in heaven. I wasn't ready to hear it."

"I would have thought it would make you feel better."

"I was angry. I'm not sure with whom. I looked at Christians as the enemy. You were telling me something I couldn't stand, something I didn't want to hear."

Vicki wanted to quote Mrs. Waltonen a million verses, but she held back. "How about now?" Vicki said.

"Well," Mrs. Waltonen said, "I've slipped into your church a few times."

"You're kidding!" Vicki said.

"I saw the tape your former pastor made. I've got it all down."

"So now what?"

"I want to believe like you so I can see my family again. But it's all too fantastic, too hard to believe."

"Harder than to believe your family was taken right out of their clothes?"

Mrs. Waltonen leaned back, and her chair squeaked.

Security was tight at the graduation ceremony. From behind the curtain, Judd watched Global Community guards herd everyone through metal detectors. Some parents forgot their tickets and still expected to get in. They were turned away, furious.

Someone tapped on Judd's shoulder. He was surprised to see Coach Handlesman.

"Hey," Judd said, "what are you doing here?"

"I'm out on good behavior," he said, chuckling. "I couldn't miss such an important night for you. I'm really proud. Can't wait to hear what you're going to say."

Judd shook his head. "Mrs. Jenness hacked everything important out of my speech. I wanted to really say something."

"You'll sure have an audience," Mr. Handlesman said. "Those are network news cameras. I hear that CNN is airing the Global Community guy live."

"I'm on just before him," Judd said. "I might just say what I want."

"Whatever you do," Mr. Handlesman said, "know that we're behind you."

Mrs. Jenness came through the curtains and clapped. The honored graduates came to attention.

Mr. Handlesman was gone.

———————————

Vicki and Bruce sat near the front. Camera crews partially blocked their view. Mary Lee Manwether, brown hair perfectly in place, jotted notes and spoke with her producer.

"If they stick with the time on the program," the producer said, "you'll have about a minute to fill before Fortunato speaks."

Mary Lee didn't look up.

As the strains of "Pomp and Circumstance" filled the room, Judd and Marjorie followed Mrs. Jenness and the faculty advisors onstage.

"Who put up the new curtain over the stage?" Mrs. Jenness whispered. "Very nice."

Leon Fortunato, dressed in a sleek, dark suit, slipped in at the last moment with an entourage of bodyguards. The audience tittered, then broke into wild applause as he was led to a chair on the stage. He bowed slightly to the crowd, then was seated.

"I can't believe I'm in the same room with him," Marjorie Amherst gushed. "He actually works side by side with Nicolae Carpathia! Am I pale, Judd? I might just keel over."

"Down, girl," Judd said. "He's just a man."

"If I get too nervous, can you take my place?" she whispered. "I don't know if I can do this."

"You'll be fine," Judd said.

"I'm serious, Judd. I think I'm going to be ill."

"How about I let you go first," Judd said. "If you have a problem, I'll come up and help."

Marjorie squeezed his hand with a look that oozed her thanks.

Judd scratched the plan to Mrs. Jenness on the back of his program and passed it to her. Mrs. Jenness frowned and looked at Judd. He stuck his finger in his mouth and pointed at Marjorie. Marjorie weaved in her seat and looked like a ghost. Mrs. Jenness pursed her lips and nodded.

———————————————

Vicki gave a little wave, but Judd didn't acknowledge her. He looked toward someone in the graduating class, nodded, then sat back. Vicki looked at the row of seniors in front of her and noticed John a few seats away. He had in his hand some kind of a control device with an antenna.

"What's going on?" Vicki mouthed when she caught his eye.

John put a finger to his lips.

———————————————

Judd tried to calm Marjorie as two students sang an original song about their years at Nicolae Carpathia High School. Mrs. Jenness beamed as one strummed a guitar and the other sang:

> *Nicolae, you and I have shared so much together.*
> *We will sing, we will work to make this world much*
>   *better.*
> *Till the day that I die, I will not forget*
> *Nicolae. Nicolae. Nicolae.*

Mr. and Mrs. Amherst applauded before the song was over. They stood, but no one else did until Leon Fortunato also rose. Mrs. Jenness alerted the audience to a change in the program and introduced the valedictorian.

Marjorie was shaky. She made it to the lectern, turned to curtsey to Leon Fortunato, and fell in a heap at his feet.

Her mother and father rushed to the stage, but Global Community guards blocked them. Marjorie was taken backstage. Mrs. Jenness, flustered, introduced Leon Fortunato next instead of Judd. The man looked at his program, then stood and thanked the audience for a standing ovation.

Vicki saw the frantic look on the reporter's face.

"Give it to us now, he's up," Mary Lee Manwether told her producer.

"They just went live to another report from New Babylon," the producer shot back. "What happened?"

"The program's out the window because the girl flopped," Mary Lee said. "Can't somebody get this guy to wait?"

"The tape's rolling," the producer said. "We'll be OK."

Someone shushed the two as Leon Fortunato began. Vicki thought he looked more like a character actor than a politician. He was thick and swarthy with his hair slicked back, and he had the air of someone used to being the center of attention. He had an accent, but Vicki couldn't place it.

"I bring you greetings from New Babylon and the man this school was named for, Global Community Potentate Nicolae Carpathia."

The audience applauded.

"Graduates, your parents and teachers have invested countless hours in your education. Today, we salute you all."

"Slick," Vicki said.

"Too slick," Bruce whispered.

Fortunato looked at the graduates. "I speak for Potentate Carpathia and the entire Global Community when I extend an invitation for you to help us answer the question that has plagued this world since time began.

"In this extraordinary moment in world history, we have within our grasp the opportunity to, as your singers suggested, 'make this world much better.' "

———————————

Mrs. Jenness got Judd's attention. She shrugged and said, "Be ready. You're next."

Judd nodded and glanced toward John in the audience. Judd lowered his head and coughed into his gown. John nodded slightly.

Judd knew he would never have this opportunity again.

———————————

"And so I thank the faculty and staff of Nicolae Carpathia High School," Leon Fortunato said, "for staying true to the cause Potentate Carpathia and I strive for daily. May your efforts bear fruit for the sake of peace, for the sake of this country, and for the sake of our world."

As the audience stood in wild applause, Vicki saw a red light on the camera. Mary Lee Manwether said, "We're ready with a videotape of a speech from Nicolae Carpathia's right-hand man—"

As Mrs. Jenness rose to introduce Judd, the producer gave Mary Lee the "stretch" sign. Something was wrong.

"All right," Mary Lee said. "We'll get to that in just a moment. Meanwhile, let's listen to one of the students of Nicolae Carpathia High, uh . . . this is Marjorie . . . no . . . I'm sorry, this is Judd Thompson, the salutatorian."

Judd took a deep breath. Leon Fortunato politely applauded and looked at his watch. Judd caught a glimpse of Vicki and Bruce, spied Coach Handlesman toward the back, and glanced at teachers who had lived through the most tumultuous year on the planet.

It was decision time. Judd saw the CNN camera trained on him. He could do only what he believed was right.

37

JOHN and Mark had studied the sound system in the auditorium. If Judd deviated from his script, Mrs. Jenness would intervene. They had to have an alternate plan.

Mark and John had rigged an auxiliary microphone, hidden under Judd's graduation gown. If his podium microphone was turned off, the auxiliary bypassed the mixing board and went straight to the huge overhead monitors. Then, the only way to keep Judd from being heard would be to cut the speaker cable.

A thousand images flashed through Judd's mind as he stepped to the lectern. Empty seats on the plane. Losing his parents. Bruce. Pastor Billings's tape. Vicki and Lionel and Ryan.

The crowd stared, and the red light on the television camera beckoned. Whatever the cost, whatever the outcome, he felt God had called him to this moment.

Judd remembered a few techniques from speech class.

He let the audience settle, then paused another second. The auditorium stilled as he folded his notes and placed them inside the lectern. He would speak from memory and from his heart.

"I made a promise to myself in this room one year ago. I vowed to deliver a message tonight. And I thank G—I'm thankful I'm able to do that."

No looking down. Judd looked at their faces.

"When we graduates started our junior year, we had no idea that many of our friends would not join us tonight. Kids we went to grade school with. Kids we played T-ball with. We felt as close to some of them as to our own families. But now they're gone.

"I would like to remember them now with a moment of silence."

Judd stepped back and bowed his head. He turned slightly to see Mrs. Jenness and Leon Fortunato looking at the floor. So far, so good.

"We remember those who are not with us," Judd finally said softly. Then his voice rose. "And now we embark on a new road. As Mr. Fortunato said, we have an opportunity to promote peace. To make this world much better."

Judd grabbed the lectern and with the fervency of an old-time preacher belted out, "We have an opportunity to follow the mandate of the Global Community and its leader, Nicolae Carpathia."

Vicki, stunned, looked at Bruce. Applause filled the auditorium. She saw Leon Fortunato lean down and say something to Mrs. Jenness. Mary Lee Manwether pointed to herself, but her producer rolled a finger in the air and said, "Let it go. This is good."

Bruce said, "Carpathia has certain powers of control. Maybe his right-hand man has learned from him."

Vicki glanced at John. He was smiling.

———————————

Judd's heart pounded. He took another breath to calm himself. He made the students laugh with memories of familiar sights and sounds on campus. He poked fun at the keyboard teacher and gave statistics on how many frogs they had dissected in biology class. The faculty laughed along.

"They say confession is good for the soul," Judd said, "and if it's good for the soul, it ought to be good for the Global Community."

Judd looked around and saw Leon Fortunato chuckle. Mrs. Jenness quickly leafed through Judd's script.

"Last year after some of our friends left us behind, someone published and distributed an underground newspaper. It contained some rather outlandish statements."

Mrs. Jenness frantically scanned pages and threw them aside. She stood.

It's too early to be shut down, Judd thought.

Judd continued, "For those who don't know, our administration cracked down on these would-be journalists, and I think it's appropriate to give a round of applause for our principal, Mrs. Jenness."

335

Mrs. Jenness was caught off guard. She glared at Judd. Then, realizing the camera was on her, she smiled and waved. Reluctantly, she sat.

———————————

Vicki held her breath. Was Judd going to give up his friends?

———————————

"This is really cool," Ryan said as he and Lionel listened to the applause. "Wish we could be there."

"No way we'd have gotten in," Lionel said. "The place is packed."

"This isn't what he wrote," Ryan said. "This is the speech he didn't show them."

"And how do you know that?" Lionel said, suddenly interested.

"Found it," Ryan said. "It's goin' on the Web as soon as he's finished."

———————————

"I carry a secret tonight," Judd continued. "I know the identity of the one who printed, wrote, and helped distribute that paper. One of our teachers last year took the fall for the real culprit, and I feel bad about that. The truth is, the culprit was . . . *me.*"

———————————

Vicki heard someone say, "I don't believe it."

"I knew it all the time," another said.

"What's he doing?" Vicki said as Judd called for quiet.

The camera was still on. The CNN producer told Mary Lee to sit down.

Bruce said, "It looks like Mrs. Jenness is ready to pull the plug."

Judd glanced back as Mrs. Jenness turned to Leon Fortunato and Leon assured her with a wave.

Judd continued. "A year ago I knew the truth and didn't want to accept it. I have come to believe that the truth will set you free."

Judd told about his plan to run away and about the plane ride to Europe on which scores of passengers disappeared around him.

"We've learned a lot at Nicolae High. We owe a debt to our teachers and parents. But if we gain a whole world of knowledge and miss the most important thing in life, what good will our education be? What if we gain the world but lose our souls?

"You will make many decisions in the future. But tonight I tell you that there is ultimate truth. If you believe it and act on it, your life will change forever. If you dismiss it, the road ahead is grim."

Judd heard Fortunato say, "OK, that's enough," and Mrs. Jenness approached. He kept going.

"There is one way, one truth, one path to life and peace, and that is through Jesus Christ."

Mrs. Jenness said, "Stop." She drew a finger across her throat at the control board, and AV techies turned knobs, flipped switches, pulled cords, and shrugged.

337

"I beg you to consider him! He died that you might live."

"Judd, step away from the microphone," Mrs. Jenness said.

Judd stayed where he was. He pointed behind him, and instantly the curtain fell, revealing a banner with the text of a Bible verse, John 3:16.

"For God so loved the world that he gave his only begotten Son, that whoever believes in him should not perish but have everlasting life."

"Someone turn the microphone off!" Mrs. Jenness yelled. Global Community guards approached. Though the microphone was dead, Judd could still be heard.

He heard a scattering of boos and hisses. Judd moved to his right at the edge of the stage and looked into the faces of the graduating class.

"You've read the *Underground*," he said, his voice even louder now through the hidden microphone. "You know that what the Bible predicted is coming true."

Mrs. Jenness screamed through the dead microphone, "Turn him off!"

But Judd's voice rang clear through the hall. "I'm not a rebel," he said. "I'm a truth teller."

Global Community guards rushed the stage. Judd moved left and was blocked from the stairs. He ran right as Fortunato rose and avoided Leon like a running back slipping a tackler.

"God will hear you if you ask him to forgive you," Judd shouted as he ran, breathing heavily now. Students hooted and cheered as he eluded the guards. The CNN camera followed him. He slipped into the plants at the edge of the stage. Before him was the drop to the auditorium floor. Guards were upon him.

"If you believe in your heart that Jesus was raised from the dead and confess with your mouth that he is Lord, you will be saved. Don't wait. Pray now!"

Judd heard the footsteps. Mrs. Jenness still shouted. He glanced to see an angry Leon Fortunato escorted by a cadre of bodyguards. A GC guard reached for Judd but got only the edge of his robe. Judd pulled away, heard a rip, and lost his balance. He flipped in the air and landed hard on his feet as he fell to the floor. Pain shot through his right foot.

Vicki jumped out of her seat, but Bruce grabbed her arm.

"Let me go!" she said.

The audience fell silent now. Students craned their necks to see Judd lying under the John 3:16 banner.

"Uh, just another indication of the religious diversity in the country," Mary Lee Manwether said. "And now, I think we have the tape of the remarks made tonight by the Global Community's Leon Fortunato."

As the guards converged upon him, Judd forced himself to speak through the pain.

"Give your life to Christ right now," he gasped. "Pray with me. God, I know I have sinned. . . . I need your forgiveness. Come . . . into my life now . . . change me . . . I accept you now."

As the guards yanked him to his feet, he forced himself into one last act of commitment. One last show of resolve. Judd rolled on his side and put his weight on his good leg. Slowly, painfully, he stood.

"Thank you," he said as the Global Community guards grabbed him and led him away.

———————————

Vicki could not hold back her tears. Bruce put an arm around her.

The room was silent except for Judd's heavy breathing into the microphone. The guards were not gentle. One called him a name. Another cursed and told the others to keep quiet.

Then, through her tears, Vicki saw something wonderful. On the other side of the auditorium stood a lone figure—a faculty member.

"Who is that?" Bruce said.

"Mrs. Waltonen," Vicki said.

In the back Coach Handlesman stood and clapped. Bruce and Vicki stood. Then John and Mark in their graduation robes. Throughout the auditorium students and parents stood, some clapping, some weeping. Some sat in silence. Others booed.

Vicki shook. A guard roughly ushered Mrs. Waltonen from the room.

38

JUDD was expelled, given no credit, and barred from any college or university. A Global Community officer looked at him with contempt.

"I hope you're happy," the man said. "You'll never be anything now!"

After hours of detainment, Judd had signed a statement agreeing to cease making public statements of disloyalty to the Global Community. Otherwise he would be sent to prison.

"Do you mean to keep that promise?" Bruce asked as he drove Judd home early the next morning.

"I can keep that promise and still talk about my faith," Judd said. "But if it comes to that, there are worse things than a reeducation camp."

"I hope Coach Handlesman and Mrs. Waltonen agree," Bruce said. GC peacekeepers concluded that Mr. Handlesman was to blame for the device that allowed Judd to override the sound system.

The broadcast had been live, so news of Judd's speech spread. He was a hero to believers and a sad figure to others. Fortunato called the event "an isolated incident," but leaked reports said he was furious with the news producer who had called the shots and had her fired from her post. Judd only hoped Nicolae Carpathia heard about it.

Judd didn't want to go to college anyway, not with only a few years left. Bruce asked him to go with him on more trips abroad.

But John wanted to go to college.

"Seems like a waste to me," Mark said. "We have less than seven years left. We ought to make the most of them."

"And your answer is the militia?" John said.

"You bet. The *Underground* helped us get our message out. Let's take it to another level."

Bruce shook his head.

"Tomorrow night we're simulating an attack," Mark said. "I can't say much, but the militia is big. I think God is going to use it to overthrow Carpathia."

"That doesn't square with Scripture," Judd said.

"What are we supposed to do, roll over and play dead?" Mark said. "Come out and go through an exercise with us, Judd. Your ankle's healed."

"I'm not worried about my ankle. I just don't think this is the answer."

"And I think you're chicken."

Vicki jumped in. "And what do the women in your militia do? Stay home and bake cookies?"

"Come along if you'd like," Mark said. "All of you. Bruce, too."

"Cool," Ryan said. "What time do we leave?"

"Sorry," Mark said. "Too young."

"I'll be there," Judd said.

"Me, too," Vicki said.

———————————————

Vicki put on combat fatigues. She painted her face the same colors and surprised Chaya, who was studying in the den.

"You went a little heavy on the green and black," Chaya joked. "What're you trying to prove?"

"Judd and I hope we can show Mark how silly this all is."

The moon was full as they drove north. The air was hot and muggy, but the wind felt good as it rushed through the cab of Mark's truck. The militia had grown in the last year, and Mark explained their network. The Midwest was one of the strongest outposts in the country.

"But Carpathia has gathered all the nuclear weapons," Judd said. "What chance could you possibly have? It's like a slingshot against a bazooka."

"You think Global Community has all the nukes?" Mark said with a smile. "The GC won't know what hit 'em. Besides, look what God did once with a slingshot."

They parked in a wooded area in Wisconsin and covered the truck with brush.

"Is this necessary?" Judd said.

Mark didn't answer. He led them through a half mile of woods into a clearing, where a few hundred men in fatigues stood talking. Vicki noticed few women. Major Stockton Evers, a well-built man with close-cropped hair, stood on a small hill to address the group.

"Tonight we simulate a battle strike," he said. He suddenly noticed Judd and Vicki and clenched his teeth.

"Who are these two?"

"Friends of mine," Mark said. "I've told you about—"

"*Anyone* who attends has to go through protocol," Major Evers interrupted. "Especially a meeting as sensitive as this one."

Mark said, "This is Judd Thompson, the one who stood up to Leon Fortunato on television."

Major Evers raised his eyebrows.

"And this is Vicki Byrne, our friend."

"And we can trust them?"

"I would trust my life to them, or I wouldn't have brought them."

Several clapped and patted Judd on the back, but Vicki noticed a few scowls.

"Next time, you check with me before you bring anyone, understand?" Major Evers said.

The man led each squad through grueling paces as they moved through the woods.

"No wonder you're in such good shape," Vicki said as she tried to keep up. Some behind her were laughing.

"You're doing good," Mark said. "Watch for branches and holes up ahead. Don't twist that ankle again, Judd."

An hour into the exercise, Vicki heard something strange and recognized the *thwop-thwop-thwop* of helicopter blades.

"You guys really make this thing realistic," Vicki said.

Mark looked concerned. "Stay here."

The rest of the squad looked confused. First one helicopter, then another appeared. Bright lights shone down as Judd and Vicki shielded their eyes.

"Impressive," Judd said.

Mark ran back to them. "This way," he said, and hurtled through the woods.

"Halt! Stay where you are," a voice boomed from the sky. "This is an unlawful assembly. Lie down with your hands over your heads."

People screamed. A few lay down while others ran.

"This is a joke, right?" Judd yelled, as he and Vicki caught up with Mark.

"No joke," Mark said. A burst of machine gunfire cut small trees in half ahead of them. Mark veered left and shouted, "Keep your heads down and follow me!"

Vicki ran, but her legs felt like lead. Nothing she had ever experienced, not even the disappearance of her family, compared with this terror.

Mark led them to the edge of a cliff. Vicki saw only rocks, then darkness below. A third helicopter now pursued, its lights scanning the trees behind them.

"Come on," Mark yelled as he jumped into the ravine.

"Mark, no!" Vicki screamed, then covered her eyes.

Judd grabbed her arm. "You're next."

In the moonlight Vicki saw Mark below, suspended from a rope. She jumped to a ledge and grabbed the rope. Swinging back and forth, she and Mark made their way down. Halfway to the bottom, Mark disappeared into the face of a rock.

Vicki's heart pounded as first she, then Judd followed Mark into a huge cave just as the helicopter passed.

She tried to catch her breath.

"Mark, come to your senses," Vicki said.

Mark held up his hand. Something was moving behind them. A light shone in their faces.

"You made it," Major Evers said.

"Yes, sir," Mark said. "How about the others?"

"We're checking," Major Evers said. He sat and turned off his light. Vicki heard water trickling and muffled voices deep in the cave.

"The GC means business," Mark said.

"We knew they were onto us," Major Evers said.

"Then why did you take the chance?" Vicki said.

"We let the GC find us. Carpathia will hear there's a couple hundred guys doing push-ups in the woods. He thinks small potatoes. Meanwhile, we plan our assault."

"When?" Judd said.

"I wouldn't tell you if I knew. When the time is right, we'll strike, and with a vengeance."

"Is it true President Fitzhugh is involved with the militia?" Judd said.

Evers squinted at him. "You know I can't divulge that. But our objective is to have him back in the Oval Office within a couple of months." He shook his head. "The way Carpathia has treated that man . . ."

"Why is Carpathia doing this?" Vicki said. "Who do you think he is?"

"I know religious types think he's the Antichrist. Frankly, I don't know, and I don't care. He's taken our country from us. I'd die to get it back."

"If we don't stand up to him," Mark said, "he'll take everything."

A man with a walkie-talkie led Major Evers and the kids to a communications post. Four militia members had been shot. The GC were sending troops on foot and were only a few miles away.

"I'm sorry," Mark said. "If I'd have known, I wouldn't have brought you."

"Try to make it back to your vehicle and get out of here," Major Evers said. "If you get caught, we were just roasting hot dogs."

Mark made the climb up look easy. Judd favored his ankle. Vicki slipped once, but when Judd grabbed her arm, she glared at him and wrenched away.

"I can do it," she said.

As they reached the truck, Mark slid behind the wheel. "Something isn't right," he said. "That was too easy."

He slipped out of the truck and with catlike motion climbed an enormous tree. In a few moments he was back. "It's a trap," he said. "We'll have to find another way out."

"We could hoof it," Vicki said.

"Can't leave the truck," Mark said. "GC would trace it." He pulled a map from the glove compartment. "Head east on foot. After a few miles, you'll come to a stream. Follow that south just across the Illinois border. If I make it through, I'll meet you here, at this overpass."

"Shouldn't we stick together?" Judd said.

"If they catch you," Mark said, "it's off to the reeducation camp. Get going."

Judd heard helicopters in the distance. He and Vicki started off.

"I don't think we convinced him of anything," Vicki whispered.

"Those guys have made up their minds," Judd said.

39

EVERYONE made it home without incident, but the next day they argued. "What happened last night proves we're doing the right thing," Mark said.

"How can you say that?" Judd said, hardly able to control himself. "It was foolish. All three of us could have been killed! And for what? What did we accomplish?"

"You don't understand," Mark said. "Things are about to change."

"The change has to be spiritual," Judd said. "There are so many constructive things you could do."

"You don't call fighting the Antichrist constructive?" Mark said.

Vicki said, "We're just concerned about you, Mark."

"Think about Lionel and Ryan, too," Judd said. "You're influencing those guys."

Judd slept until afternoon, then headed to the church. He was surprised to find Vicki at the front door. "Keeping watch?" he said.

"You haven't heard about the wedding?" Vicki said.

Vicki explained the romance Judd hadn't seen. He knew Chloe Steele and Buck Williams were seeing each other and even guessed that they might get married. But he hadn't guessed about Amanda White and Rayford Steele. She was a tall, handsome woman about Mr. Steele's age; she had streaked hair and impeccable taste in clothes.

"And it was the most romantic proposal I've ever heard of. Buck surprised Chloe at Amanda's office and proposed to her in one room while her dad was proposing to Amanda in the other. The only problem is, now we're losing Chloe. She and Buck will live in New York."

Judd and Vicki crept to Bruce's office and listened outside the door. Bruce told the couples where to stand and led them through the double ceremony.

"I'm not going to preach a sermon," Bruce said. "You've heard enough of those. But I do want to challenge you. With what lies ahead, with the uncertainty all around us, cling to each other. Love each other. Forgive each other. Put each other's needs ahead of your own, as Christ did. And let no one, *no one* come between what God has divinely joined."

Judd heard Buck say his vows. Buck's voice was trembling. "Chloe, I promise to love you, and you only. I will honor you above all others, above even my own life. . . . "

Chloe responded with her vows.

Then Rayford pledged himself to Amanda, saying, "I will treasure the gift God has given me in you."

"And I am yours, Rayford," Amanda said, "whether in sickness or in health, for richer or poorer, until death separates us."

Bruce finished by praying, "For this brief flash of joy in a world on the brink of disaster, we thank you and pray your blessing and protection on us all until we meet back here again. Bind our hearts as brothers and sisters in Christ while we are apart."

Judd and Vicki stepped outside the church.

"Makes you wonder, doesn't it?" Judd said.

"Wonder what?" Vicki said.

"You know," Judd said, pawing the ground with his foot. "That kind of stuff."

"What kind of stuff?"

"You know."

"Judd Thompson, this is the first time I've seen you blush."

Vicki let him stammer, then came to his rescue. "You know Captain Steele and Amanda are moving to New Babylon."

"You're kidding," Judd said.

"Carpathia wants all his staff there."

Judd turned to Vicki. "I've always wondered whether—"

But Bruce and the couples came out of the office. "Hey, kids," Bruce said. "I'd like you to meet Rayford and Amanda Steele, and Chloe and Buck Williams."

Vicki looked at Judd and smiled.

Judd and Bruce flew to Australia. In Melbourne thousands of believers crowded the local stadium to hear the American pastor speak. In Sydney the crowds were even greater, but Judd also saw more Global Community peacekeepers.

When they arrived in Jakarta, Indonesia, a team of translators met them and set up their schedule. Judd tried to pick up a few words of each new language they encountered. On the island of Sumatra he tried to say he was Bruce's right-hand man. The locals laughed as the translator informed Judd that he had said, "I am the hand of a chicken."

Judd and Bruce arrived in the middle of dry season. In one stadium Judd looked out over the sea of people and noticed smoke rising in the distance.

"That is our volcano," an interpreter said. "But don't be alarmed. It has not been active for years. It is only showing off."

People stood in the searing heat to hear Bruce. Muslim leaders in traditional garb stood at the back of the service. At the end of one message, the men tore their robes, cried out, and ran to the front of the stadium.

Judd rushed to Bruce. "Get out of here! They're going to kill you!"

"Wait," Bruce said. "Look."

The men were on their knees, crying out to God. Judd was amazed at what a simple message could do. People were hungry for God.

Bruce spoke freely of the judgments to come. He

urged people to accept God's forgiveness before it was too late. He also taught how to start home churches for when public meetings would be outlawed.

Judd missed his friends and was torn by what he felt for Vicki. Bruce kept him busy with many E-mail messages from around the world. With Bruce's help Judd typed answers.

"You have a question here from Rayford about the fifth and seventh?" Judd said. "What does that mean?"

"He's talking about the judgments predicted in Revelation," Bruce said. "We have to be careful. The GC could intercept these, and Rayford would be in danger."

"What are those judgments?"

"Many are clear, but the fifth and seventh are difficult. In his vision, the apostle John sees under the altar in heaven the souls of those who had been slain for the Word of God and for their testimonies. They ask God how long it will be until he avenges their deaths. He gives them white robes and tells them others will be martyred first. So the fifth Seal Judgment costs people who have become believers since the Rapture their lives."

"That could include you or me."

"Any of us," Bruce said.

"What about the seventh?"

"That's a mystery. It's so awesome that when it's revealed in heaven, there is silence for half an hour. Whatever it is, it seems to progress from the sixth seal, which is the greatest earthquake in history, and brings in more judgments, each worse than the one before it."

Judd tried to list the other judgments. "A world war, famine, martyrdom—"

"Don't forget plagues and the death of a quarter of the earth's population," Bruce said as he replied to Rayford's message.

Judd looked over Bruce's shoulder as he typed: "He who dwells in the secret place of the Most High shall abide under the shadow of the Almighty."

Vicki and Chaya followed Bruce and Judd's travels on a world map. A red pin marked each place the two visited.

Judd also uploaded pictures of crowds and interesting sights from each place. In one picture Bruce and Judd wore nervous smiles as they sat at a dinner table. In front of them was an overflowing dish of what looked like small biscuits. Judd held one up and winked at the camera.

"What were those things you were holding in the picture?" Vicki wrote.

"A delicacy," he wrote back. "Sheep's eyeballs."

Chaya gagged and Vicki wrote, "You actually ate those things!?"

"It would have been impolite not to," Judd said. "For sheep's eyeballs they weren't bad."

Chaya answered the door as Judd wrote Vicki their schedule. "Bruce and I are having lunch with some important people who just had to see us, and then we're heading home. Can't wait to see you."

Just then Chaya stepped back from the door and gasped. "Mother!"

The waitress spoke in broken English. "Man in corner buy meal for you, mister sir."

Bruce and Judd looked, but there was no one to thank. Bruce shrugged and turned back to the several guests at his table.

"Doctor Barnes," the interpreter at the table said.

"Please," Bruce said. "Call me pastor. I'm not a doctor."

"Yes, pastor," the man said. "The others want me to thank you for teaching us. But they ask, what do they do now? Many thousands have believed your message."

"Get your people into the Bible," Bruce said. The interpreter rattled off the translation. "Study the Scriptures daily. Nothing is more important. We must be ready for the return of Christ."

On the plane that night, Bruce sat next to a businessman from Chicago. Judd closed his eyes and leaned against the window as he listened to Bruce describe what had happened to him during the disappearances.

"That might be good for you," the man said, "but your faith is too exclusive, saying there is only one way to God. Enigma Babylon says all paths to God are valid. Just like there are a lot of planes you could take to Chicago."

"It's true that the message of the Bible is different from Enigma Babylon," Bruce said. "Let me show you."

Judd drifted off as he heard Bruce's Bible pages turning. He awoke to shouting.

"Somebody do something!"

"What's wrong with him?"

"Is he dead?"

Bruce slumped in the aisle. A flight attendant rushed to him.

"He didn't look good, and I told him so," the man said. "Then he just passed out."

"We should be in Chicago in two hours," the attendant said.

"He looks pretty bad," the man said. "Can't you do anything?"

Judd unbuckled and leaned over Bruce's body.

Bruce's color wasn't right. His lips moved. Judd leaned closer.

"Give it to him," Bruce managed.

"Give who what, Bruce?"

"My Bible," Bruce whispered. "Let him read it for himself."

"Excuse me, I'm a doctor," a woman said, and the aisle cleared.

40

MRS. STEIN had changed since Vicki last saw her. Her eyes had dark circles, her hair had thinned, and she looked tired. Chaya invited her in, and Vicki excused herself.

"No," Mrs. Stein said. "I'd like you to stay if Chaya doesn't mind."

The three sat in the living room in strained silence until Mrs. Stein spoke. "I've come to the point where I don't care what your father thinks. He told me not to come. He said seeing you would just upset me more."

"What's wrong, Mom?"

"I had a routine checkup," Mrs. Stein said. "But the doctor found a lump. He said it was likely nothing to worry about." Her eyes were vacant, and her chin trembled. "It wasn't routine. I have cancer."

She broke down. Chaya put her arm around her mother. "I had no idea," she said. "I'm here for you, Mom."

By the time the plane landed in Chicago Bruce was sitting up and feeling better. The man beside him would not take Bruce's Bible, but Judd got his business card and promised to send one from Ryan's stash.

Loretta, the church secretary, met them at the airport and was upset about Bruce's condition. "I'm taking you straight to the emergency room."

"Nonsense," Bruce said. "I'm fine. I need to get back to the church. If I'm not feeling better tomorrow, I'll see a doctor."

After debriefing at home, Judd learned from John the latest about Mark.

"Three more militia exercises in the last week," John said. "They're gearing up for something. Mark won't talk specifics, but he called our relatives who live near Washington, D.C. and told them to leave and stay out of major East Coast cities."

"But if Bruce is right," Judd said. "The uprising against the Antichrist will be crushed. And if Mark gets involved, he doesn't have a chance."

"Your father has been telling me to forget about you," Mrs. Stein said. "But I can't. Plus I'm scared, and I feel something is missing in my life."

"God loves you, Mom. He can give you peace. You can know that your sins are forgiven and that you'll spend eternity with him."

"You can't know!" Mrs. Stein said. "It is arrogant to say such a thing."

Vicki grabbed a Bible, and Chaya read from the book of John. "And truly Jesus did many other signs in the presence of his disciples, which are not written in this book; but these are written that you may believe that Jesus is the Christ, the Son of God, and that believing you may have life in his name."

"This is what Rabbi Ben-Judah was talking about on TV," Mrs. Stein said.

"Exactly," Chaya said. "It's what I discovered. We Jewish people have been looking for Messiah. But he has already come."

"If your father knew I was talking to you—"

"You said you didn't care what Dad thinks," Chaya said. "Please, Mom, let me show you more."

Vicki made lunch while the two talked. Chaya told her mother about her friend at the University of Chicago who had explained who Jesus was and what he had done. At times Mrs. Stein argued, but each time Chaya gently led her back to the Bible.

Before they ate, Vicki thanked God for Mrs. Stein and prayed for her upcoming surgery. "Give her the peace that passes all understanding."

When she looked up, Mrs. Stein was crying.

―――――――――――――

When Judd called Bruce later that afternoon to tell him about Mark, Bruce sounded weak. "You OK?" Judd said.

"I can't talk long," Bruce said. "But don't worry. I'll be

all right. And so will Mark. He has to make his own decisions."

Mrs. Stein thanked Vicki and gathered her things. Her surgery was set for Friday morning at Northwest Community Hospital. "Don't come to see me until the next morning."

"Dad can't keep me from seeing you."

"Please," Mrs. Stein said, "we can talk Saturday."

"Mom, don't go into surgery without settling this."

"That is between God and me. I will take it up with him in my own time."

Judd and John met secretly with Vicki and Chaya late the next night, and they brought each other up to date.

"Mark's ready to give his life for the militia," John said.

"When a person is that committed," Judd said, "there's no way to stop him."

"Tie him up and stick him in the basement," Vicki said.

Judd laughed.

"I'm serious," she said. "Give him something that puts him to sleep, and lock him up till this blows over."

"And how long are you going to keep him?" Judd said. "He'll never trust us again."

"We'd only be doing it because we care," Vicki said.

"And if it works, we use it as a new evangelism tool," John said. "Lock all non-Christians in Bruce's basement 'til they see the light."

Vicki said, "He's your cousin! I'd think you'd care more about him than that."

John stared at her. "I do care. I want to knock some sense into him, and I'd do it if I could. He's bigger than me, and all that training has made him hard as a rock."

"Have you thought about going to the authorities?" Chaya said. "I know it's drastic, but if they know about it beforehand, they can stop it, and no one gets hurt."

"I couldn't think of giving him over to the Global Community goons," John said.

Judd had been quiet. "If the militia is really planning a strike against the Global Community," he said, "one of their targets has to be Nicolae Carpathia."

"Of course," John said. "They wouldn't be able to restore President Fitzhugh if they don't take him out."

"Which puts whose life in danger?" Judd said.

"Rayford Steele's!" Vicki gasped.

"Bingo," Judd said. "Maybe Mrs. Steele's, too. I wonder if that would change Mark's mind?"

"It wouldn't," Mark said, and everyone jerked to attention. "Hi, everybody. Thanks for inviting me."

Judd didn't know what to say. John stared at the floor.

"I don't want anyone to die, and I don't want to die. Captain Steele knew the risks when he took the job.

"Have any of you considered the possibility that I'm right? I'm going to fight the enemy of this country and the enemy of our souls. People are going to die no matter what. You ought to support me and be thankful the militia is willing to put it all on the line."

"Nobody questions your motives," Judd said. "We just don't want you to throw your life away."

Chaya said, "Isn't Scripture clear that no uprising will stop the Antichrist?"

Mark shrugged. "That's your interpretation," he said. "If God calls you to do something, you've got to do it no matter what other people say. I thought you'd be behind me. If you can't support me, fine. But don't get in my way."

The phone rang, and Vicki handed it to Judd. It was Loretta. When he laid the phone down he felt sick to his stomach.

"What is it?" Vicki said.

Loretta found Pastor Bruce on the floor of his study," Judd said. "They're taking him to the emergency room!"

Judd raced to Northwest Community Hospital in Arlington Heights. He found Loretta with an elder from New Hope Village Church.

"Bruce was disoriented," Loretta said nervously. "He didn't want us to bring him, but he looked so pale."

Eventually a doctor told them, "We're going to monitor him here tonight. His heart rate is erratic, but he's resting. Could be a heart attack, or he may have picked up something overseas. You can see him if you make it quick."

Judd was shocked to find Bruce hooked up to tubes and monitors. Judd took Bruce's hand, which was limp and unusually cold.

Bruce's eyelids fluttered. He whispered, "So tired. I wanted to surprise them Saturday."

"Surprise who?" Judd said, but Bruce didn't respond.

Bruce's Bible lay on the stand by the bed. Judd opened it to one of Bruce's favorite passages, and his voice broke as he leaned close. "He who dwells in the secret place of the Most High shall abide under the shadow of the Almighty."

STOP treating us like little kids," Lionel said at breakfast Friday morning. "It's not right to have meetings without us."

Ryan was furious. "Mark is our friend, too," he said. "We've got a right to know what's going on."

"I was afraid you'd want to follow him," Judd said. "What was I supposed to do?"

"Let us go see Bruce then."

"Can't. Sorry."

"See," Ryan said. "This is the same thing."

"They won't let you in," Judd said. "Maybe when he's feeling better."

"I'm going to send him a card," Ryan muttered as he slammed the door.

Judd called Loretta for the latest on Bruce. She said, "He rested through the night and told me he wants to be out in time to meet Rayford and the rest tomorrow."

"So that's what he meant about meeting people for

lunch," Judd said. "Is Captain Steele flying Carpathia into the country?"

"I don't have a clue."

Vicki drove Chaya to the hospital Friday morning and saw Chaya's mother and father walk in. Chaya left a bouquet of flowers at the front desk for her mother. They asked about Bruce, but the nurses were tightlipped.

Patricia Devlin, the head nurse, said, "Family members?"

Vicki said, "Daughter."

"No change," the nurse said. "Check back later."

"I can't even see my own father?"

Ms. Devlin peered at Vicki over her glasses. "You look a little old to be his daughter," she said. "But anyway, his doctor says no visitors until his illness is identified."

John and Mark were at Judd's that evening when Ryan handed Judd a card with a beautiful picture of clouds on the front.

"It's for Bruce," Ryan said. "I hope he likes it."

"I'm sure he will," Judd said, "but I can't promise when he'll get it."

"Then I'll take it to him myself."

"You can't," Judd said. "I told you that."

Judd answered the phone, and a mysterious voice asked for Mark.

When Mark took it, he said, "We are? When? Where? I'll be there."

"Hey, I got a hot date I forgot about," Mark said. Judd and John didn't smile. "Can you give John a ride home?"

Judd nodded.

Mark paused at the door. "You guys take care of yourselves, OK?"

The phone woke Vicki Saturday morning. Judd was frantic.

"I need your help," Judd said. "Ryan isn't in his room. He's gone."

"Where could he be?"

"He talked about going to see Bruce."

"That's a long way on busy streets," Vicki said. "What can I do?"

"Come help me look for him," Judd said.

"Will do. Chaya and I are heading to the hospital to check on her mom, anyway," Vicki said. "We'll look for him there. How's Bruce?"

"Loretta says he called for his laptop, which was good news, but then she found out they were moving him to Intensive Care. She thinks he had a premonition."

"A premonition?" Vicki said. "About what? He's not that sick, is he?"

"I don't know," Judd said. "Bruce asked her to print out everything from his hard drive."

"By the way," Judd added quickly, "John said Mark didn't come home last night."

367

Ryan pedaled faster. He hated shutting Phoenix up at the house, but there was no way he could take him. He wanted to stay on less crowded streets, but to get his bearings he had to follow the main roads.

He asked directions several times and was relieved when a woman told him to cut through her yard. The hospital was on the other side of a grassy knoll.

Ryan parked his bike and locked it to a post near the emergency room entrance. Finding the hospital was the easy part. The hard part would be making it to Bruce's room.

An older woman at the information desk told him Bruce was on the fourth floor in Intensive Care. "But you won't be able to go up there, son."

Ryan waited until the elevator was empty, pushed the button for the fourth floor, then hit floor five as well.

On the fourth floor Ryan saw the nurses' station and noticed three nurses pushing a man in a wheelchair. The doors closed, and Ryan rode up to five.

From there he hurried to the stairway, walked down one flight, and watched the nurses through the small window.

When everyone seemed busy he opened the door and slipped down the hall. He found Bruce's room and made sure no one was watching as he entered.

Ryan wasn't sure it was Bruce, there were so many machines and tubes hooked up to him. When he finally saw his face, Ryan knew.

"I brought you something," Ryan said softly.

Ryan held the card in front of Bruce's closed eyes. "It looks like heaven, or at least what I think heaven might look like," Ryan said.

He heard voices and a cart outside. Ryan hit the floor and rolled under the bed as someone entered, took something, and left.

Ryan rolled out from under the bed. He touched Bruce's face. "If it hadn't been for you," he whispered, "I don't know what would have happened to me."

Ryan pulled up a chair, sat, and laid his head on the bed beside Bruce.

Ryan felt something on his shoulder and flinched. He was afraid someone had discovered him. But it was Bruce's hand, barely moving, patting Ryan's shoulder.

Loretta was ashen when Judd found her at the church. She sat alone, staring at the computer as the printer worked away.

"That young man taught me more about the Bible than I learned in all my years of Sunday school," she said.

"What's happened?" Judd said.

"I just got off the phone with the hospital. Bruce has slipped into a coma."

Vicki saw no sign of Ryan. Chaya's mother came through surgery, but they wouldn't know for a few days if the last-ditch effort was successful. Chaya visited her mother, while Vicki headed for Intensive Care.

Vicki briskly walked past the nurses' station, hoping

she could find Bruce's room quickly and ask him if Ryan had been there.

The writing was poor on the clipboards on each door. Vicki bent close to read, when the door opened and an orderly nearly knocked her over.

He eyed Vicki suspiciously. "This is Intensive Care. You shouldn't be here."

"Is this Pastor Barnes's room?" Vicki said.

"It is, but . . . "

"I'm his daughter."

"You're Vicki?" he said.

"You know my name?"

"Pastor Bruce told me about you before he slipped into a coma."

Vicki gasped.

He pulled her inside the room and shut the door. "I'm sorry. I assumed you knew."

Vicki heard the beep of the monitors fastened to Bruce's chest. Tubes ran everywhere, and an oxygen mask covered his face.

"What did he say?" Vicki said, choking back tears.

"First thing he wanted to know was if I knew Jesus. He was in and out after that. Might have been dreaming. Mumbled something about a wedding."

Vicki nodded.

"He opened his eyes and asked me if I was Vicki. I said I didn't know who Vicki was, but I sure hoped she didn't look like me. He said you were his only daughter now. Then he went back to sleep. The next time I came in, he was in a coma."

Bruce's Bible lay on the nightstand. Beside it was a card with clouds on the front.

"You'd better get back to the waiting room," the orderly said.

"Wait," Vicki said. "You didn't see a boy up here, did you?"

"No boys in this room. Just doctors and nurses, and me, of course. Now come on."

"One more thing," Vicki said. "How did you answer? Do you know Jesus?"

The orderly smiled. "You're Pastor Bruce's daughter all right."

Vicki met Chaya in the lobby.

"Mother actually had a Bible open," Chaya said. "But she was afraid Dad would walk in."

Vicki asked at the front desk, but no one had seen a boy on a bike. As she and Chaya were getting into the car, a plane flew low over the parking lot.

Seconds later, a huge explosion erupted.

———————————————

Judd felt the earth shudder at the church before the loud rumble. Windowpanes crashed in the back. From the parking lot he saw black smoke rise in the distance and bombers from all directions. Another explosion, then a bigger one, hurtled plumes of smoke high into the air.

He jumped in his car and headed toward the hospital. He dialed his house on his cell phone. Lionel answered.

"Any sign of Ryan?" Judd said.

"Not yet. Did you hear that noise?"

"I heard it. Take cover in the basement."

Fire trucks, ambulances, and police cruisers swirled around Judd. The radio gave the sports report, then the weather.

"Come on, come on, what happened?" Judd said.

Finally a voice interrupted. "This breaking story! An explosion in northwest suburban Arlington Heights. We have a reporter on the way. Wait, excuse me. I'm told we have a woman on the phone who's at the scene. Hello? Ma'am?"

"There were planes and then *kaboom!*"

"Planes? This was some kind of an attack?"

"An attack. That's exactly what it was."

"And where are you?"

"Near the old racecourse off Euclid," she said. "They're still comin' in and droppin' their bombs."

"Don't you know the target?"

"No, but it was south of me. I can see the smoke from my front window."

Judd saw the same mushroom cloud and then the fire. Traffic stopped. He parked and took off on foot. He called Lionel again. Still no sign of Ryan.

Judd called the hospital but couldn't get through. He could smell the acrid smoke and feel the heat. Fire trucks and ambulances sat in the middle of the street. He dialed Vicki at home. No answer.

Running, he saw a boy on a bicycle. "Any other kids come by here?" Judd yelled.

"No," the kid said. "And stay away from the hospital. It's like a war zone."

"They're taking the wounded there?"

"It was hit!" the kid said. He rode away, pale and clearly terrified.

Judd's head spun, and the smoke made it difficult to breathe. He cut through a parking lot, then past a grassy area. Judd's heart sank as he came over the rise and saw the hospital. Part of the full height of the structure was still intact, but much of it was rubble. A few white-uniformed workers scurried about.

He heard a plane directly overhead and looked up in time to see it deliver its payload. The bomb wobbled in the air, then straightened out. The plane veered off with a deafening roar as Judd hit the ground and covered his head.

The earth shook with the force of the explosion. No more planes. Only sirens and the crackling fire and the sobs.

And the sobs were his own.

42

AS THE smoke cleared Judd ran full tilt toward the hospital. Police and firemen were just arriving. Bodies lay scattered. He heard the faint cry of a newborn in the rubble, and four officers began lifting concrete.

Judd couldn't believe anyone could have survived. Part of the structure looked normal, but the other half looked like a mashed toy. Girders protruded. Water sprayed from broken pipes. Hospital equipment lay charred and twisted on the ground.

Bruce was in there somewhere. Judd had to find him. As more emergency personnel arrived, Judd acted like he was supposed to be there. He kept his head down and walked toward what used to be the Intensive Care unit.

Vicki and Chaya were just pulling away when the first plane struck. They ran through the parking lot and into backyards. As planes roared overhead, Vicki and Chaya jumped fences and ran around swimming pools.

Just when they thought they were far enough away, a terrific blast shook the earth. Streetlights shattered, and houses exploded a block away. With fire and falling debris around them, they kept going, dodging cars that had run off the road. People screamed in terror as the planes kept coming.

Vicki and Chaya sprinted ten minutes until a woman called out to them from her house. She took the girls to her basement, where they listened to the thunder overhead.

"Who would attack us?" the woman said. She turned on the television. The Cable News Network/Global Community Network correspondent was broadcasting live just outside Washington, D.C.

"The fate of Global Community Potentate Nicolae Carpathia remains in question at this hour as Washington lies in ruins. The massive assault was launched by East Coast militia, with the aid of the United States of Britain and the former sovereign state of Egypt, not part of the Middle Eastern Commonwealth."

Chaya shook her head. The once beautiful view of Washington, D.C. was now a disaster area.

"Potentate Carpathia arrived here last night and was thought to be staying in the presidential suite of the Capital Noir, but eyewitnesses say that the luxury hotel was leveled this morning.

"Global Community peacekeeping forces immediately retaliated and have attacked a former Nike base in suburban Chicago."

"What's a Nike base?" Vicki said.

"That old building near the hospital," the woman said. "Nike is a type of missile. They had training fields over there, barracks, lots of jeeps. But it's been closed for years. People say the militia was using it."

The report switched to Chicago. A man at a news desk stammered through the information.

"Uh, we have reports of civilian casualties in the surrounding suburbs, and uh, a colossal traffic tie-up is hampering rescue efforts. Please, if you are anywhere near the suburbs of Arlington Heights, Prospect Heights, Mount Prospect, or Rolling Meadows, take caution. Find a safe place for you and your family.

"Here's what we know right now about the strike on the Nike base. We are told that Global Community intelligence has uncovered a plot to destroy Potentate Carpathia's plane at O'Hare."

"Mr. Steele!" Vicki said.

"The attack on the Nike base was effected without nuclear weapons," the man continued. "Again, *without* the use of nuclear weapons. A statement from Global Community command says there is no danger of radiation fallout in the Chicago area."

The station switched to a network reporter. "Egyptian ground forces moving toward Iraq have been wiped out by Global Community air forces, thwarting an obvious siege upon New Babylon. Global Community forces are now advancing on England. Ah, please stand by. . . .

Potentate Carpathia is safe! He will address the nation in a few moments."

Judd's cell phone rang.

"Judd, it's John." He sounded awful. "I think Mark was at the Nike base."

"Oh, no!" Judd said. "The hospital was hit, too."

"I'm a few blocks away," John said. "I'll meet you there."

To Vicki, Nicolae Carpathia sounded calm, as if commenting on a golf tournament rather than World War III.

"Loyal citizens of the Global Community," Carpathia said, "I come to you today with a broken heart, unable to tell you even from where I speak. For more than a year we have worked to draw this Global Community together under a banner of peace and harmony. Today, unfortunately, we have been reminded again that there are still those among us who would pull us apart.

"It is no secret that I am, always have been, and always will be a pacifist. I do not believe in war. I do not believe in weaponry. I do not believe in bloodshed. On the other hand, I feel responsible for you, my brother or my sister in this global village.

"Global Community peacekeeping forces have already crushed the resistance. The death of innocent civilians weighs heavy on me, but I pledge immediate judgment upon all enemies of peace. The beautiful capital of the

United States of North America has been laid waste, and you will hear stories of more destruction and death. Our goal remains peace and reconstruction. I will be back at the secure headquarters in New Babylon in due time and will communicate with you frequently.

"Above all, do not fear. Live in confidence that no threat to global tranquility will be tolerated, and no enemy of peace will survive."

A correspondent for CNN/GCN recapped Carpathia's statement. "And this late word: Anti-Global Community militia forces have threatened nuclear war on New York City, primarily Kennedy International Airport. Civilians are fleeing the area.

"And now this from London," he said, touching his hand to his forehead. "I'm sorry. A one-hundred-megaton bomb has destroyed Heathrow Airport, and radiation fallout is threatening the area for miles."

"It's the end of the world," the woman said to Vicki and Chaya.

———

Judd avoided eye contact with the growing number of police and emergency workers. He saw several people lifting bodies to a makeshift outdoor morgue.

"We're getting a patient list and an employee record from the office," Judd heard a man say to rescue workers. "When we get it, we need to reconcile that list with the ID bracelets."

"Any survivors?" another man asked.

"Three women," the man said. "Two nurses and a

doctor. They were outside for a smoke when the bombing started."

The men scattered. Judd looked at the row of lifeless bodies. He went to the first and slowly lifted the white sheet. A woman. *Who was she?* Judd wondered.

Next was a young bald man, probably a cancer patient. The third was an elderly man with white hair.

Judd stood over the fourth body and heard the workers returning. He lifted the sheet and gasped.

Vicki and Chaya waited until they were sure the bombing had stopped. The lady begged them to stay.

"My mother was at the hospital," Chaya said. "And Vicki's father. We have to go back."

By the time they reached the hospital, police barrier tape had been stretched around the campus. Guards patrolled the area.

Chaya pointed excitedly toward the debris. "It's Judd," she said.

They both yelled at him and waved as Judd was led from the area by two guards. As he got closer, Vicki could see Judd crying.

He ducked under the police tape and fell to his knees. "I saw him, Vick'."

"Who?" Vicki said. "Ryan?"

"Bruce. They just brought him out and laid him in the grass." Judd looked up at Vicki. "Bruce is gone. Dead."

Vicki and Chaya burst into tears and embraced Judd. Why would God take Bruce now? Vicki shook. The man who had taken her in, who had given so much to teach them the truth of God's Word, had fallen.

"My mother," Chaya said. "How will I find out about my mother?"

"They're identifying bodies," Judd said. He suggested they stay while he went to find John at the Nike base. They would try to find Mark. Judd left Vicki his cell phone and asked her to keep in touch with Lionel.

Judd met John near the Nike base. Smoke rose from the building and small explosions still erupted inside. Judd approached an officer. "What happened?"

"Global Community took out the militia," the officer said. "Their stash of weapons is blowing up now."

"Any survivors?" John said.

The officer raised his eyebrows and shook his head. "In there? Anybody who survived the bombs would have been vaporized by the heat."

John hung his head.

"Don't give up," Judd said. "You never know."

They jogged toward Judd's car. Traffic was backed up as far as he could see.

"Cut down this alley," John said. "There's a convenience store down here Mark talked about. The owner might know something."

When they pulled off the street, Judd noticed Mark's truck parked in the back.

John ran toward the vehicle. He skidded to a stop and

peered through the window. Judd fell in behind him. On the seat of the truck, flat on his face, lay Mark.

"Oh no," John said.

When Judd opened the door, Mark sat up. He wore his battle fatigues, and his face was painted green and black.

"Don't say it," Mark said. "You were right."

"Are you OK?" John said.

"They're all gone," Mark said.

"How did you make it out?" Judd said.

"Major Evers sent the younger guys out just before the attack. He must have known."

"Come on," John said. "This area will be crawling with GC in a few minutes. Come back for the truck later."

Judd brought his car around and hustled Mark into the trunk.

Tears were Vicki's first response to Bruce's death. The more she thought of him, the more she felt like she had been kicked in the stomach. There were no words for the pain. Bruce had never asked to be called "Dad" or "Father," but in many ways she felt closer to him than to her real dad. Now Bruce was gone, and she wanted to scream. At the same time she was overcome by a stillness and a peace she couldn't explain.

After a few minutes she realized there was more to do. *Ryan,* she thought. Vicki called Lionel, but there was still no sign of him. She and Chaya held each other and wept as they waited for word about her mother. Suddenly Vicki spotted Chaya's father running toward the morgue area. Officials shooed him away. He stood behind the yellow tape and stared at the ground.

A nurse finally led Chaya toward the temporary morgue. Vicki watched as Mr. Stein ran to Chaya. The nurse checked her clipboard and led them stiffly away. Vicki saw Chaya look at her father, but it appeared he did not return her glance.

Vicki thought about Bruce. He had treated her like she was his own, and now he was gone. *Gone.* When Vicki allowed that thought, she staggered. The pain cut so deep, it was almost unbearable. There would be a time of grieving, she knew. Now she had to concentrate.

Vicki called Lionel. "Ryan?" she said.

"His bike is gone," Lionel said. "And he left Phoenix."

Chaya returned without her father, beaming through her tears.

Judd weaved through traffic and onto side streets. He had to get Mark to safety before the GC resumed their search. Judd saw a roadblock and turned down another side street. Global Community peacekeepers were scouring each car.

After nearly an hour, Judd pulled into his garage. Mark was exhausted. He tore off his fatigues and ran past Lionel for the shower. Judd found him a change of clothes.

"Vicki said Chaya identified her mom's body," Lionel said.

Judd slumped into a kitchen chair.

Chaya put her head on Vicki's shoulder and wept.

"I'm so sorry," Vicki said.

"She looked so beautiful."

"How is your father?"

Chaya shook her head. She held up a crumpled piece of paper, the note she had given her mother that morning.

"Mom always wrote everything down," Chaya said. "We'd find notes all over the house."

Chaya turned the paper over, and Vicki saw Mrs. Stein's handwriting.

"Forgive me, God. Help me live for you and for your Son, Jesus, the Messiah."

Everybody met at Judd's house that evening, and he stood before pale, frightened faces. What would they do without Bruce? How would they find Ryan? And would they have to face further conflict in the future?

"This is a terrible day," he said. "And we have to face the fact that Ryan may have been—"

"Don't write him off yet," Lionel said, his voice quavering. "He's tough."

"Bruce said once that one of the hardest things you ever have to do is let go of someone you care about," Judd said.

384

"I'm telling you, don't count him out!" Lionel sobbed.

"I'm sorry," Judd said. "All we can do is try to stay safe and honor the memory of our friends by telling everybody the truth about God, no matter what the cost, no matter what anybody does."

"I'm in," John said.

"Me, too," Chaya whispered.

Vicki nodded, and Mark cleared his throat. "I want to fight the enemy," he said. "This time, I want to do it the right way."

Lionel rose and moved slowly toward the stairs.

"Lionel?" Vicki said, worried as much about him as about how she was going to cope with fresh grief.

He turned. "You all can rah-rah about the future, and yeah, you can count me in. But don't include me in cryin' over Ryan, 'cause I'm not buying that yet. He'll be back."

ABOUT THE AUTHORS

Jerry B. Jenkins (www.jerryjenkins.com) is the writer of the Left Behind series. He owns the Jerry B. Jenkins Christian Writers Guild, an organization dedicated to mentoring aspiring authors. Former vice president for publishing for the Moody Bible Institute of Chicago, he also served many years as editor of *Moody* magazine and is now Moody's writer-at-large.

His writing has appeared in publications as varied as *Reader's Digest, Parade, Guideposts*, in-flight magazines, and dozens of other periodicals. Jenkins's biographies include books with Billy Graham, Hank Aaron, Bill Gaither, Luis Palau, Walter Payton, Orel Hershiser, and Nolan Ryan, among many others. His books appear regularly on the *New York Times, USA Today, Wall Street Journal*, and *Publishers Weekly* best-seller lists.

Jerry is also the writer of the nationally syndicated sports story comic strip *Gil Thorp*, distributed to newspapers across the United States by Tribune Media Services.

Jerry and his wife, Dianna, live in Colorado and have three grown sons.

Dr. Tim LaHaye (www.timlahaye.com), who conceived the idea of fictionalizing an account of the Rapture and the Tribulation, is a noted author, minister, and nationally recognized speaker on Bible prophecy. He is the founder of both Tim LaHaye Ministries and The PreTrib Research Center. He also recently cofounded the Tim LaHaye School of Prophecy at Liberty University. Presently Dr. LaHaye speaks at many of the major Bible prophecy conferences in the U.S. and Canada, where his current prophecy books are very popular.

Dr. LaHaye holds a doctor of ministry degree from Western Theological Seminary and a doctor of literature degree from Liberty University. For twenty-five years he pastored one of the nation's outstanding churches in San Diego, which grew to three locations. It was during that time that he founded two accredited Christian high schools, a Christian school system of ten schools, and Christian Heritage College.

Dr. LaHaye has written over forty books that have been published in more than thirty languages. He has written books on a wide variety of subjects, such as family life, temperaments, and Bible prophecy. His current fiction works, the Left Behind series, written with Jerry B. Jenkins, continue to appear on the best-seller lists of the Christian Booksellers Association, *Publishers Weekly*, *Wall Street Journal*, *USA Today*, and the *New York Times*.

He is the father of four grown children and grandfather of nine. Snow skiing, waterskiing, motorcycling, golfing, vacationing with family, and jogging are among his leisure activities.

Coming Spring 2004

The next two books
in the Young Trib Force Series!

www.areUthirsty.com

well. . . are you?